HORSE PLAY

a horse play novel ~ book one

a novel by
A.D. RYAN

Ryan, A.D.
Horse Play / A.D. Ryan

(Horse Play Series ; 01)

ISBN 978-1517002466

Text and Cover design by Angela Schmuhl
Cover Image: Shutterstock, © Kiuikson

CONTENTS

ACKNOWLEDGEMENTS

Readers, the ones who stuck with me back when some of my stuff was posted online in it's roughest form and those who've just joined me on this crazy life journey: you mean the world to me. Seriously. None of this would be happening if you weren't all behind me, supporting me and pushing me to be better. Thank you.

For Ryan and my kids, you all have been so incredibly patient and tolerant while I pursue this crazy little dream I have. Boys, Mama promises to write you a story one day soon. You're both so understanding when I tell you I can't read one of my books to you, so I promise you that one day, you'll have your very own book that we can read together. I love you, I love you, I love you. *kisses*

Brothers, sisters, Mom, and Dads ... your love and support mean the world to me. You were my first cheerleaders, and you gave me the confidence I needed to pursue something I love doing. Thank you for always being interested and for never holding me back.

My bestie, you've been there for me since I posted my first story online (remember that hot mess?). Thank you for holding my hand through the stressful times, and high-fiving me through the happy ones.

Tiff who fell in love with this story when she first read it YEARS ago, I appreciate all that you do, even if we don't talk often. It's actually incredible that we can go weeks and months between emails and messages and it feels like no time at all has passed!

I'm adding a new name to my roster with this novel: Marla. Thank you for taking a chance on an unknown wannabe author and helping everything make sense. I'd heard nothing but good things about your editing services, and I'm so glad you were able to fit me in!

And finally, to the pre-readers and my street team; you are all so incredible. I have this very real problem with anxiety, so the idea with sharing something as dear to me as the characters I've created is almost crippling. You've all been so lovely, accepting not only my personal brand of crazy, but for loving my characters as much – if not more than – I do.

Thank you all. So much.

UPSIDE DOWN

Birds chirped in the tree outside my open bedroom window, and a cool morning breeze wafted in and tickled my feet. At some point in the night, I must have kicked them free from my duvet. One at a time, I opened my eyes, looking around my room groggily. My clothes from the day before were draped over the edge of my hamper, my laptop was half-open on my desk, and my curtains were open wide, allowing the early morning sun to filter in.

My house was eerily quiet, and I lay in bed staring at nothing in particular as I tried to find the energy to roll out of bed. The sun was shining in through my window, and it made me giddy for today's training since I was likely going to be able to ride outside. Suddenly, it occurred to me that it was far too bright to be before six in the morning—which was when my alarm clock was supposed to go off.

Looking to my right, I noticed it was almost seven. I bolted upright and ran over to grab my jeans from yesterday and a fresh shirt. After quickly pulling them on, I ran to the bathroom where I brushed my teeth and pulled my long blond hair up into a haphazard ponytail before heading for the door. I slipped my paddock boots on, quickly lacing them, and then rushed out of the house.

As I ran all the way down my front walkway, I prayed that my father wouldn't be too upset with my tardiness. I threw the front gate open and looked over at my dad's house on the right. No one was home, which meant he was already at the barn.

"Shit!" I cursed breathlessly as I picked up the pace in an effort to make up for lost time. When I reached the large barn, I was gasping for air, and the sound of my boots hitting the pavement between the stalls startled several of the horses that had been tethered there for the morning lessons.

"Madi?" a familiar voice called out.

I looked up and saw Thomas Young, my dad's life-long friend and our lead horse trainer. He pushed his black hair off his dark skin as he walked beside the small chestnut mare and toward me. He was smiling wide, his dark eyes not holding even a glimmer of annoyance toward me, while I tried to regulate my breathing.

"Oh," I wheezed, looking up at him. "Hey, Tom. Have you … seen my dad?" My chest felt tight and hot as I continued to suck in breath after excruciating breath.

"Not since he helped me muck out the stalls," he replied.

I shot Tom an apologetic look. "Damn it. I'm so sorry. I overslept. I should have been here. I'll make it up to you, I promise."

Tom smiled. "Nah, don't even worry about it. It's what I get paid for, right?"

I shrugged and patted him on the shoulder before I went off in search of my father. "I guess. Listen, I need to go find my dad and see just how much trouble I'm in, all right?"

"I wouldn't worry too much," Tom assured me. "He didn't seem too upset."

I narrowed my eyes teasingly. "See, it's that "too upset" that has me nervous."

Tom laughed loudly. "Come on, Madison. You're a

grown woman. How much trouble could he possibly give you?"

He had a point, but I also knew that my dad had a habit of keeping our personal relationship out of our business one. "He's my boss, Tom. A lot." I had just turned to go check the paddocks for my father when an old Harley drove past the barn door. The engine was loud, alarming some of the horses that were grazing nearby. The driver wore a helmet and sunglasses, so I couldn't make out his face as he sped around the far corner of the barn, disappearing from sight.

I didn't give much thought to the vehicle as I went off in search of my dad. They probably just got turned around and would be heading back out to the highway soon enough. As I neared the closest paddock to the barn, I could clearly make out my father's shape standing in the center with a large Thoroughbred mare I'd recognize anywhere. Picking up the pace, I made it to the metal fence and slipped between the bars.

"Hey Dad," I greeted nervously as I watched him kneel down next to Halley's right foreleg. His blond hair, a shade darker than my own and sprinkled with gray, shimmered in the sun as he turned and acknowledged me with a nod. His dark brown eyes were warm, and I didn't sense any irritation behind his expression. It was a relief.

"Hey kiddo," he replied as he ran his hand down the length of Halley's shin. "Swelling's gone down. The vet says she might be ready for some light training."

"Really?" I couldn't believe it. About two months ago, Halley and I had been working on going over some higher rails in preparation of the upcoming show season, and she had landed wrong after the jump, pulling the tendons in her leg.

Standing up, he brushed the dust from his jeans and faced me. At a slim five-foot-ten, Wayne Landry wasn't overly intimidating. He was a sweet man who'd made a living helping abused and injured animals. We specialized in mostly horses, but we'd had a few dogs over the years that we'd also nursed back to health.

Dad patted Halley's neck. "Hear that, girl?" he asked her softly, moving around to face her. "You up to it?"

As if understanding what he was saying, Halley nudged her nose into his chest, sending him back a step. With a light laugh, he turned to me and handed me Halley's red lead. "Take it easy on her."

"I will," I promised him excitedly as I rushed forward and ran my hand up the white blaze that adorned Halley's black face before scratching between her ears. She leaned her head into it greedily.

My father turned to walk away, and I started to follow him when he stopped abruptly in his tracks and turned to face me. "And let's be clear, you're not off the hook for being late this morning."

"I know. I'm sorry. I must have forgotten to set my alarm clock," I told him honestly. "It won't happen again." I hoped I was able to assure him that I wasn't going to make a habit of what happened.

Landry's Equine Rescue and Rehabilitation Facility had been a successful business just outside of Savannah, Tennessee for over forty years, when my grandfather started it. Dad had been running the family business for the last two years since my grandfather passed away. He had always helped Grandpa out when he wasn't teaching, but he never really felt that the ranch was his calling. Not until the ranch was left to him in the will. After going over the paperwork with the accountant, Dad realized just how lucrative this place was. It was a lot of work day-in and day-out, but with my offer to help him out, he decided to give it a go ... for his dad.

Ever since I could remember, I loved coming out here on

the weekends and riding. Grandpa had given me my first horse; a thirteen-year-old gelding named Oscar that he'd bought at an auction. When I got a bit older, I would learn that Oscar was to be sent to slaughter because he was older and wasn't a purebred. No one saw any value in him. But I did. Oscar was great, but as I grew over the years and became a more experienced rider, I found that he just didn't challenge me as much as he once did. I told Grandpa that I wanted him to be used as a beginner lesson horse in his final years, because I couldn't bear to see him leave the ranch he'd grown to know as home.

In addition to rescuing unwanted animals, my grandfather also recognized good bloodlines in his horses when he saw them, so he chose to breed them. So, seven years ago, when I turned eighteen, my grandfather let me have first pick of the foals being born that year. It didn't take me as long as I thought it would to find her, either. When I saw her running around after her mother in the paddock, her black coat warmed by the sun, I knew I had to have her. She had a thin blaze that started as a point in the middle of her forehead and got progressively wider as it trailed down at an angle, ending in a huge burst of white over the entire right side of her muzzle. It looked like a comet shooting through the night sky against the color of her coat. I'd always been fascinated with astrology, so when Grandpa asked me what I wanted to name her, I knew immediately that Halley's Comet was most fitting.

He worked with me as often as I was able to make it out, without disrupting my college course load, until she was trained. I finished my four years of college, majoring in Business so I could one-day help run the ranch. It had been my dream for as long as I could remember.

While there was always a time and place in my life for a good old western saddle, I'd always been a fan of English rid-

ing. With that in mind, that was primarily how I started training my new horse. Within her first two years, Halley was
green-broke and fairly trustworthy, but she still needed a lot
of ground work before I could even think of jumping her.

By the time Halley and I had taken our first jump together, my grandfather had fallen ill, and he passed away one
month later. In the two years since his death, I had been
working with Tom, who had been the ranch's head trainer for
the last twenty years, and had once upon a time, competed on
a professional level. He even helped me line up a sponsor a
couple years ago, and I'd toured some of the pro competitions
up until Halley got hurt.

My grandfather's absence wasn't forgotten, though. I
was surrounded with his legacy. Hell, I lived in his three-
bedroom house on the grounds while my father lived in the
smaller guest cottage next door. Dad said he had no use for
the main house and that I should have it. He said Grandpa
would have wanted it that way. I had always been close with
my grandparents, but working with him and Halley several
times a week definitely brought us even closer. His death
wasn't just devastating to my father, but to me as well.

I walked with a hop in my step a few paces behind my
dad with Halley at my side, her limp completely gone. As I
went to lead her into the barn, I noticed my father lift an arm
and wave to a man standing next to the Harley I had seen
earlier. I had to wonder how Dad knew him and why he was
here. Even from far away, I couldn't help but admire the
stranger. The way the sunlight made his brown hair glimmer
in the sun, the strong angles to his jaw, not to mention his tall,
muscular build ...

*Get a grip, Madison! He's probably just stopping for direc-
tions. Not to mention, you've sworn off men, remember? Dane only
just moved out a few weeks ago ...*

"You mean since I kicked him out," I corrected myself

out loud as I continued on my way into the barn to tether Halley. When I entered the locker room to grab my brushes and tack, I found Tom coming out of the viewing gallery on the other side.

"Hey, Madison. Did you find your dad?" he asked as he approached me to help me hoist my saddle out of the top locker.

I stepped back, tucking my blond hair behind my ear, and allowed him to carry it for me. "Oh, yeah. Everything is good. He said I could ride Halley today."

He smirked. "Explains the gear." We walked together until we reached Halley, and Tom set the saddle on the blanket rack outside her stall door. "Can I do anything else for you? Your dad said I should ask before I head to the feed store to pick up more grain."

"Uh," I said, dragging the word out as I thought of anything else that needed to be done. "Nope. Go ahead. I'll take care of anything that comes up."

"Cool. I'm going to take the truck, if that's all right?"

I nodded as I grabbed my curry comb to begin grooming Halley. "That's what it's there for. Though, it's been acting up, so just watch out for it, okay?"

"Has it?" Tom asked, sounding a little stunned. He was the one who kept the old thing running, and he was a pretty decent mechanic. "I'll take a look at it when I get back."

Tom left us then, and I stood with Halley in the empty barn. "Good ol' Tom, hey, Hails?" I cooed to her as I ran the rubber comb over her body in circular motions. Her skin flicked beneath the comb, and she shook her head, rattling the halter.

Once I had finished with the first comb, I reached down into my tattered box for the hard-bristled brush and began flicking away the dust I had stirred up with the first. Halley's posture relaxed and she rested her left hind leg as I continued to work. Grooming Halley was something I did every day. It was something that both of us truly enjoyed. I brought out the last brush. It was full of super-soft bristles and really made her shine. When I finished with her body, I moved to her face and laughed softly when I saw her eyes looking rather sleepy. She perked right up when I dropped the brush in the box and reached for her saddle pad.

Halley's eyes widened as I walked back to her left side and slid the pad into place; she seemed to be just as excited about our long-overdue ride as I was. I then grabbed the sleek, black leather saddle and placed it on her back, dropping the girth over to her right side so I could grab it beneath her and fasten it.

Once it was on tight enough, I put a set of therapeutic boots on her. We'd bought them for her after the accident in hopes they'd help with her recovery. They were supposed to absorb some of the pressure and keep her from injuring herself any further. The vet highly recommended them if we ever wanted to use her as anything more than a broodmare in the future. When I reached for her bridle, I found myself growing more excited; it had been two long months since I had ridden her. I had been helping Tom train the other horses we had, but it just wasn't the same. They weren't mine ... well, I guess *technically* they were. It was just different.

With the bridle on, I untethered Halley and took her to our outdoor arena. Chances were, Jillian was teaching a morning class inside anyway, and I wanted to take advantage of the gorgeous weather.

Once inside the arena, I closed the gate and mounted her. I sank into the supple leather saddle, and with a sigh, I was home. We walked around the arena for fifteen minutes to warm her up, and I counted the perfectly spaced beats of her gait. *One. Two. Three. Four.* She wasn't favoring her leg, so I decided we would pick up into a trot. *One. Two. One. Two.* I rose on every other beat, and Halley flipped her head slightly and snorted with delight. When I felt she was ready, I nudged her forward into a steady lope.

As we cantered around the arena, I kept my seat in the saddle, keeping her going by pushing forward. When we hit the corner, I turned her so we could change direction. Her flying lead-change was seamless and she instantly flipped to the opposite lead. We moved smoothly around the low cross-rail that had been set up for last night's beginner jumper class and continued on.

We made a few more laps around the arena, and as we approached the entry, I saw a man with a head of unruly brown hair watching us. I instantly recognized him as the man who had met with Dad a little while ago.

He leaned over the top rail of the fence, his posture relaxed and his right leg bent so his foot could rest on the bottom rung. He was wearing a pair of jeans and a white T-shirt that showed off his muscular physique. His right arm was tattooed starting at his wrist and disappearing beneath the sleeve of his shirt. I found it extremely sexy — which surprised me since I wasn't really a fan of tattoos — and I kind of wanted to see more of it.

As Halley and I drew nearer, I took in the deep blue color of his eyes and the way they sparkled like sapphires in the sun. I was instantly mesmerized. Halley continued to lope around the arena, and when I caught the stranger's gaze again I got lost in his eyes once more. There was something in the way he was watching me that made me smile, and he returned that smile with one that caused an unexpected flurry of butterflies to erupt in my belly. Completely distracted by his smirk, I hadn't even realized that Halley was headed for the small cross-rail just off the trail until we were nearly upon it.

Instinctively, I leaned forward in preparation for her to

take the jump, but as I did, Halley stopped … and I kept on going. The ground came up to meet me far too fast, and all I felt was pressure in my head as I landed hard on my back.

THROWN

After a few seconds, I opened my eyes and started to sit up. My entire body ached as I struggled to inhale deeply, and my head was spinning so fast, my vision blurred.

"Holy shit! Are you okay?" a deep voice called out to me. At first it sounded kind of hazy—like a dream. Everything soon became clear when I heard the disruption of the arena dirt and sensed a body next to me.

"Uh ... yeah," I groaned as I started to push myself up. The stranger slipped his left arm around me while I gripped his right hand with mine, and he helped me stand. I teetered slightly on wobbly legs, but his hand firmly gripped my waist as I struggled to keep my balance. As soon as I was on my feet, I looked around frantically for Halley, only to find her standing on the other side of the low fence looking at me like she was confused about what happened.

"Madison!" Dad's panicked voice rang through the yard, and I looked up just in time to see him hop the fence with more ease than a fifty-three-year-old man should be capable of. "Kiddo, are you okay?"

With my body still in such close proximity to the stranger—*the beautiful, beautiful stranger*—I suddenly felt embarrassed. I pulled free of Mr. Blue-Eyes, pushing the stray hairs that had fallen from my ponytail off of my forehead and looked between my dad and the man who was looking at me like I was going to collapse any minute.

"Yeah. I'm fine," I assured them both.

Dad breathed a sigh of relief before narrowing his eyes at me, and I shied away from his glare. I'd seen it before. I knew what was coming next. "What the hell were you thinking, Madison? I told you *light* training with Halley. She's not ready for jumps! Are you trying to put her back out of commission?" he shouted.

"What? No, of course not! It … it was an accident," I argued softly, not really relishing the fact that I was having my ass chewed out in front of a complete stranger.

"Wayne, I saw the whole thing," Blue-Eyes said. "It looked as though the mare had just gone off track a bit. I don't think … Madison —"

"Madi," I interjected out of habit, preferring my nickname.

"My apologies. I don't think Madi intended for this to happen." He looked down at me with concern again. "Why weren't you wearing the proper gear?"

Any gratitude I felt toward this man instantly fizzled as a frosty barrier slammed down in its place. He was just like any other man I'd ever known — a know-it-all who thinks they can tell me what to do.

Needless to say, I reacted angrily upon hearing his words. "Excuse me? And just who the hell are you?"

My dad shook his head before gesturing toward the brown-haired Adonis — *the jerky, brown-haired Adonis* — that was reprimanding me. Granted, I should have been wearing a helmet, but it wasn't as though I had anticipated taking a jump … by myself. "I'm sorry. Madi, this is Jensen. Our new ranch hand. I just hired him this morning."

I could feel my annoyance flare at my father for not consulting me on this. Yes, he was the boss, but this was also a partnership. Since when did he not run this sort of thing by me? I narrowed my eyes at this *Jensen*. "Can you ride?" I inquired snidely, eyeing him up and down, being careful to take note of his designer jeans. The tattoos didn't exactly seem like something a ranch hand would spend their money on. Clearly he wasn't farm material.

"Since I could walk, actually," he replied confidently, crossing his arms across his chest in challenge. "My dad's a vet, your vet, actually. He and my mother used to live in the country, and we've always been around horses. It was important I learn. In fact ..." He let his words hang for a moment while a cocky smirk graced his stupid, delicious-looking lips. "Maybe I could teach you a few things."

My mouth fell open in shock, and just as I was about to say something extremely unladylike, Dad laughed and clapped Jensen on the back. "Son, Madi's been riding since she was a toddler. In fact, this is the first time I've seen her fall off her mount in years," he said through his hysterics.

My rage suddenly spiked, and I crossed my arms defensively. "We don't need a ranch hand," I said pointedly. Mostly to my father, but also to Mr. Conceited. "We have Tom."

"Madison, we're getting busier, and Tom is already responsible for so much. We need someone else," Dad tried reasoning.

"We have me." I was mildly insulted.

My dad stepped into my line of sight as I continued to glare at this jerk that was coming onto *my* ranch and acting like he was King Shit of Turd Island. "Madison, you know how busy we get this time of year. People bringing their horses to be boarded for the winter? All the new rescues? What do you think we spent the entire spring and summer building the new barn for?"

I clenched my teeth and rolled my eyes as I exhaled an

exasperated breath through my nose. "You're right," I told my father quietly. "Fine. He can stay. But he's on probation." After making my point, I turned on my heel and grabbed Halley's reins before leading her for the exit.

"I'm hitting the trails. I'll be back in a half hour."

"Um, Madi?" Jensen called after me. "Don't forget a helmet this time, okay?"

I held back a rage-fueled scream as I led Halley to the barn so I could grab my helmet. As infuriating as his belittling was, he was right; it probably wouldn't have been good if I fell off and was knocked unconscious in the middle of nowhere — and let's face it, if it were to happen to anyone, it'd be me.

Once my helmet was secure on my head, I mounted Halley and we headed for our favorite trail. My body was a little stiff from my fall, but I knew a nice soak in my tub tonight would help loosen all the tension.

Halley and I walked down a trail beneath a canopy of branches with autumn-colored leaves, letting the early morning breeze waft over us. It was always refreshing to go on a trail ride, and while I went on them often, this was my first time in months with Halley.

Being in the fresh air with my horse calmed me down. It allowed me to think back to my accident and realize that maybe I had reacted immaturely. I was sure Jensen hadn't meant anything by his comments; he seemed genuinely concerned. Sure, his tone implied a holier-than-thou attitude, but then again, so had mine. Perhaps I'd been a bit too quick to judge.

It didn't seem like we had gone very far before I had to head back. Halley was starting to favor her foreleg, so I had to get her brushed down and rub some cooling gel onto the area before turning her out for a bit. When we returned to the barn, I took Halley's bridle off and refastened her halter before removing her saddle and taking everything to put it away.

After washing off the bit, I headed into the locker room, stopping dead in my tracks when I saw Jensen standing with his back to me. Then, I saw a slender hand appear on his arm, running up and down its length. A familiar giggle sounded in the small room, and I chuckled softly. I should have known that Jillian would take notice of the fresh meat.

Jillian Walker was our twenty-four year old instructor. During the winter months, we kept her on staff in the evenings and on weekends, but during the summer, she upped her lesson load substantially since most of her students were out of school. It was no secret that she liked to have a good time; she was always telling stories about her many suitors, and she told them without the slightest hint of regret to her tone.

Twirling a lock of her chestnut-colored hair around her finger, she smiled up at Jensen with her perfect teeth. She was a very beautiful girl with her big doe eyes, shiny long hair, and athletic body.

Jensen quickly snapped his head around, looking flustered because I had clearly just caught them flirting. "No need to worry. We don't care if you feel the need to fraternize. Just keep it professional when on the job, and should it not work out ... well, don't let it affect your work." I tried to keep the experience on the subject from my voice, but I wondered if a little of it had maybe slipped out. If so, I chose to ignore it.

Without a word to me, Jill turned and headed toward the viewing gallery with a little extra bounce in her step. She opened the door to the indoor arena and disappeared from sight.

Rolling my eyes, I pushed past Jensen as he stood there, stunned, and stopped in the far corner where my locker was.

Lifting the saddle over my head, I tried to slide it onto its mount, but unfortunately, at five-foot-five I was too short, and the stepladder had gone missing a few weeks ago. I grunted and stood on my tip-toes, but I was still unsuccessful. Suddenly, two warm hands brushed mine, and I could feel the heat of a body directly behind me as I gripped the pommel of the saddle and tried not to pass out from the bizarre fog that instantly filled my head.

I was acting like a swoony little schoolgirl at the scent of his cologne, and it should have bothered me.

"Allow me," Jensen crooned, the warmth of his breath dancing across the exposed skin of my neck. My skin prickled all over my body. Apparently my brain hadn't passed the memo along to the rest of me yet that I had sworn off men, because I was instantly overcome with the need to do very, *very* bad things to him. A lot.

Once the saddle was secure on its rack, I quickly ducked out from under his arm. "Uh, thanks. I should, um … get back to Hails," I stammered as I backed out of the locker room, leaving Jensen there staring at what I could only assume was a cloud of dust shaped like my retreating form.

When I reached my mare's side, I rested my forehead on her neck and took several deep breaths to calm my nerves. I couldn't understand it, but when his hands touched mine, a tiny current of electricity had passed through us. I could only wonder if he felt it, too.

"Halley, huh?" Jensen said from behind me, shocking me once more.

I turned around abruptly, causing Halley to throw her head up in fright. "Wh-what?" I stammered.

Jensen stepped closer to me, his deep blue eyes locked on mine. His eyelashes were thick and dark, accentuating the color of his eyes. I was sure women were envious of them. I kind of was.

When he lifted his arm, I watched nervously as it got closer to me, and then passed me to run over Halley's face. Now that it was right in front of me, I was able to see the tattoos on his arm a little better. The colors were vibrant and the designs exquisite in the way they all tied together to tell a story I was suddenly curious to learn more about.

Halley exhaled heavily through her nostrils, and I turned to look at her. Her eyes lulled shut as he stroked the white streak and chuckled. She trusted him within seconds, and I knew she was generally a pretty good judge of character ...

If only he hadn't been such a jerk earlier.

"Like the comet. Clever."

"I tend to be, yes," I quipped, turning away from him so I could groom Halley and go about my day.

"So, is there anything I should know before I officially start tomorrow?" he asked, still petting Halley's face as her breathing deepened.

I laughed. The sound echoed through the barn, startling the barn cats that were sleeping peacefully in a vacant stall. "No, I think you pretty much know everything, now don't you?"

"Touché," he replied with a chuckle. "Well, I'm just going to walk the grounds and learn where everything is at so I can properly navigate with little to no instructions needed." Jensen headed for the doorway before turning back. "I look forward to working with you, Madi."

My knees threatened to buckle as the low vibrato of his voice moved through me. Instead of answering, because I couldn't trust my own voice to remain steady, I raised my hand without turning to him and waved it dismissively so I could finish up Halley's grooming. Once she was cleaned up, I knelt down next to her and rubbed her ointment on her leg before wrapping it with bandages and putting her in her paddock.

Once she was happy and feeding, I headed to the viewing gallery to check on Jill's lesson. Everything seemed to be running smoothly as four girls ranging from ages six to ten, rode around the arena at a steady trot, coming down the middle over the trotting poles that Jill had spaced out. It made me nostalgic for when I used to teach before I decided I wanted to compete and help my dad rescue and rehabilitate. After waving at Jillian, I headed outside just as Tom pulled into the yard. He was backing the truck up so he could unload the feed, and when he stepped out of the truck, Jensen came jogging over with a smile on his face.

"Hey, there. You must be Tom. I'm Jensen, the new ranch hand."

While the two of them got acquainted, I decided to help Jill out. "Um, I'm going to go grab the next round of lesson horses for Jill, and then get Starla ready for today's session," I explained. "Meet you in the outdoor arena in about an hour, Tom?" Tom nodded once before opening the tailgate and slinging a bag of feed over his shoulder, and I walked in the opposite direction.

I checked the schedule and grabbed the two horses that Jill would need for her lesson. On my way to the barn, I found my dad in the outdoor ring, setting up a small course for my session.

"Madi," Dad greeted as he set the final oxer in place. "I figured since you were so gung-ho to jump, maybe you and Starla would like to try a course."

Annoyed, I glared at him as I slipped between the fence rails. "Dad, I told you it was an accident. I feel bad enough."

He laughed and wrapped an arm around my shoulder, tucking me into his side. "Aw, Madi, I'm only teasing."

I heard the crunch of gravel heading our way and saw Tom making his way toward the arena. "Why don't you go and get Starla ready and we can get started a little early."

Confused, my eyebrows pulled together.

Tom smiled. "That new ranch hand of yours has quite the initiative. He was quick to offer to put the feed away."

Hearing this made me reevaluate Jensen's earlier attitude again. Perhaps I'd been a little too defensive given how my last relationship ended. I was even more certain now that he probably hadn't meant to sound as judgmental as he did. Maybe I should have given him the benefit of the doubt. After all, he wasn't Dane Hall. Just because my ex was a complete and utter waste of space didn't mean that all men were. Jensen seemed genuinely concerned when I fell off Halley, and he'd been nothing but helpful when I got back from my ride.

I owed him a huge apology, and I planned to make it up to him the next time I saw him.

Hoping to find him in the barn, I headed there. I didn't see him on my way to grab Starla's halter and lead, and I didn't see him on my way out to her paddock. My apology would have to wait unless he found me while I was tacking her up.

He didn't.

As soon as she was ready, I grabbed my helmet and led Starla to the arena.

"Glad to see you remembered a helmet, Madi," Tom teased as I hopped into the saddle.

"Har har," I dead-panned as I started Starla's warm-up.

During the entire session, Starla was a dream. She was still young, and this was her first time completing a course, but her gaits were smooth, her transitions seamless, and her warm-up jumps perfect. She refused a couple of the oxers the first few times, but she eventually grew comfortable with them, and after a couple of awkward deer-hops over them, she sailed like a pro.

Tom instructed me on my course order, and Starla took

the first three low rails like a champ. However, when we rounded the corner and headed to the low brush fence, I caught a glimpse of Jensen carrying a bale of hay right past the arena fence. I didn't miss the way his muscles tensed beneath the weight of the bale, and I may have even sighed, or moaned, or something equally as wistful. Whatever the sound was, it could only mean trouble.

Apparently, Jensen had this pull over me because before I knew it Starla veered right, and I went left, landing on my left side with a solid thud.

I looked up, silently cursing my luck today, and saw Jensen drop the bale he was carrying and hop the fence, beating Tom by a few paces. "Damn, Madi. Today's just not your day, huh?" He reached out to help me up, but I denied his help, slapping his hand away, and pushed myself to my feet. My pride was hurt, and I was trying to rebuild it by denying anyone's help.

"Apparently," I practically sneered.

"Are you all right, Madi?" Tom asked as he held my face and checked my eyes.

I nodded, pushing his hands away. "Yeah. I'm fine."

Tom checked his watch and then looked over at Starla who had stopped near the abandoned bale of hay and stretched her head through the fence to feed on it. "What do you say we call it? I think Starla's had enough. Go comb her down, we'll have lunch and prep for our afternoon session with Ransom."

"Okay, but if I fall off again, I quit," I half-joked through clenched teeth as I sucked in a painful breath. I brushed the dirt off my jeans and headed over to where Starla was currently stuffing her face. As I grabbed the reins and coaxed Starla's head away from the hay, it didn't escape my notice that Jensen was right behind me. He opened the gate for me, and I nodded my thanks.

"Um, don't forget to take the rest of that bale into the barn," I instructed, not even taking a beat to look at him. I didn't mean for it to sound rude, but I was embarrassed about falling in front of him twice in one day. I must have looked like an amateur, and not someone who'd been riding for her entire life. My apology could wait until I'd had a chance to stitch my pride back together.

"Yes, ma'am."

After tethering Starla, I removed her saddle and set it aside. I brushed her down and gave her a small bucket of grain before turning her out to her usual paddock. I cleaned up my mess in the barn and put the saddle away before heading to my dad's place for lunch.

Having lunch with Dad, Tom, and Jill gave us a chance to discuss what was going on with the ranch and map out the rest of our day. We were all so busy at any given hour that this one hour was crucial to running our business.

The entire way over to Dad's, I thought about Jensen. Horrible thoughts. Then remorse and regret set in. Soon, everything quickly turned into confusing and dirty thoughts when I remembered the strain of his biceps as he carried that bale of hay earlier and the warmth of his hands over mine.

I tried to shake it off when warmth spread beneath my skin, a dull tingle working its way down my body. It was probably a good thing I had an hour to regroup before I had to see him again.

"Dad? I'm here!" I announced as I untied my boots and left them next to everyone else's.

"In the kitchen, sweetheart," he replied.

As I made my way down the narrow hall, I could smell something being cooked. This confused me because I always prepared lunch. When I turned the corner, I stopped as soon as I spotted Jensen standing over the stove.

So much for that hour …

3

BEEN THERE, DONE THAT

"Have a seat, Madi. Jensen's offered to make us lunch to-day," Dad said, kicking my usual chair out for me.

I sat down, my eyes never leaving Jensen as he stood at the stove and did my job. It was hard to not feel the resentment that slowly started bubbling inside me again. He'd been here all of one day and had already inserted himself into our lives. Sure, he seemed nice enough—most of the time—but I felt like I was being replaced. Was that a ridiculous thought? Absolutely, but I wasn't exactly known for maintaining rational thought every second of every day.

I liked to think it was just part of my charm.

When Jensen turned to offer me a smile, I returned it awkwardly. He was throwing off the balance of my perfect little world. It was the only explanation for how discombobulated I was all of a sudden.

As I burned holes in the back of his head—while also briefly checking out his ass—I was only vaguely aware of the conversation going on around me. It wasn't until Dad asked me if I was all right after my recent mishap with Starla that I tore my eyes away from the mess of brown hair and focused.

"Yeah, I'm fine. I don't know, I think I just lost focus is all. She spooked, and I didn't see it coming until it was too late," I explained, shifting my gaze from the subject of my irritation-slash-attraction to my father.

I stood up and headed for the sink so I could wash my hands before lunch. As I stood there, letting the water run over my hands, I looked over at Jensen and watched him grill the sandwiches he had made. He lifted his eyes to mine, and I immediately grew flustered and looked back down at my hands.

By the time I had taken my seat again, Jensen had placed the sandwiches on the table and sat in the chair right next to mine. His denim-clad knee brushed mine, and my breath hitched slightly. If men weren't such assholes, I might have found him remotely attractive. Oh, who was I kidding? I definitely found him attractive, even if he was an asshole. Besides, just because Dane turned out to be Mr. Wrong, doesn't mean all men are dicks.

The room was silent as we all began to eat, and I had to admit, Jensen was a halfway decent cook. Sure, it was just a grilled cheese sandwich, and anyone could likely make it, but I had to commend him for it. As I ate, Dad and Tom began to talk about their upcoming fishing trip, with Jill chiming in every once in awhile.

"How is it?" Jensen asked, turning his head slightly to face me.

Still not wanting to feed his obvious ego, I shrugged. "It's all right," I said flippantly.

He chuckled and picked up his empty plate to put it in the dishwasher. "Yeah, that's why you haven't spoken two words since starting lunch."

"Yes, and my lack of talking had nothing to do with my unwillingness to discuss fishing." I turned back to the table and stood up, smiling. "I'm going to go get Ransom ready and warmed up. I'll meet you in the arena in a half hour, Tom?" I tossed the remainder of my lunch, leaving my plate in the sink.

"Sure thing, Madison. Hey, why don't you take Jensen with you? Show him the ropes," he suggested.

I forced a smile on my face and looked at Jensen. "It would be my pleasure," I ground out.

The both of us put our boots back on before I led him to the barn to grab Ransom's lead. On our way to Ransom's paddock, I stopped to check on Halley.

"What happened to her?" Jensen asked quietly as I knelt down to feel her leg.

I turned my head toward him and cocked an eyebrow. "What? You mean you don't actually know everything?" Jensen seemed taken aback, and I instantly regretted my tone. He crossed his arms across his chest, leaning on the fence as he waited for my response. "We were working on her jumping, she landed funny and tore the ligaments in her leg. The vet doesn't seem to think she'll ever be the same again, but I think she will be. She's already been through so much."

"I'm impressed." His tone indicated that his sincerity was true, and I thought I was finally catching a glimpse of Jensen's other side. Until he continued. "Based on your inability to remain in the saddle today, I didn't peg you as a pro."

Even though he was probably just teasing me, I was offended. I stood quickly and forced my way past him. "Screw you," I sniped.

Jensen closed the gate behind me and followed as I gave him the rundown of the barn's operations. As usual, he was cocky and overly-confident, telling me that we operated as he would have expected.

Never had I wanted to kick a man in the balls as much as I did him. And yet, I still found myself oddly attracted to him. *Well,* I pondered silently as I took in his striking features again. *Maybe not* oddly ...

I started to wonder if I was PMSing. My hormones were all over the place. Or perhaps I was just a little jaded because of how the last man in my life treated me.

Jensen walked with me out to Ransom's shared paddock and then came with me to catch the young stallion. Ransom's dark brown coat gleamed in the afternoon sun, and as soon as he caught sight of me with the lead, he took off running.

"Damn it," I cursed under my breath, and just as I started forward, Jensen grasped my arm, causing fireworks to shoot through my veins again, and held out his other hand.

"May I?" he inquired smoothly.

I laughed at his assuming he would be able to catch Ransom any better than Tom or me and held the lead out to him. "Be my guest, but he's not going to be easy."

Jensen gave me a wink, and my heart fluttered. My body was reacting the exact opposite to how my mind figured it should be acting to this arrogant newcomer, and it upset me. He took the blue lead from me and held it behind his back as he clucked and walked slowly toward the bay stallion. Ransom whinnied and then took off at a full gallop. I couldn't help but laugh as I perched myself on top of the fence so I could watch Jensen try again.

He turned his head to me and smirked again before running his fingers through his messy, sex-hair. He looked back at Ransom and started making the same clucking noise as before, and this time only took two steps before stopping in the middle of the paddock. Confusion swept over me as I wondered what he was doing. How on Earth did he expect to catch a horse from there?

My eyes widened as I watched Ransom calm down and stare at the strange man standing before him. He tilted his head to the side and perked his ears forward as he took several curious steps toward Jensen. I stared in awe as Ransom dropped his head into the halter that Jensen held and allowed a stranger to lead him toward me.

"What? How?" I couldn't wrap my head around it.

Jensen smiled and held his free hand out to me to help me down. I didn't take it and jumped to the ground, stumbling in the process and forcing Jensen to rescue me, anyway. It would appear that I was entirely too clumsy today. Okay, every day.

"Now, if you'd have accepted my help in the first place, that wouldn't have happened," Jensen teased as he released his firm hold around my waist.

It was comments like that, that made me crazy. While I could admit I was definitely a little touchy, his snarky comments weren't helping his case. I shot a bitchy smirk at him and snatched Ransom's lead as I failed to come up with a decent comeback.

As I tacked Ransom up for his training, Jensen and Tom's son, Jeff, took the ATVs out to the far pasture to check on the horses out there before going to the new barn to check on the last few things to be done. Every once in awhile, I'd catch a glimpse of Jensen as he walked through the yard, wiping sweat from his brow with the back of his arm. The white shirt he wore was smudged with dirt, and as if that wasn't enough to send my libido into overdrive, his tanned muscles glistened with sweat as the hot sun beat down on him while he worked.

"Madison! Pay attention to Ransom!" Tom shouted, and I shook my head to get it back in the game.

"Sorry!" I apologized as I looked down to see that Ransom was leading with the wrong leg, causing him to stumble when he rounded the corner. I was able to right myself for the first time that day and remained seated, and I quickly told Ransom with my legs that he needed to switch leads. He did so perfectly, and Tom and I worked on more of his groundwork for another half hour before he said Ransom had done enough for today.

After brushing Ransom down, I put him out in his pad-dock before going about my evening chores. I was just help-ing little Mallory Edwards tack up her pony when my dad found me and pulled me aside.

"Madi, I've noticed you watching Jensen today," he started.

I swallowed thickly, heat blazing like hellfire beneath my cheeks. "Y-you have?" I stammered.

Dad nodded once. "How do you think he's doing?"

Relief poured out of me as I realized he had seen me *watching* him ... not *ogling* him. "Oh, well aside from being on the overly-cocky side, he's been doing an all right job."

Dad beamed. "Good! I think he'll be a good addition to our team." I laughed and shook my head at his enthusiasm. "Um, how would you feel if I asked him to stay on the prem-ises? He just moved into the area and was actually staying with his sister until he found a job and an apartment. I fig-ured this might just be easier than the commute."

It made sense, I suppose. I clapped Dad on the shoulder and smiled. "Whatever you say, boss."

"I'm glad you're on board with this, Madison. Why don't you call it a day? I'll finish up with the guys," Dad offered, and even though I had gotten a late start, I couldn't help but love the idea of taking a really hot bath and resting my bruis-ing backside.

"Thanks, Dad. I'll be here first thing in the morning," I promised, stepping up on my toes to kiss his cheek. "Call if you need me, though. Okay?"

"Will do, kiddo. Go, rest. I have a feeling you'll be hur-tin' tomorrow." As I walked away, I heard him laugh, and I could only shake my head.

When I stepped through my door, I made sure to turn the deadbolt before I checked my messages. I went into the kitchen and hit the button on my ancient answering machine and listened as a familiar male voice sounded through my house.

"Hey, babe. It's Dane calling. Again. I don't know why you won't return my calls. I said I was sorry. Please, call me back. I want to talk to you. We can work this ou — "

Because that shit wasn't going to happen in a million years — or longer if I could help it — I deleted the message before it was even finished and headed toward my bathroom. After turning the tap on, I sat on the edge of the over-sized antique claw-foot tub that my grandparents had specially ordered when they built the place and poured in my Epsom salts and some coconut scented bubble bath before I started stripping my jeans and T-shirt off. When I lifted my shirt over my head, I felt all the muscles in my left side tug and pull painfully. It even felt like it might have been deeper than just my muscles.

I stood to survey the damage, and one look in the mirror told me that tomorrow would not be a good riding day for me. The entire left side of my ass and ribs were already bruising. It started dark in the center and lightened as it spread across my body. By tomorrow, it would be completely black and blue. With a sigh, I released my hair of its messy ponytail and slid down into the tub.

I turned off the tap before settling back onto the rounded edge of the tub and closing my eyes. The salts effervesced in the water, making my skin tingle slightly. The heat of the water caused my skin to redden, and the bubbles ... well, they just smelled good. They really served no other purpose.

Every time the water would begin to cool, I'd lift the plug, allowing a little to escape and turn the hot water tap on with my foot. I did this several times in the hour I remained in my warm, steamy bathroom, and finally decided it was time to wash my hair and get out once my fingers and toes started to prune.

After drying off my body, I padded to my bedroom naked, using my towel to dry my hair. I rifled through my dresser and found a pair of simple black shorts and a dark purple fitted tank. I pulled them on, and then grabbed my overflowing hamper and hauled it to my laundry room down the hall. With my laundry started, I went to the kitchen in search of something to make myself for dinner.

I found some tomato, lettuce, cheese and bread, so I pulled it all out and made myself a sandwich before heading to the living room to eat. I had just settled into my leather sofa when there was a loud knock at the door. Placing my uneaten sandwich on my glass coffee table, I stood to go and find out who it was.

As I got closer to the door, I feared it might be Dane, coming back to beg forgiveness. I mentally prepared myself, because he had this nasty habit of making me believe he didn't mean to hurt me. My habit of taking him back was even nastier, and I was trying to change my ways. What I wasn't expecting when I opened the door was to see Jensen standing there. And I most certainly wasn't expecting to see him holding bags with what I assumed contained his clothing.

"Hey, roomie," he said with a crooked smile.

4
MAYBE I WAS WRONG

"Excuse me?" I demanded. What the hell was he talking about? He couldn't possibly think—

"What the hell are you talking about?" I asked, cutting my own thoughts off as my brain tried (read: *hoped*) to interpret his words to mean something else entirely.

"Well, I'm just getting back on my feet after ..." He paused, looking uncomfortable with the idea of sharing too much. "I had a string of bad luck recently, and your dad has been gracious enough to give me this job, and said I could stay on the ranch. For convenience," he replied. Nope. His words held no hidden meaning, and meant exactly what I feared they did.

His eyes were mesmerizing, and I wanted to get lost in them. What was it about him that made my knees weak and my heartbeat quicken? He seemed so confident—too confident, actually.

Jerky. Yeah, that's right. Now I remember ...

Giving my head a quick shake in order to clear it, I cocked an eyebrow and crossed my arms beneath my breasts. "Yeah, and?"

His eyes shifted down momentarily before he cleared his throat and raised them back to mine. *Interesting,* I thought, smirking slightly.

"He said since his place is just a one bedroom, that I could stay here. He said you had plenty of room," Jensen continued. "He didn't tell you?"

My eyes widened and my lips formed a hard line as I inhaled slowly. I threw on my work boots, not even bothering to lace them up in my haste to find out just what the hell was going on. As I raced through the yard with Jensen hot on my trail, I stumbled on a small divot in the road and fell. Pain shot up my side and through my bruised ribcage as I landed, and the gravel tore up the skin on my knees.

"What the hell is wrong with my feet?" I shouted as I turned over, brushing the debris from my flesh and inspecting the scrapes.

Jensen laughed as he knelt before me and laced up my worn-out boots. "Maybe if you'd have taken the time to properly lace your boots, this wouldn't have happened." Our eyes locked as he finished lacing the second one, and his hand moved up, grazing my calf in the process. I inhaled sharply, my heart pounding wildly in my chest. I was momentarily stunned into silence, and it wasn't until he broke eye contact with me and spoke again that I found my voice.

"Although, I seriously doubt that."

"Oh, great. Another safety lecture from the help. Fantastic," I sniped as I pushed myself to my feet.

Standing right with me, Jensen eyed me carefully. "Madi, I'm only teasing. Why are you fighting this?"

It was unclear exactly what he meant … or maybe it was unclear what I was fighting. All I knew was, me shacking up with some guy — a guy who was drop-dead gorgeous to the millionth degree, who oozed charm and charisma and sexuality — was a bad idea. A very, very bad idea. Especially since we worked together. I had both been there and fucking done that. I refused to do it again.

Jensen took a step forward, his eyes burning into mine, causing the flurry of butterflies that still hadn't left my insides to flutter faster. He was waiting for an answer, but for some reason my brain couldn't remember what the question was.

Think, brain, think! Oh! Fighting! "Because—"

I was about to explain that he didn't belong here with his cocky attitude and know-it-all behavior, not wanting him to think I didn't want him here because all I seemed to be capable of doing when he was around—besides fall off my horse—was ogle his body and imagine doing things I was positive defied the laws of physics. It wasn't a lie. He *was* cocky. And a know-it-all, actually. But, just as I was about to speak, Dad interrupted me. "Madi, what the hell are you doing out here ... in *that*?"

Looking down at my attire, I remembered that it wasn't much of anything as I hadn't actually intended on going out after my bath. Nervous, I cast my eyes between him and Jensen, whose eyes were now looking up and down my near-naked body; it was the second time in the last fifteen minutes that I had caught him eyeballing me. A breeze picked up, and I pulled my arms tight across my chest to hide the telltale sign that the temperature had dropped a few degrees.

Remembering why I was out here, I glared up at my father. "So, guess who was shocked to find out she had a new roommate?" I said firmly, nodding my head in Jensen's direction—who shook his head, finally removing his eyes from my barely-covered ass. When Dad didn't respond, I got angry. "Me! What the hell is going on?"

Dad grabbed my bicep gently and tugged me away from our audience. "Why are you so upset by this? You agreed when I said he should stay on the ranch."

"You didn't tell me where he'd be staying!"

Dad gave me the dad-look. "Madison, where else on the

ranch would he stay? My place?"

"For one," I fired back.

Dad cocked an eyebrow and grumbled. "I live in a one-bedroom guest cottage. I'm not going to have him sleep on the sofa. You have two extra rooms in your house. I thought you understood that when I discussed it with you."

I dropped my eyes to the ground. "I just don't think it's a good idea after what happened last time." I was too disappointed in my past actions to look him in the eye. I opened my mouth to say more, but Dad nipped it in the bud. "I can understand your apprehensions, Madison. But Jensen, he's ..." Dad paused, looking over my shoulder at Jensen and considering something before making eye contact with me again. "He's a good guy. I've known his parents a long time."

There were so many reasons that my father should have known better than this. Okay, well *one*. Dane. True, it was my own fault for getting involved with him when working relationships rarely worked out. But still! Dad continued to stare me down, and I knew that I was fighting a losing battle. Ultimately, he was right. It did make more sense for Jensen to stay on the ranch, and my house *was* the only place with enough room.

"Fine," I said through gritted teeth. "But do me a favor? Next time you're going to bunk me with someone, don't be so cryptic when asking me if I'm okay with it, all right?"

Dad laughed and rubbed the top of my head, messing up my wet hair even more than it already was. "Whatever you say, kiddo. Now, get inside before you catch a cold. I'll see you in the morning."

"Goodnight, Dad." With my teeth now chattering, I turned back to Jensen, who was smirking at me knowingly. "Come on, I'll show you to your room."

"That would be great," Jensen said sincerely, making me want to believe *that* was the person he was ... but I was sure he would say something in the next three seconds to screw up my perception. His personality kept switching from hot to cold ... or, maybe that's just how I was seeing it.

As soon as we walked through the door, my phone was ringing, so I quickly undid my boots and kicked them off so I could go answer it. When I picked up the handset, I didn't recognize the number. I never answered numbers I didn't recognize just in case it was Dane, but I also didn't want Dane leaving a message that Jensen would overhear over my dinosaur of an answering machine. So, I hit the on button and held the phone up to my ear.

"Hello?" I inquired nervously.

"Hi, is Jensen in, please?" a woman asked in a soft, delicate voice. I think I even detected a bit of a British accent.

Flirting with Jillian, being all mysterious and flashing those bedroom eyes at me ... and he's got *this* woman hanging by his every word. Jensen was a piece of work. I let out a disgusted breath as I turned to find him standing in my kitchen with me.

"Yeah. Hold on." I held the phone out to Jensen with a scowl. "It's for you."

When he took the phone from me, his fingers brushed the back of my hand and sent chills running up and down my spine. It irritated me that every time I was ready to label him a prick, all he had to do was speak in that smooth tone or touch me in some completely innocent way, and I melted like butter before him — after a *day*.

I quickly retreated to the living room where I remembered my sandwich was waiting for me. Flicking on the TV, I sat back and was quickly engrossed in an old episode of *True Blood*. I was barely ten minutes in when I heard Jensen's hushed voice growing louder.

"Yeah. I know. I'll call you tomorrow ... I love you, too."
I took an angry bite of my sandwich, my nose scrunching up

in disgust as he hung up the phone and walked over to set it on the coffee table.

"So, how does your girlfriend feel about you shacking up with a woman you just met?" I asked before taking another bite of my sandwich.

Jensen smiled crookedly. "I don't know. I'll have to jump off that bridge when I come to it," he said with a flirtatious tone in his voice. He must have sensed what I was going to say next, because he spoke first. "That was my mother. I haven't had a girlfriend in a very long time."

"Oh," I responded quietly, my cheeks instantly warming with embarrassment.

"Look, it's been a long day. Would you mind showing me to my room and then the shower?" Jensen requested coldly. Clearly I had insulted him, and it made me feel terrible. Which made no sense at all; he had been nothing but rude and bossy all day. So why did I feel bad?

"Um, yeah. Sure." I stood from the couch and walked toward him as he continued to watch me.

When I reached him, I was forced to brush past him in the narrow doorway to lead the way to his room. We walked down the hall, and I showed him each room as we went.

"This is my room," I said, stepping inside so he could see. It was pretty basic; bed, dresser, desk, closet. The linens were gray, and the walls white. I then showed him the two other rooms in the house, one of which was bigger than the other, and let him take his pick.

"What's this?" Jensen asked.

I turned around in time to see his fingers tracing the huge dent in the drywall between the bedroom and bathroom. I shook my head, unable to look at the cracks for too long before I felt nauseous.

"Nothing," I told him, not wanting to get into it. Pushing the resurfacing memories aside, I forced a smile. "So which room do you want?

He chose the one across from mine, which was the smaller of the three. The master bedroom at the end of the hall, which was my grandparents' room, remained empty for guests. I preferred it that way, because then they had their own private bathroom.

From the doorway, I watched as he set his bags on the bed and opened them up before removing several articles of clothing. He must not have realized I was still standing there because he lifted his used-to-be-white shirt over his head and stood half naked with his back to me. My eyes raked over the muscles on his upper body as they rippled and flexed with each move he made, and I let out a tiny groan. Jensen turned quickly to see me gawking at him from the doorway of his room.

"See something you like, Madi?" he inquired with a cheeky grin.

"You said you wanted a shower. It's this way," I told him, flustered and a little bitchy because I got caught. I walked down the hall and stood by the open bathroom door, waiting for Jensen to catch up.

He emerged from his room, and I found myself gawking at his near-nakedness again before reminding myself that he was a cocky ass in order to keep my thoughts in check. Jensen stepped into the bathroom and eyed everything before turning to face me. He was close—so very close—and he smelled good. Like cologne, and man, and horses and … *man*. I had to fight the urge to close my eyes and inhale deeply as we stared into each other's eyes.

"Thanks, but I think I've got it from here … unless you were hoping to join me?"

My eyes widened and my mouth dropped open in shock. "Ugh! You're … I can't even … UGH!" My inability to form a coherent sentence seemed to amuse Jensen, and I rushed back to the living room to watch my show.

"What are you watching?"

Startled, I nearly choked on the bite of my sandwich when I looked up to find Jensen in a pair of plaid pants and a fitted, white T-shirt. His hair was dripping wet, and he ran his fingers through it as he walked to me.

"True Blood."

"I don't get it. What's the draw?"

After calming my racing heart from nearly jumping out of my chest, I spoke. "If you're not a fan, please feel free to watch the thirteen inch black and white TV in your room," I offered glibly.

"Well, it's got to be better than … holy shit! Are those tits?" He flopped down next to me and relaxed into the couch.

We sat in an oddly comfortable silence and watched the rest of the show. When it ended, I stood up to take my plate to the kitchen, wincing as I straightened my body against the increasing ache in my left side.

After placing it in the dishwasher, I grabbed a glass of water and took a sip while I walked back to the living room. Jensen had his feet up on the table and was busy flipping through the channels on my flat screen. I set my glass down and stretched with my arms above my head, grimacing as the pain in my back and ribs continued to remind me of my stellar day.

I noticed Jensen's eyes go wide as I relaxed my body. "What?"

His eyes froze on the bare sliver of my abdomen, and I felt every inch of my flesh heat as I blushed. My heart fluttered wildly behind my ribs as he continued to gape at me … for the third time since I answered my door.

"Madi, your body—"

As soon as he spoke, I snapped back to reality. "Holy

crap! Get a hold of yourself! I'm not now, nor will I ever be, looking for you to jump my bones," I said, momentarily forgetting about my injuries and flopping back down on the couch.

Jensen laughed and tossed the remote on the table. "Lean forward and lift your shirt," he instructed smoothly.

Had I not been in my right mind, I'd have felt compelled to do anything he asked me to. Based solely on just how liquid-smooth his voice sounded.

"Ex-excuse me?" I stammered, furrowing my brows.

"Just do it," he commanded with a little smirk while rolling his eyes. When I refused to move, Jensen huffed exasperatedly. "I saw the way you flinched, not to mention the bruising that was visible between your shorts and shirt. Please, let me look?"

I sighed in defeat—and, if I was being completely honest, disappointment—and sat forward on the couch, lifting the back of my thin tank top so he could see what I knew was already there. I felt the couch dip as Jensen scooted over, lifting his left leg so he could slip in behind me. My heart started to beat nervously when I felt him shift closer to me, a heavy pulse working its way between my thighs.

Pulling my bottom lip painfully between my teeth to keep from whimpering as his flannel pajama pant-clad groin pressed flush against my ass—which, remember, wasn't covered by much fabric itself—I closed my eyes tightly. With my hands clenched together in fists as he shifted again, I had to fight with myself to stay still. There was something about him sitting behind me, though, that just felt so damn right. I suppose it could've been that I hadn't had sex in months, and being this close to a good-looking, *available* man reminded me of that fact.

I felt desire roll deep in my belly, swelling and joining the heavy pulse between my legs. *Shit, it's been so long,* I

thought, suddenly enjoying the tender attention of the opposite sex — even if it wasn't *meant* to be sexual.

Jensen sucked in a quick breath, and I wanted to imagine
the look on his face to be the same one I wore as his hands
lightly touched my ribs. His eyes would be hooded with lust
as he fought with himself to rip my sorry excuse for a shirt
from my back and ravage me on the wide leather couch, the
sweat from our bodies would cause us to slide against one
another ...

I moaned as Jensen touched my ribs with a little more
pressure, shying away from his hands. "I'm sorry," he whispered, pulling his hands back quickly. "Does it hurt?"

"A ... a little," I confessed shakily, my head still kind of
foggy from the vivid images I had conjured up moments ago.

Jensen's hands ghosted over my flesh, occasionally grazing it with the very tips of his fingers. "I have to touch. It
might hurt, okay?"

Pulling my bottom lip between my teeth again, I nodded
and waited for the blinding pain. I was pleased when he only
pressed lightly, causing a very minimal sting to shoot
through my chest. However, as soon as he touched my bottom rib, I sucked in a sharp breath. Seeing white, I cried out
and slapped my hand down on his thigh to grip onto something.

"Okay, that's it. Get up, let's go find you some clothes,"
Jensen said, placing his cool hands gently on my hips.

"What? Why?" I stammered. It was a stupid question; I
knew what his answer would be.

Jensen helped me to my feet, keeping his hands on my
waist as he pushed me gently toward my bedroom. "I'm taking you to the hospital."

I shook my head and turned around to move away from
him. "Don't be ridiculous," I said, holding my left arm tightly
to my side to keep the pain at bay. "I'm fine. I'll *be* fine, I just

need to relax and let it heal. I swear."

"It's just a precaution." Jensen paused and looked at me with resolve. "Let's just go and make sure you're okay."

"Like I said, I'm fine. I've fallen off my horse before. This is nothing, I swear." It was sweet how concerned he seemed, but it was misplaced. I knew I would be okay with a little rest. "I'm tired; I think I'm going to turn in. I'll see you in the morning?"

Jensen nodded once, still eyeing me skeptically.

"Feel free to, um, stay up and watch TV," I offered as I continued to back away from him. Something flashed in his eyes, sending shivers through me. I had to wrap my arms around myself to try and harness it.

"Thanks, but I think I'll turn in, too." Jensen's voice was low and gruff, and the sound of it spread through me, causing goose bumps to cover my body.

I turned from him with a nervous smile and walked quickly to my room. "Goodnight," I stammered, closing my door as Jensen stood across the hall in his room smiling.

"Goodnight, Madi."

That night, I had very pleasant dreams of Jensen Davis.

JUST MY LUCK

When I woke the next morning, every muscle in my body ached. I sat up slowly, trying really hard not to cry out as I stretched. The pain wasn't any less, but on the bright side, it wasn't much worse either. That had to be good for something, right?

Upon exiting my room to wash up, I noticed that Jensen's door was closed. Even though I knew it probably bordered on creepy, I placed a hand on the solid wood panel and leaned in, debating whether or not I should knock to see if he was awake. When I heard shuffling, I decided against it and continued toward the bathroom.

Once behind the closed door, I lifted my tank top to view my injuries and cringed when I saw the deep purplish-black marks. They started just under my breast and travelled down my ribcage until they disappeared beneath my shorts. Carefully, I moved the waistband of my shorts and looked down in horror when I realized that the bruise reached my upper thigh and covered half of my ass cheek. I tried to touch them gently, but even the faintest touch caused me to whimper.

As much as it pained me to admit it, Jensen was right. I should have gone to the doctor. Unfortunately there was no time for that today. There was far too much to do around the ranch before Jeff left for school in the fall. Telling myself over and over again that I would be okay, I replaced my shirt and brushed my teeth before exiting the bathroom.

The smell of coffee hit me hard when I stepped into the hall and back to my room to get dressed. Seeing Jensen's open door and his bed made caused those damn butterflies to wake up and flutter wildly in my stomach. It was a feeling I hadn't had in quite some time, and I rolled my eyes at myself because of the promise I made when I threw Dane out.

After I pulled on my jeans and a T-shirt, I made my bed and followed the heavenly smell all the way to the source. From his position in my chair at the table, Jensen's stunning blue eyes rose from yesterday's paper, and he offered me a wide smile. "Good morning, sunshine," he greeted.

"Hey," I responded in a raspy voice as I opened the cupboard to find a mug. "Did you sleep well?"

"Like a rock."

With a laugh, I shook my head, standing on the tips of my toes and reaching for a cup. "I never understood that saying." I had just grabbed my cup when suddenly I felt Jensen's presence next to me. The cup slipped from my grip, and Jensen caught it before it hit the rustic wood countertop and broke.

"Thanks," I breathed, turning to face him. I could feel the blood rush to my cheeks, and I dropped my face, nervously tucking my hair behind my ears.

"I'm sorry. I didn't mean to startle you. It's just, you were reaching, and I saw your bruise. Would you mind … ?"

I nodded as his words trailed off, and I brought my eyes back to his. They were a soft shade of blue with little flecks of gray and green, and they drew me in. His breath was fresh, which led me to believe he had been up before I stopped outside his door to listen in. *Okay, okay: spy.*

Completely lost in his gaze, I slowly backed up until the

small of my back hit the kitchen island. I lifted my shirt so he could see, but his eyes didn't leave mine for the longest time. I wondered what he was thinking. I knew what *I* was thinking, and let's be honest, it wasn't entirely innocent. No, it involved pulling Jensen to me until he had me pinned against the refrigerator. His hands would grasp at my heated flesh as he kissed me with so much passion it left us both breathless. Finally, they would glide down my body; I could practically feel them as they roamed across my neck, over the swells of my breasts, trailed over my stomach and then between my legs ...

Pulling my lip between my teeth, I closed my eyes and tried to calm my unsteady breathing before he realized just how turned on I was ... over nothing. I mentally chastised myself for such lurid thoughts.

I was pulled from any lustful feelings I was having when Jensen's chilled hands touched my ribs, and I recoiled instantly, slamming my right hip into the wooden island counter.

"Madi ..." he whispered, dragging out my name when he spoke, his tone smooth like silk against my skin.

I yanked my shirt down and then avoided the area all together as I turned from him and focused on pouring my coffee. "I know what you're going to say, Jensen. And I'm fine. There's no time for a trip to the doctor right now."

With a sigh of defeat, Jensen backed up toward the table, holding his hands up before him in surrender as he sat back down. "Okay. Okay," he relented. "Just, promise me one thing?" I nodded as I turned to join him at the table. "Be careful. Don't do anything reckless today."

"Ugh," I grunted. "I'm a klutz one day. I fall off my horse—for the first time in years, I might add—and you've got me pegged as a walking accident. Fantastic."

Jensen's eyes softened and his forehead wrinkled with ... worry? "Just be careful. I don't like the looks of it."

"What are you, a doctor now?" I scoffed, sipping my coffee slowly.

"No. But, my mother is, and I've seen this sort of thing before. Please, just—"

"Fine." I groaned in exasperation, rolling my eyes. "I'll be careful."

Jensen relaxed, standing once again. "We've got a bit of time, you hungry?"

"Uh ... yeah. Sure."

As Jensen passed by me for the fridge, my eyes landed on his backside, and I found myself ogling ... again. I really was pathetic. Though, I couldn't really help that it was so fine. This was really his fault. If he didn't do—well, whatever it was he did to make it look like that—then I wouldn't even be in this predicament.

I pulled my knees to my chest and continued sipping my coffee while I watched him. My imagination started to run away with me again as I wondered what his ass looked like naked. Would it be just as tan as the rest of his body? Toned? Yeah, probably.

"So, you've got eggs and bread," Jensen said, standing quickly—catching me staring at him with googly eyes. I knew he caught me too, because that damn cocky smirk played at the corners of his mouth, and I was blushing fiercely. Thankfully, he didn't say anything. "I could make closed Denver sandwiches?"

"Yeah," I croaked, still terribly embarrassed. "That sounds great."

Jensen grabbed what he needed from the fridge before closing it and walking over to the counter by the stove so he could begin prepping breakfast. I picked up the paper, even though I had already read it, and kept my eyes trained on the small black font. I couldn't find it in myself to absorb the words before me, instead my mind kept focusing on the sight of Jensen's chiseled chest, and how great his jeans fit.

"Here you go," Jensen announced, sliding my plate in front of me. Had I really been thinking about him so long that he'd had time to prepare a meal? I hope he hadn't been trying to start up a conversation.

I set the paper down beside me and eyed the toasted sandwich. It looked amazing. The fluffy omelet had an assortment of vegetables in it with shredded cheddar stuffed inside. How it looked was no comparison to how it tasted. They were only eggs, but I had never tasted anything so incredible.

"This is really good. Thank you," I said after swallowing my first bite.

"It was my pleasure."

"Where did you learn to cook like this?"

Jensen's eyebrows furrowed, and he averted his eyes. "I recently worked in a kitchen for a few weeks before we ... parted ways. I picked up a few things."

The way he skirted how he left his last job gave me pause. I wanted to inquire further, but figured it was none of my business.

By the time we finished our breakfast, it was almost six, and I knew we'd have to get to the barn to turn the horses out and clean their stalls. After doing our dishes — I washed while Jensen stood beside me and dried — we put our shoes on.

"Don't forget to tie those," Jensen teased. "You did promise to be careful today, after all."

I rolled my eyes and laughed. Next to my foot was an old work glove, so I picked it up and tossed it at his head. "Shut up."

Jensen's eyes narrowed. "If you weren't already injured, you'd be so dead, Landry."

"You don't think I could take you?" I inquired, to which Jensen's jaw gaped open. It was then that I realized how he took my playful threat. Instead of showing my embarrassment, I winked. It was time to make him squirm for once.

As we sat there, bantering back and forth playfully, I let all of my preconceived notions about Jensen slip away. It was nice to let go of the animosity I felt toward him yesterday, having caught a glimpse of how genuine he was. Maybe his attitude yesterday was due to nerves or was a way of protecting himself, while I suspected mine was due to my past blinding me and turning me into this jaded person who saw everyone as the enemy.

Jensen and I walked to the barn, and when we arrived, Jeff, Tom, and my dad were already busy leading a few of the horses out.

"Good mornin', kids. Sleep well?" Dad asked as he passed by with Oscar. I reached out and ran my hand down my first horse's back as I continued past him.

"Like rocks," Jensen snickered, elbowing my arm as he passed by and headed to Ransom's stall.

I shook my head and laughed, which caused Dad's eyes to brighten at seeing Jensen and me getting along. "I see you've made nice?"

"For now," I joked, opening Halley's stall. I grabbed her halter and slipped inside to find her waiting for me. "Good morning, girl." She huffed softly, pushing her head into the open halter. "We'll go for a ride later, okay?"

I led Halley out of her stall and toward her paddock. I gave her a kiss on her muzzle before releasing her and watched her trot off toward the trough in the far corner. When I exited the pen, locking it behind me, I saw Jensen walking my way with Ransom. Watching him interact with one of the more ornery horses we owned was fascinating. I was able to bond with Ransom, but he still pulled the strings some days, making my job tough. But the way Jensen was able to catch him with no trouble the day before, and how he was able to walk calmly next to him, whispering to him as he stroked the length of his face was ... well, it was mind-blowing.

Jensen raised his eyes to meet mine, offering me a warm smile, and I returned the gesture, smiling twice as wide. A flurry of butterfly-rific activity flourished in my stomach again, and I had to mentally kick my own ass to remind my-self that I vowed to never get involved with an employee again.

There was so much to get done around the ranch that morning, so Jensen and I never spoke again. It definitely made it easier for me to stop wondering just how soft his lips might be.

Once all the stalls were empty, we got rid of the old straw so we could lay fresh stuff down. It didn't occur to me at first, but every stall I cleaned, Jensen was directly across, watching me closely; it didn't take me long to figure out why. Every time I would maneuver my pitchfork, pain would ex-plode through my body. There were a couple of times he would straighten up and move to run for me, but I assured him I was fine with just a look. The way he seemed concerned was sweet, but also a little overwhelming and foreign.

With the five of us working in the barn, it didn't take more than an hour to get all the stalls cleaned and re-watered. There was still a little time before Jillian's first lesson started, so I grabbed a few halters for the lesson horses she would need.

"Mind if I tag along?" Jensen asked, jogging to catch up.

I wasn't stupid. I knew it wasn't just him "tagging along." He was keeping an eye on me.

"Sure. We have to go to the paddock past the new barn to collect the lesson horses for Jillian's first class," I informed him, handing him one of the halters I had grabbed. We caught two of four horses before heading back for the last couple.

We had just tethered the last two lesson ponies in the barn, when I heard footsteps approaching. I turned around to see Tom strolling through the barn.

"Hey kids," he greeted enthusiastically. "Madison, your dad's looking for you. Jillian called in sick. She can't teach her lessons. Your dad was wondering if you could handle her classes today?"

"What about training with Starla and Ransom? Plus, Glory still has a long way to go before we can use her in lessons," I said. I preferred to be riding than training. It's where I felt more myself.

"Madi," Jensen interjected, focusing his smoldering gaze on me. "I think after your day yesterday, that maybe taking it easy isn't such a bad idea."

Even though we'd been getting along, being told what to do—by someone who I barely knew, at that—grated on my nerves. I was annoyed with him all over again. And just when I thought we were making progress.

"Look, I told you—I don't know how many times—I'm *fine*." My rage bubbled just below the surface.

"You keep saying that, and yet I don't seem to believe you. You promised," Jensen continued, his voice dropping into a low whisper and his eyes pleading with me.

"Madison, I have to agree. You can't be feeling completely up to par after falling off twice yesterday. I'd probably be hurting after the first," Tom told me. "Take it easy today, and if you're still feeling antsy tomorrow, we'll train all day."

As soon as I started to consider his offer Jensen opened his mouth. "I don't kn—"

"Zip it, Davis," I said through clenched teeth, my eyes narrowing. He instantly backed off, and I turned to Tom. "Okay. I'll take today off. If you see Dad before I do, let him know I'll teach the lessons."

Tom gave my arm a squeeze as he passed by, leaving me and Jensen alone in the barn. I turned for the lesson schedule to see who all I was expecting first, and Jensen followed. As I stood, looking up at the white board above my head, Jensen nudged my right arm lightly until I looked up at him.

"Thank you," he said softly.

"I didn't do it for you. So, don't flatter yourself." I nudged him with my elbow and shot him a little smirk.

He chuckled. "If you say so."

We exited the small room together, and I slid open the large arena door to make sure all the jump standards and poles were properly stored so we didn't have any early morning mishaps.

Jillian's first lesson of the day was an intermediate jumping class, so I would need to arrange a few jumps. I headed to the far corner where the standards were and placed my hands on either side, ready to pull it across the arena.

"What the hell do you think you're doing?" Jensen shrieked. Yes, shrieked. I may have giggled a little.

"Um, setting up for my class?" I retorted.

"Tell me what you need. You're going to do more damage to yourself if you go around lifting heavy shit all the time."

I exhaled heavily, admitting my defeat. "I'll need six standards moved down the center of the arena. I want it set up so I can do a single and an oxer combination. Two full strides between each obstacle. Think you can handle that, superstar?" I teased.

Something challenging flashed in his eyes. "You'd be surprised just how much I can handle, sweetheart."

"Irk." Yeah, I had no idea what that was supposed to mean. All I knew was that it was a high and squeaky sound that escaped my strained vocal chords as he continued to stare into my eyes.

"What's the matter, Madi?" he inquired, moving behind me until his right hand rested on my right hip and squeezed as he leaned down to whisper in my ear. "Still think I'm not *up* for it?"

Honestly? I had no idea ... but I really fucking hoped he was. No, not for the set up for the lesson ... but for other things. Lots and lots and *lots* of other, much dirtier things.

"I ... um ... I ..." I stammered unintelligently.

"I'm waiting."

The door to the arena suddenly flew open, and I flung myself away from Jensen as his breath continued to waft over the exposed skin of my neck. Dad stepped down onto the dirt floor, and in a sure sign of my guilt, I kept my eyes averted from Jensen's as I turned to face him and give him instructions on what I needed. "So, yeah. I need that combination set up before my class starts. Just, lay the poles on the ground between the standards, I'll warm everyone up over them before I raise them," I said, my heart beating so painfully loud that it was all I could hear in my own ears.

Through my periphery, I noticed Jensen give a nod, and I think he said something along the lines of "Yes, of course," but I still couldn't hear anything. I inhaled deeply and closed my eyes before turning to Dad with an insanely wide smile on my face. I felt like The Joker.

"Getting down to it, I see?"

"What?" I squeaked, and I heard Jensen curse as a pole fell on his foot. Clearly, he had understood my dad's words to mean the same thing I had.

Dad looked between us for a minute, eyebrow raised and suspicious. I could almost hear the gears in his brain turning and coming up with a theory and knew I had to cut it off at the pass.

"Yeah, totally. My side is still a little sore, so I asked Jensen to help me set up a combination for my lessons. I don't know exactly what Jill had planned for today, but being intermediate I figured a combination would be good to start," I rambled without taking a breath. *Smooth, Madi. Real smooth.*

Dad still seemed uneasy regarding what exactly he walked in on, but he went with it. "Good to hear. Jensen, when you're finished with my daughter ..." I choked on my own saliva, coughing and sputtering to clear my air passage "... I'd like your help in the new barn."

"Oh, sure, Wayne." While I really didn't want Jensen to go off and do other things, in case I needed him, I knew that he had a job to do, too.

Dad pulled me aside and looked down at me. "How are you feeling, Madison? I noticed you moving like your side was bothering you more than just a little."

I shook my head and smiled. "I'll be okay. I'll refrain from riding today, and Tom said if I'm feeling better tomorrow I can get back in the saddle."

"Good. Well, take it easy. I don't need you hurting yourself any more, all right?"

"Yeah, yeah. I can't really get into too much trouble here, now can I?" I asked sarcastically.

With a laugh, Dad rolled his eyes. "If it were anyone but you, Madison, I'd probably agree." I couldn't argue; the man had a very valid point. "Okay, I'll leave you two to it. Jensen? I'll see you out at the new barn when you finish up here."

I turned to watch Jensen nod his compliance as he positioned the last standard in place before going back and retrieving the poles I would need. The air in the arena after Dad left us alone was thick. And, not just with the dust that had been stirred up from moving the standards and poles through the loose dirt. The sexual tension that we had encouraged between one another was heavy.

Once Jensen finished double checking the distance between the obstacles I asked him to set up, he walked over to me, his forehead still furrowed with worry. "Okay, I'm going off to see your dad ... in an empty barn ... with tons of tools and places to hide a body. Does it go without saying that I'm so sorry? The things I said ... they were borderline harassment. I was only joking around with you because you ... well, not to sound like a first-grader, but you started it."

My mouth fell slack, and my eyes went wide as I gaped at him. "*I* started it? What about you? With the smolder and ... and the sex-voice?"

That seemed to erase the lines of worry from Jensen's face. Now the corners of his eyes were crinkled as he grinned at me. Yeah, it was pretty sexy. "Sex-voice?"

"Oh, don't even pretend you don't know *exactly* what I'm talking about, mister."

"I assure you, I have no idea. Please, enlighten me," he prodded, taking a step toward me.

Laughing hysterically, I shook my head, backing away from him with every step he took. "Forget it! Now, go. My father's probably waiting to castrate you." Jensen actually whimpered, and I couldn't help but laugh harder when he hung his head and left me alone in the middle of the arena.

The hour-long lesson went great. I actually forgot just how much I enjoyed teaching. April, sixteen, and her thirteen-year-old brother, Carl had so much promise. April even got pretty excited when she realized I was teaching their class today. She assured me she loved Jillian as an instructor, but to have someone who had competed internationally was "beyond awesome." It was quite flattering, and made me promise to maybe do a little more of it. April did have an amazing grace about her when she rode, and I knew that in the next few years, she could probably compete internationally, too. We'd just need to work with her a little more to hone her skills and find the perfect horse for her.

As the lesson wore on, I was definitely grateful for Jensen setting up my jumps for me. Even just lifting the poles into their cups caused me more pain than I'd have liked. I was glad I only had a couple of jumper classes today, and that they were all in the same level; it definitely saved me from having to set up an entire course and move things around. I had barely seen Jensen, and I knew that Jeff was probably busy with them as they did whatever needed to be done in the new barn. I was able to handle rolling more poles over, using my feet, for a beginner class to use as trotting poles, so that wasn't so bad.

As I stood in the center of the arena during the last fifteen minutes of my final lesson of the day, I could feel my exhaustion settling in. My side started to throb, and I was really looking forward to another nice, hot bath.

"Okay, guys," I said to Maria and Lucy as they trotted their horses around the arena. "One more lap and then slow to a walk and let Oscar and Gwen cool down. While they do, we'll do a few stretches."

The two young girls giggled and chatted for a bit before I started instructing them on how to properly stretch while they cooled down their mounts. As they leaned diagonally across and reached for their right toes with their left hands, I took the opportunity to lift my arms above my head to stretch my good side, hoping to not upset the left. The pull felt good, until it reached across my back.

When I opened my eyes, I saw Jensen in the viewing gallery with the girls' mothers—alive and well, as it would seem. The two women cast a look in his direction and stared a little longer than I was entirely comfortable with.

Completely ignoring them, he offered me a smile, while also shooting me a look that asked if I was feeling all right. With a nod, I assured him I was fine, and he waved before taking off to do his job.

I helped Maria and Lucy dismount before opening the

arena door so they could go and brush Oscar and Gwen down. After assisting them with their tack, I made sure to stick around until they finished up and their parents joined us. Their mothers were also fans of the sport and gushed about how incredible it was that I was teaching their daughters. As they retreated, I also heard them comment on the attractive new "stud." I knew they weren't talking about Ransom.

Cougars. They weren't just a threat to our livestock.

After returning Gwen and Oscar to their outdoor paddock, I saw Dad coming out of the new barn and waved. "Hey, Dad. How was today? I feel like I barely saw you."

"Really busy. We're a lot closer to finishing the barn, though. Come on, take a look." Even though I was exhausted, he was so excited, so I tagged along with him. When we stepped into the enormous space, I was stunned. It had been a couple of weeks since I had been in here, when it was nothing more than beams and dirt. But now? Now there was a concrete aisle like the original barn, and there were walls and doors on each of the stalls.

"Wow, Dad! It looks great!" He gave me a tour of where the wash stalls and supply rooms were. I still couldn't believe just how huge it was.

"Yeah, we just need one final inspection and we should be able to start boarding in here."

We were one of the more popular riding stables in the area, so to be able to offer the space for more potential clients was a giant step for our business. It could easily push our yearly projections far past what we had ever projected—or even experienced.

"How were your lessons?" Dad asked as we exited the new barn.

Remembering how fantastic my day was—even with my sore ribs—I beamed. "So good, actually," I reported. "I'd forgotten just how great teaching was. I think I want to do it more often. In fact, April, from my first class is amazing, and I think with a little extra work, she could compete in a couple years' time. I'd like to talk to her and her parents about working with her privately — with Jill's permission, of course."

"Good for you, Madison. I always wondered why you stopped teaching."

I shrugged. "Too busy working on my own career, I suppose."

Nodding his understanding, Dad stopped outside the main barn. "True. Well, I'm glad you had a good day. Why don't you head on home and relax. You worked hard today. Jeff and Tom are here for a bit, they can help me bring in all the horses."

"You're sure? That's two nights in a row."

"Yeah, you're still walking like you're in pain. Go home. Rest up," Dad instructed, pulling out the dad-voice.

"Okay. I'll see you in the morning. Goodnight."

After kissing my dad goodnight, I headed home. On the way, I didn't see Jensen, so I just assumed he was off helping Jeff or Tom with something. I was curious to see if maybe Dad had said something to him — if he'd seen more than I had hoped. Sure, Dad hadn't said anything to me, but I could only imagine that would have been uncomfortable for him; talking to his one and only daughter about relations with the opposite sex.

I opened my front door and removed my boots. If I listened hard enough, I swear I could hear the tub calling my name, and I figured I should get that done before Jensen got home. After grabbing a fresh towel from the closet across from the bathroom, I turned the knob and let myself in.

Steam poured out of the bathroom, which confused me at first. Until it cleared, anyway. As the fog lifted I watched, wide-eyed as Jensen stepped out of the shower. I had trouble tearing my eyes away from his body. His hot, steamy, naked, *wet* body. We both stood there, the pause both awkward and maddening, and I was embarrassed to admit I didn't focus on his upper body. No, I'd already seen that. Instead, I decided to focus on the lower half.

Nay-ked. Yup, two looong drawn out syllables for that bad-boy.

Of course, his legs were *nothing* in comparison to what was between them.

Holy mother of —! A sound escaped me — though, if I was to try and describe what that sound was, I wouldn't be able to.

Jensen smirked ... well, I think he smirked, I was still looking at ... at ... there was no name for what I was looking at. If I called it a penis, or a dick, or a cock, well that would just class him with all the rest. No, Jensen was hung. Like, *really* hung. Super hung. *Dude.*

"Umm, Madi?" My eyes snapped up to his, and I was right, he *was* smirking. "Mind closing the door, sweetheart? Unless, of course, you planned on taking me up on last night's invitation to join me?"

"Uhhhhh ..."

6

TALK ABOUT AWKWARD

"Um, Madison?" Jensen repeated, but for some reason, I was frozen in place, my eyes still locked between his strong thighs.

Naked. Jensen's naked, and I can't seem to stop staring at him. This is going to be awkward. No, wait. It already is.

I shook my head like a maniac before finding my strangled voice. "Oh my God!" I fumbled for the doorknob so I could exit and shut the door behind me. I tripped over my own feet as Jensen reached for his towel to cover up his body — his glorious body — but I finally made it into the hall. Clutching the doorknob tightly in my hand behind me, I pressed my back against the solid door. Breathing was difficult as I continued to think about Jensen's impressive length.

Don't forget girth. I groaned silently — at least, I hoped it was silently — and palmed my face. "Oh God, was there girth." Not a question. *Definitely* a statement.

"What's that?" Jensen called from the other side of the bathroom door, and I hissed at myself for speaking aloud.

He mustn't have known I was leaning against it, because the door opened quickly, and I was on my ass before I knew it. Pain shot up my left side as the bottom of my bruised ass cheek connected with the ceramic tile of the bathroom. That wasn't the worst of it, though.

On my way down, I had grasped for something to catch me before I landed, only to grab a handful of terrycloth. Yup, Jensen's towel. So, there I was, sitting on the ground, eye-level with Jensen's dick. As I stared just a little bit more—because, clearly I hadn't had enough the first time—Jensen scrambled to find something else to cover himself with. Finally, I closed my eyes tightly, rolling to the right and hugging the wall so he could make his escape.

When I heard his bedroom door close, I picked myself up and closed myself in the bathroom, parking my bright red self on the edge of the tub and groaning with embarrassment into my hands. A light rap on the door pulled me from my humiliation.

"Go away!" I mumbled into my hands, only to have Jensen knock again.

"Madi, it's really fine."

Understatement. There was nothing "fine" about naked-Jensen. He was un-fucking-believable.

"No, it's not." I got up and ripped the door open to find him in another fitted T-shirt, this time black, and a pair of gray flannel pants. "What the hell were you doing here, anyway?" My eyes travelled down his body, remembering what I'd seen. I smiled before mentally slapping myself upside the head.

Jensen looked at me, confused. "Um, I live here now, Madi."

I reached out and slapped his chest, lightly. The instant my hand touched his solid pecs, I wanted to let it roam up until I fisted his dark hair hard enough to force his face to mine. I was so screwed. Not literally. Well, maybe—No! My will power was wavering with every passing millisecond, and a raging war of emotions and common sense ensued deep inside me. "That's not what I meant! You should have been working!"

With a chuckle, Jensen explained. "I'd been working all day in the new barn. Putting up the stall doors and a few of the other finishing touches. Your dad said I could take off early, and that's when I came to see you in the arena, but you were still with your last session. I figured I'd hurry home and shower before you got back—clearly, that didn't work out so well."

My eyes went wide again as the memory slowly replayed—because I didn't want it to "flash." Trust me, nobody would.

"We really need to stop talking about this. It was one thing when you were being all sex-voice, smoldery guy, but now ... Jensen, I've seen you *naked*." I whispered the last word.

"Yeah, and?" he paused for a moment before smirking. "Madi ..." He drew out my name teasingly before continuing, going the extra mile and poking the ribs on my good side playfully. "Have you never seen a naked man before?"

"What?" I asked, my voice cracking like a pre-pubescent boy. "Don't be ridiculous! Of course I have. But, we work together."

"Mmm hmm, and?" Jensen said, taking a step forward. My heart skipped a beat, and I felt a lump in my throat as the distance between us lessened more and more.

I began to breathe heavily, his lips mere inches from mine. I wanted him. So badly. But I shouldn't.

"Well, I'd be lying if I didn't admit to wanting to take things further with you." Jensen's voice was soft and low as it vibrated beneath my skin.

His fingers grazed my cheek before moving through my hair to the back of my head. My eyes closed at the tingling sensation of his fingers on my scalp, and I sighed before holding my breath in anticipation as his lips barely brushed mine.

"I'm going to kiss you now," he informed me.

There was a spark as his bottom lip connected with mine, and in a flash, I backed up, covering my mouth with the tips of my fingers. "We can't," I told him breathlessly.

Jensen watched me back into the still-hazy bathroom until my legs hit the edge of the tub. "We can't?" I shook my head softly and he looked as though he understood. "You don't want to?" *Or not ...*

Internally I screamed, *"Yes!"* but, out loud, I lied. "No. I don't."

Jensen looked into my eyes, his own narrowing knowingly in an instant. "You're lying." That panty-melting, crooked smirk appeared, and while I considered telling him he was right—that my pants were most definitely on fire—I held firm.

"Think what you want, Jensen. I just got swept up in the moment. We both did. There's nothing here."

He still wasn't buying it. In fact, he said the one thing I never, in a million years, would have expected. "Does this have something to do with Dane?"

"Wh—what?" I stammered.

"Well, I assume he's an ex?"

I nodded. "How do you even know about him?"

Jensen shrugged, a tiny sliver of his abdomen showing for a fraction of a second. "He called while you were out."

"You spoke to him?"

"Nah. He left a message." Jensen said, shaking his head simultaneously. "You didn't check the machine?"

"Not yet. I was going to have a bath because my back is killing me."

Concern flashed across Jensen's face again and he stepped back toward me. I was already pinned against the tub and moving at half-speed, so unless Scotty was going to beam me up, I had nowhere to go.

Yeah, I just referenced *Star Trek*. What of it?

"Can I see how it looks?"

I cocked an eyebrow at him. "Are you going to tell me to go to the doctor?" I was glad that the sexual tension was gone — well, for the most part, anyway.

Jensen chuckled. "I make no promises."

"Nice," I said, turning to the right so my left side was more easily accessible to him. "So you expect promises to be made to you and kept, but you don't make them yourself? I think that borders on hypocrisy."

Jensen laughed. "No, I think it qualifies as full-blown hypocrisy. It's okay; I can own it."

I raised my left arm, bending it and resting my forearm on the top of my head. I had just crossed my right arm across my torso to lift my shirt, but Jensen had already dropped to his knees and was pushing my shirt upward.

Fuck my life. Just when I thought the sexual tension had mostly cleared, a brand new wave of it steamrolled right over me. He sat eye-level with my bare stomach. I could feel his breath across my flesh as he looked over the tender spots that covered my ribs, and I had to bite the inside of my cheek and clench my eyes to keep from moaning or whimpering — basically any noise that would let him know that my pants were now on fire for an entirely different reason than lying.

"Wow, it's really up there," Jensen whispered, causing me to snap my head to him, eyes wide and nervous.

"What?" I cried out, my eyes falling to his flannel-covered crotch.

Jensen smirked. "The bruise, pervert."

My entire body was about to break out in embarrassing red blotches. "I knew that."

"Again with the lying, Landry. One of these days your pants are going to spontaneously combust."

Too late.

In order to keep myself from jumping him right there, I changed the topic back to the situation at hand. "How is it?"

"I don't know; I can only see a small portion of it. You can say no, but it'd be easier for me to tell if you took off your shirt?" He phrased it as a question, probably expecting me to huff, yank my shirt down, and storm out of the bathroom.

Instead, I smirked. "And this has nothing to do with you wanting to get me naked for seeing you naked? Level the playing field?"

"All in due time, sweetheart. All in due time." And just like that, he turned the tables on me again.

Very carefully, I lifted my shirt over my head, discarding it to the floor, leaving me in only my plain, white bra. When my hands dropped to unbutton my jeans, I watched Jensen's eyes widen.

"What are you ... ?" he croaked.

I continued to push my jeans down over my hips. "My bruise goes down past my hip." My jeans fell to a heap around my ankles, so I stepped out of them, using Jensen's shoulder to balance myself. His right hand snapped to the small of my back to steady me when I teetered, and sent a wave of lust directly to my lady-bits.

So, there I stood in my most basic white bra and panties with Jensen kneeling next to me. His eyes were still wide as he looked up and down my body, and my stomach knotted as the realization of my actions finally caught up with me. I quickly turned my face from his to hide the blush I felt warming my face, neck, and finally chest.

"Wow," Jensen said breathlessly as I felt his hands gently touch my ribs before trailing down my side and over my hip. A delightful tremble worked through my body when the tips of his fingers grazed the flesh of my ass that wasn't covered by white cotton.

This was such a bad idea, I thought to myself, swallowing

thickly.

"Madison." I turned back to him and looked down into his eyes. They were no longer wide with shock, but full of worry. "I don't like the looks of this. Please let me take you to the doctor."

"Don't ..." I started to say, watching as Jensen slowly stood until he towered over me again. "I'm going to be fine. I just need to rest. Maybe have a bath."

Nodding hesitantly, Jensen leaned forward, and I inhaled sharply as I expected him to kiss me. He didn't, though. Instead, he continued on until he was leaning over the tub to start my bath.

"Okay," he whispered, straightening once more. "You relax. I'll go start dinner."

Jensen turned from me with a smile and exited the bathroom, winking at me as he turned the lock on the inside of the door before closing it behind him. Once on the other side of the door, he jiggled it to make sure it was locked. "Just checking," he called through the door.

Rolling my eyes, I laughed and added my salts and bubble bath before removing my two remaining articles of clothing and stepping into the warm water. When the water level was a few inches from the curved rim of the tub, I turned it off and settled back to relax. I closed my eyes and took a deep, cleansing breath as my body released most of the tension from my muscles. Most. Not all.

With my back feeling as close to normal as it would for the next few days, I stood up, draining the tub and flipping on the shower so I could rinse off and wash my hair. I pulled the shower curtain closed to keep the water from spraying all over the floor. Letting my eyes close, I moved my face under the gentle spray of water and my thoughts instantly drifted to Jensen.

Yes, I had feelings for him, but not all of them were contempt. Sure, he was an arrogant jerk sometimes, but he was also sweet and caring. My thoughts instantly took a turn, and soon I was remembering how his skin looked bathed in the post-shower steam. The way the beads of water trailed down his body. It dripped from his water-darkened hair, onto his shoulder where it proceeded to trickle down his chest until it rolled down his well-sculpted abs and reached that yummy V-shaped muscle that led to the motherland.

There was a dull ache between my legs that suddenly needed attention. I ran my hands through my hair, allowing them to rest on my shoulders for a moment as I pulled my bottom lip between my teeth. Removing my face from the water and opening my eyes, I eyed the door nervously. I was wound like a friggin' top, and if I didn't get the release my body so desperately craved, I was sure to implode.

My hands had just begun their journey south when a knock at the door ripped me from the fantasy I'd started to weave.

My hands flew to my face, pushing the droplets of water away. "Yeah?"

"Dinner's going to be ready in about ten minutes."

"Okay. I'm almost done." Jensen's shadow disappeared from under the door, and I rinsed the conditioner from my hair.

I wrapped my towel around my body and stepped out of the shower before walking over to the mirror and using my hand to clear it. Using my wide-toothed comb I untangled my wet hair before unlocking the door. Barefoot, I proceeded to my bedroom to find some comfortable clothes.

I settled on a pair of blue plaid-patterned mid-calf pajama pants. They were silk and so soft against my clean skin, and I paired them with a tight, white camisole that showed off a teensy bit of my midriff. After towel-drying my hair a little, I hung the fluffy green towel behind my door and headed to the kitchen to find Jensen was just pulling a casserole from the oven.

"That smells delicious," I told him as I moved to his side and inhaled deeply. I hadn't realized just how close I was until he shifted and the back of his arm grazed my right breast, causing my nipples to react. Yes, he noticed. And yes, I blushed.

"Thanks. It's my mom's recipe. It's a vegetarian dish— that won't be a problem, will it?"

I think that was when I fell in love with him—or, at least, deep like, because I'd only known him for two days now. "Not at all. I'm a vegetarian, too." I don't think I ever really understood exactly what *swooning* felt like, but I definitely did now. In fact, I think I had just gone pro.

"Go on, sit down. I'll bring it over."

I did as Jensen instructed, sitting in my usual seat and waiting patiently for dinner to find its way into my belly. Jensen placed the casserole in the middle of the table, and I licked my lips in anticipation.

Jensen took his seat next to me and waited. I raised my eyes to him and noticed him watching me. "What?" I asked softly, self-consciously tucking my damp hair behind my ear.

Shaking his head, he smiled. "No, it's nothing. You just look so relaxed, is all."

I laughed nervously, remembering what almost went down during my shower. "Oh, uh, yeah. The bath really helped."

"Your side feels okay, then?" he inquired, reaching over and dishing out some of the casserole for me before filling his own plate.

"Um, yes?"

Raising his eyes to me, he cocked an eyebrow. "Madi..."

"Save it." I stabbed a piece of the broccoli casserole and ate it. "Mmmm," I mumbled, closing my eyes to savor the taste of what had to be a homemade cream sauce. "This is incredible."

When I opened my eyes, Jensen was staring intensely at me as I shoved another forkful into my mouth. "What?" I asked, covering my mouth to conceal the food in it and feeling self-conscious all over again.

Chuckling, Jensen shook his head. "Nothing."

"Look who's the liar now." I teased, lightly nudging his leg beneath the table. "So, you're a vegetarian, huh?"

Jensen swallowed his food and nodded. "Yeah. Cooking at your dad's place yesterday was a challenge. The man doesn't really have much to offer in his fridge that was entirely vegetarian friendly."

"Tell me about it. I mean, I eat eggs and some dairy, but that's about it. Dad refuses to eat dinner over here most nights because I never cook anything *substantial*." I lowered my voice to offer the best impression of my father as possible, making Jensen laugh. I leaned forward and indicated with my index finger to come closer so I could tell him a secret. Yes, I realized we were the only two in the room; maybe I just wanted to be closer to him, all right? "Can I tell you something?"

Jensen nodded, moving his chair over slightly, his knee brushing against mine under the table, making those pesky butterflies flourish again. Our eyes locked. "I've done something really bad. Do you promise not to tell anyone?"

"I thought we covered where I stand on making promises," Jensen reminded me, his tone soft and teasing.

"Just do it. I'm your boss."

Nodding, he conceded. "Okay, I promise to keep your secret."

I looked around the room unnecessarily before returning my eyes to his. "I do all of my dad's grocery shopping and, while I buy him meats for dinners and such, I buy vegan deli meats for lunches since that's when I mostly eat over there."

"You do what?" Jensen asked, his lips turning up at the corners into a wide smile as he laughed. "You are bad. Way worse than me." He sat up and picked up his fork to have another bite. "I think you might just need to be punished."

I had just taken a bite as he said that last bit, and I damn-near choked on it. The legs of his chair scraped against the tile as he pushed his chair back to stand up when I held up a hand. "No," I said through a cough. "I'm okay. I just wasn't expecting that."

Once I had my coughing fit under control, Jensen relaxed and we continued eating. "So, tell me about yourself."

"What do you want to know?"

I shrugged. "How did your parents meet?"

Jensen took another bite, and I did the same as I waited for him to continue. "After high school, my dad travelled England, met my mother, who was taking a bit of time off before going to college in the states. Their meeting was kis-met in a way. Turned out they were going to the same college."

"That's so cool," I said, totally enthralled by his parents' love story. My own mother died when I was two, so I don't know much about her, other than she was the love of my father's life.

"They got married while he was still in school because they found out they were expecting me," Jensen continued. "Mom finished up her residency by the time I was two, and they had my sister, Lilah, a few years later. We grew up on a farm just outside of Memphis, and after I graduated, I went to the University of Houston."

"What did you study?"

"Well, I couldn't settle on a major at first, which pissed my dad off. He wanted me to be a doctor or a lawyer, and while I seriously considered both career paths, it just wasn't who I was, you know?"

"I do." Though, imagining him in a suit, coming home after a long day and me stripping him of his tie, jacket, and shirt ... *Focus, Madison!*

"I finally settled on a Business degree."

"Me too!" I exclaimed, slapping his arm lightly. "Can I ask why you chose to work here instead of doing something with your degree?"

Jensen looked at me funny for a minute. "What makes you think I'm not doing something with my degree?" My brow furrowed with confusion as I tried to understand how he could possibly be putting his education to good use working as a ranch-hand.

"What do you mean?"

"Madi, I'm hoping to invest in a third of the ranch. Your dad hasn't talked to you?"

I shook my head. "No, in case you haven't noticed, things around here have been a little crazy." It was upsetting that my father was interested in selling a third of his father's legacy—especially without talking to me about it first—but at the same time, cementing Jensen's place in this company meant cementing him in my life.

Holy shit, I think I've lost my mind. It had only been a couple of days, and I was already looking for ways to keep him around.

"It's just ..." The mood in the room shifted, and he seemed nervous about something, almost like he was struggling to find his words. "I've been struggling to find work these last few months, so when I met with my father after moving back, he told me of the recent expansion and I came up with a few ideas to help out a little more." He paused for a moment as he gauged my lack of reaction to what he was telling me. "You see ... growing up on the farm when I was little. I have such fond memories of it, and I've always wanted to eventually run my own."

That jarred me back into reality, and I found myself pushing away from the table, crossing my arms across my chest as I glared angrily at him. "So, you're using *my* ranch to gain experience to start your own?" I spat. It took all of thirty seconds for me to go right back to loathing Jensen fucking Davis.

"What? Not at all. I love your operation here, and when Dad told me you guys were expanding, that's when I decided that I wanted to be a part of it. That is … if you'll have me?"

"Oh," I said softly, allowing my arms to fall slack in my lap and feeling guilty for jumping to conclusions like I so often did. "So, you don't plan on opening up your own place one day?"

Jensen laughed. "And go up against a business that's already successful? Not likely. Plus, I don't know that I could be *the boss*."

Oh, I bet you could, I thought, biting my bottom lip gently as I considered the possibilities of him bossing me around a little bit. Apparently, even having a serious conversation with him led right back to me fantasizing about sex with him. It's what he did to me—well, not the sex. Just the "me thinking about sex all the time" thing. Let's blame him for not locking the bathroom door. Yeah, that seemed right to me. It was all his fault.

"Your dad's a good man, Madi. He took a chance on me when no one else would. While I hadn't really considered this as something I wanted in a career, the more I see and hear about it, the more I want in." He paused, gauging my reaction. "So?" he inquired, his eyes looking deep into mine, trying to get a read on what my answer might possibly be.

"Honestly? I think it would be good for the ranch to have someone else on board who knows what they're doing. So, yes." Jensen smiled upon hearing my acceptance, and I returned the gesture, relaxing in my seat and picking my fork back up.

We talked a little more about him as we continued eating, and when both of our plates were empty, I stood up to clear the table. Jensen moved to help me, but I was having none of it.

"No way. You cooked, now sit back and relax."

"Madi, *you* should be the one relaxing," he reminded me. "You're injured."

Placing my hands on the table in front of him, I leaned forward to look him in the eye. His eyes glancing down my shirt wasn't missed, though. "It's dishes, Jensen. I think I can handle them."

I took our plates and put them in the dishwasher before going back for the leftovers so I could refrigerate them. As I was scooping it into a container, Jensen decided to restart the conversation.

"So, who's Dane?"

I stopped what I was doing for a second upon hearing his name. "My ex," I stated simply.

"Yeah, I got that earlier. What happened?"

After snapping the lid onto the plastic container, I opened the fridge to find a place for it. "I kicked him out."

"Because?" Jensen pressed.

"We broke up." I turned toward Jensen, who was now standing on the other side of the island across from me, his green eyes dark and stormy.

"He said in his message that he was sorry," Jensen started, his voice dropping as though he were treading dangerous waters. Which he was. "What did he do that he had to be sorry for?" I looked at Jensen completely dumbfounded. What was he trying to do? Run interference? Did he want me to call Dane? "It's just ... maybe he is?"

I laughed dryly. "I bet he is. I guess the next time he decides to have a little too much to drink, he won't become a belligerent asshole and push me against the wall before putting his fist through it because he missed my face."

Jensen's eyes widened. Glancing down, I noticed his hand was wrapped tight around the plate he was holding. His skin was turning white from the pressure, and I worried he might snap the plate in two, so I took it from him. "He tried to hit you?"

I shrugged, feeling tears burn my eyes, and turned toward the sink so Jensen didn't see how weak I was. I knew I shouldn't be crying over the end of a toxic relationship, but I was. "He said he wasn't really going to, that I was over-reacting, but given how close he got, yeah. I believe so."

The anger that flowed off of Jensen was undeniable. I'd known him less than forty-eight hours, and he was reacting almost viscerally to my breakup.

"My dad heard the shouting and came over immediately," I continued, turning on the water to start the dishes. "When he saw the tears on my cheeks, the hole in the wall, and the blood on Dane's knuckles, he did the math. I told Dane it was over, and my dad hauled him out of the house."

Jensen settled a little, though his forehead was still heavily furrowed. "How long ago did this happen?"

"Just over a month now." I sniffled and wiped the tears I could no longer contain.

"And he's still calling? Has he stopped by?"

I nodded and turned the water off. "A couple of times, but my dad won't let him near me. He knows my dad doesn't monitor my phone though." I glance up at Jensen again. "I haven't returned his calls, if you're wondering."

"Why not?"

Sighing, I placed my hands on the counter and leaned heavily. I watched the bubbles in the sink start to pop. "I don't trust myself to tell him to stay away."

"That wasn't an isolated incident." There's no inflection to his voice, meaning he was confident in his statement.

"It was the first time he acted violently," I told him. "But he always drank heavily and often said some awful things to me. He'd accuse me of cheating, then tell me that was ridiculous because no man would ever put up with my shit."

"Madison," Jensen tried to cut in.

"I'd stand up for myself, and we'd argue before I'd just go to bed alone while he passed out on the couch. In the mornings, he was always quick to offer an apology, and I was stupid enough to believe him."

Jensen laid a hand over mine. "You're not stupid, Madi. Guys like that have a way of manipulating their victims into staying with them. You're not the only one to have gone through something like this."

"I know. But that doesn't make me feel any less stupid." I paused, holding back a sniffle. "I found out a few days later that he'd been cheating on me too. With his ex. I guess he was just projecting his own guilt—or lack thereof—onto me." Jensen gave my hand a squeeze, and that familiar warmth spread beneath my skin. I'd only known him a short time, but I was drawn to him and wanted to forget my troubles in him.

But I knew I shouldn't.

Pulling my hand away, I submerged them in the dishwater. "It's why I've sworn to never engage in a workplace relationship again."

"I see." Jensen grabbed a dish towel and dried the dishes as I handed them to him.

With a sniffle, I blinked tears away before forcing a smile and turning around. I no longer wanted to think about what had happened. It was in the past. Where it belonged.

"So," I started. "Want to go watch TV?"

His sympathy flowed off of him, but I didn't want it. I just wanted to move on.

Jensen didn't move from his spot behind the island, so I went to him, grabbed his hand with both of mine and tugged him toward the living room. I pushed him down on one end of the couch, and sat on the left. After flipping the TV on, I brought my legs up and bent my knees to the right to get comfortable while I looked through the guide.

"What do you want to watch?" I asked. He looked a little embarrassed when I looked over at him as he contemplated an answer.

"Jensen?"

"Um, well, what we were watching last night was all right. Got any more of that?"

I used my right hand to shove him lightly. "Who's the pervert now?" I teased.

"Pfft," he retaliated. "These are boobs on TV; you were checking me out in the flesh — literally."

My face burned as I looked away from him and found a few episodes I'd recorded a while back. The show started, and Jensen and I sat in silence. I could feel myself grow sleepy, and my eyeslids dropped a few times as sleep tried to overpower me. Eventually, I lost that battle and passed out with my head leaning on the back of the couch.

GROUNDED

With my mind completely clouded with thoughts of Jensen these last couple days — even though we both agreed to just be friends — it only made sense that I'd dream about him every time I slept. The dreams were no different than my fantasies when I was awake. Which is to say, they were incredibly sexual and extremely vivid.

At some point in the dream, I found myself surrounded by warmth, and I felt safe. Secure. It was a feeling I hadn't experienced since before Dane turned into an asshole, and it wasn't until I woke up the next morning, fully stretched out on the couch, that I realized why.

Jensen was behind me. His gentle breaths passed over my neck, and his left hand rested on my hip. His chest was pressed against my back, and our legs were completely tangled up in one another's.

Still half-asleep, I wondered if our current position was accidental, or on purpose. Not that it mattered, because there was a part of me that really enjoyed the way his body molded to mine. With a soft hum, I closed my eyes and basked in the feeling of our bodies so close while he was still asleep.

Just as I was snuggling back into him, his fingers gripped my hip lightly before moving up until his hand lay flat against my abdomen. He held me still and firmly against him. I heard his breathing pattern change slightly, and he moaned in my ear. He shifted his hips, and even though it was against everything we'd agreed on, I pressed back, feeling every solid inch of him against my ass. And I liked it.

"Good morning," he whispered, his lips barely brushing my ear and sending shivers through my body. He didn't release his hold on me, and I made no indication that I was going anywhere.

"Hey," I responded softly, turning my head to look at him. "Sorry I fell asleep."

"Mmmm," he groaned, releasing his hold on my stomach to stretch before letting his hand fall back to my hip, his thumb brushing my ass. "S'okay. I did, too." Our eyes locked, and my heartbeat picked up. Our lips were so close to one another's, and I was so tempted to move just a fraction of an inch and give in to my deepest desire.

Instead, Jensen sat up behind me, clearly realizing our situation was inappropriate as he woke up completely. "I guess we should get ready for work. How are you feeling? Was sleeping on the couch too much for your side?"

Disappointed, I pushed myself up as well, running my fingers through my hair to tame any flyaways. "Um, no. I feel all right."

"Are you going to ride today?" he asked, standing and stretching his body tall. His shirt raised slightly and showed off the faint trail of hair leading down behind the waistband of his pajama pants.

"Yeah," I responded, knowing I would have to ride sooner or later. "I think so."

Jensen eyed me skeptically, but I think he thought better than to tell me what I should and shouldn't do. "You'll be careful?"

"Promise," I assured him, standing up. "I'm going to go

and brush my teeth, and then I'll make us some breakfast. Eggs and toast?"

"Sounds good. I'll meet you in the kitchen."

With my teeth and hair brushed and clothes on, I made my way to the kitchen, crossing paths with Jensen in the hall. We exchanged friendly smiles and went on our way. By the time Jensen was at the table, the eggs were almost done cooking, so I put the bread in the toaster. I added a bit of salt and pepper to the eggs just as the toaster popped and quickly plated everything before it got cold.

Placing the plates on the table, Jensen looked up at me with a smile. "Thank you."

"It's just scrambled eggs and toast. I think the squirrel living in the tree outside could make it," I joked as I sat down next to him.

Jensen chuckled and shook his head, and I just looked at him questioningly. Was that not what he meant?

Once breakfast was eaten and the dishes were done, Jensen and I put our boots on and headed for the barn to begin the day. However, before we walked in, Jensen pulled me off to the side. As we remained hidden from view of anyone else, I couldn't help but wonder if he was going to kiss me. And more importantly, would I let him?

"I need you to promise me," he said softly.

"Um, I already did," I reminded him.

"No, I know. It's just, I noticed that doing the stalls took a bit out of you yesterday, so promise me that if you feel like it's too much, you'll let me know?" His hand reached out and tucked a wisp of hair behind my ear.

"Yeah. Okay, I promise. Can we go to work now before my father thinks that something unsavory is going on between us?" I ribbed.

Thankfully, Jensen thought what I said was funny, and we entered the barn side-by-side to help take the horses out to their paddocks. With them all fed and watered, and their stalls cleaned out, I offered to help Jeff catch Jillian's first few lesson horses before I went off to find Tom. Of course, Jensen tagged along, keeping an over-cautious eye on me.

We had just finished tethering the three horses inside the barn when Tom sauntered in with his coffee mug. "Good mornin', Madi. You up for training Glory this morning?" he asked, placing his hand on my left shoulder.

Just the slightest pressure still caused me to bite down on the inside of my cheek and fight back a whimper. Jensen noticed this, but I quickly looked back to Tom and smiled.

"Yeah. I would be up for some light ground work."

"Great! I'll meet you outside in a half hour."

As Tom walked away, Jensen came over and stood in front of me. "Madi, are you *sure* about this?"

I nodded. "Relax. Glory's an older horse. She was used as a broodmare for years, and now Tom thinks she'd make a good lesson horse. She's super sweet and very tame. Your concern is noted, but I'll be okay."

Jensen didn't seem convinced, but he accepted it. "All right then. Just … be careful."

"I did promise, didn't I?" I started to back away so I could go and get Glory ready, leaving Jensen looking afraid. "Look, I'll see you at lunch, okay? Have a good morning."

"Okay. You, too."

Glory was brushed and tacked, and I made it to the arena at exactly the same time Tom did. The air was a little crisp on my bare arms, but I knew I would warm up as soon as I started riding. I stood to Glory's left and took a deep breath, biting the inside of my cheek so I didn't cry out when I used my upper body to mount her.

Once I was securely in the saddle, I pushed Glory forward and we made our way around the arena a few times.

"So, Madi," Tom shouted from his place in the center of

the arena. "What do you think of the new kid?"

"He seems all right. I only just met him, though."

Almost as if his ears were burning, Jensen appeared, looking disheveled from an hour of hard labor. His shirt was dusted with dirt, his biceps were glistening and straining beneath the bale of hay he was carrying toward the barn, and his brown hair was falling over his forehead.

From previous experience, I knew that too much time ogling him while on a horse never ended well. I returned my focus to Glory and her training.

"Okay, move her into a trot, Madi."

I gave Glory a light squeeze, and she hopped slightly before pacing her gait. I started to post, but the up and down movements proved to be too much. So, I pressed my seat into the saddle and tried to sit through it; that seemed even worse. My balance was uneven as I tried to mask my pain, and before I knew it, Glory got confused and just stopped. Because I wasn't expecting it, I fell to the left and landed on the ground in a heap. I saw nothing but blinding white light behind my clenched eyelids as pain tore its way up my body.

"Madison?" Tom's panicked voice called out. Dirt hit my hands as he skidded to a stop next to me. He placed his hand on my back as I rolled onto my right side and curled up into the fetal position. "Are you okay?"

I shook my head in the dirt and felt the hot tears fall from my eyes. "N-no."

Suddenly there was a shout from farther away. "Damn it!" More arena dirt dusted up around me, and tentative hands ghosted over my throbbing ribs. "Go get Wayne!" Jensen commanded.

I felt Jensen's body shift above me, and he leaned in close to speak softly in my ear. "Madison, can you get up?"

"I don't ... I don't know," I managed to respond.

"Try? I'll help." I wanted his soft, velvety voice to comfort me and make the pain stop. It didn't.

I nodded slowly, the dirt rubbing against my face, and I felt Jensen slip an arm under me. "Ow! Ow!" I cried, fresh tears falling from my eyes. "I—I think I broke something. I can't ..." I gasped for a breath. Razor blades shot through my rib cage and lungs. "I can't breathe."

Jensen cursed under his breath and continued to help me up. I sucked in another sharp breath as he helped me stand. The pain was excruciating, and I couldn't stand up straight.

"There you go," Jensen said in a proud-parent tone. "Will you let me take you to the doctor now?"

Slowly, and with a whimper, I opened my eyes and nodded. Jensen wrapped a hand tenderly around my waist and helped me walk. As we reached the gate, Dad and Tom came running.

"I'm going to take her to the hospital ... if that's all right with you, sir?" Jensen inquired.

Dad agreed quickly, reaching into his pocket and tossing Jensen the keys to his new truck. "Yeah, of course. Madi, honey? Are you okay?"

"I'm not entirely sure. I'll call when we know what's going on." My voice was weak, and I only hoped it came across as reassuring. I had to keep my breaths short. If I breathed too deeply, it caused the pain to worsen.

Jensen walked me toward the truck, helping me up into it before trying to fasten my seatbelt for me. I know he was just trying to be helpful, but I hated feeling helpless. He closed my door and ran around to the driver's side. We peeled out onto the highway and headed for town. Jensen was definitely speeding. My father wouldn't be too pleased.

"How bad is it?" he asked, glancing at me briefly.

With a controlled breath, I dropped my gaze to my hands and lied. "It's not so bad anymore."

"I thought we established last night that you're a terrible

liar." There was a slight inflection in his voice that told me, without having to look, that he was smirking.

"Oh, right. On a scale of one to ten?" I saw Jensen nod once through my periphery. "Well over ten. I think I cracked a rib."

Obviously frustrated, Jensen ran his fingers through his hair. "I told you to be careful."

His words affected me deeply. It wasn't like I meant for this to happen; I honestly thought I would be okay on Glory. The fact that I was in pain and frustrated with my own clumsiness didn't help me remain level-headed. I found myself suddenly annoyed with him being so ... controlling—even if it was borne out of his concern. My eyebrows knit together and I glared up at him. "It's my job. I not like I intended for this to happen," I snapped.

With a sigh, Jensen's clenched jaw relaxed, and he looked at me. His eyes were no longer dark and afraid, but light and apologetic. "I know. It's just ..." He trailed off before deciding not to finish that thought. "Never mind. That's not important. What's important is we get you taken care of now."

Jensen's total disregard for the posted speed limits resulted in us getting to the hospital in half the time. He parked as close to the doors as he could before running around to my side to help me out. Every movement caused me immense pain, and I bit my lip to keep from crying out.

"I'm so sorry," he whispered as he helped me stand up straight. He took his place by my side and wrapped his hand around my waist, leading me into the building.

We walked up to the admittance desk, and when the receptionist looked up at us, she smiled. "Why, Jensen! How nice to see you again."

His smile was warm, but rushed as he held me upright. "It's nice to see you, too, Mrs. Johnston. I wish we could stay and chat, but my friend here is terribly hurt, and we need to see my mother if she's available." In response to his request, she nodded before picking up her telephone and punching in a series of numbers.

"Do you want to sit?" Jensen asked as he led me toward the row of seats in the waiting area.

"Um … I don't know that I'd be able to stand up again without wanting to die." With an understanding nod, Jensen remained by my side as we waited. It didn't take long before the doors to the elevator opened and a blonde woman in a white doctor's coat stepped out.

"Jensen? Sweetheart, what's going on?" The woman approached, and the closer she got, the more I could see the similarities.

"Mom, this is Wayne's daughter, Madison. She had an accident on her horse, and she thinks she might have broken something," Jensen explained as his mother ushered us away from the waiting room and through a corridor until we were in an exam room. Jensen helped me up onto the table, and I inhaled sharply as I sat.

"Sorry," he whispered, his fingers sliding along the exposed skin of my lower back as he removed his arm from around me.

"So you're Wayne Landry's daughter." I nodded in response, still unable to really focus on anything besides the pain. "I'm Dr. Davis. But you can call me Marie." There was a brief pause before she continued. "Jensen says he works with you?"

"For," I managed to say. "Jensen works for me."

Jensen chuckled from beside me. "And here I thought we'd made nice. I guess I shouldn't complain, though; it would appear you haven't lost your spark."

"All right, Madison. Where does it hurt, honey?" Dr. Davis asked, ignoring our banter.

Indicating to my left side, I spoke. "My ribs."

"Can I get you to lift your shirt so I can get a closer look?" I lifted my shirt and watched her blue eyes go wide. "And where does the bruising start and end?" she asked.

"Um, it starts about here," I said, indicating to just beside my breast. "And ends about here." I pointed to the side of my upper thigh.

She didn't say anything more as she looked at my ribs. The bruising wasn't any darker; in fact, it had lightened some in the last day and a half.

Dr. Davis's hands reached out and touched my ribs gently. Of course, the pain that shot through my body suggested that maybe she hit me. With a sledgehammer.

"Ungh!" I cried out, my eyes clenching shut as my hand shot over and gripped Jensen's. The pain was so excruciating, I hadn't even realize I'd done it until Jensen laced his fingers through mine and started stroking the back of my hand with his thumb. It was calming.

Jensen's mother sighed. "Madison, I'm afraid I'm going to have to run some x-rays. Until then, I won't know what we're dealing with. I'm going to give you a shot of morphine to take the edge off until we know what we're dealing with."

Needles skeeved me out most days, but I was quickly on board if it meant I could breathe again. Jensen helped me lower my shirt, which should have been weird, but because he refused to release my hand, it wasn't. He then helped me down from the table, and we followed his mother to proceed with my x-rays.

It was a good thing I had been put into a wheelchair. The morphine kicked in on our way to the room where they kept the giant machine, making me feel hazy and loopy. Jensen stayed with me the entire time, only leaving once I was secure on the table to get scanned.

Once they were done, we were escorted back to our previous exam room to wait on the scans. After helping me back up onto the table, I started to wobble. I wanted to lie down.

"Wait, wait, wait," Jensen whispered as I started to lower myself onto the table. He hopped up next to me and sidled up to my right side, draping his arm behind me. I could feel his hand lightly brush my ass as he braced himself on the table.

I moaned softly, leaning to the side and resting my head on his shoulder. He removed his arm from behind me and began running his fingers through my hair.

"S'nice," I told him, my words mumbled from my current high and my scalp tingling.

"How are you feeling?" he breathed, his lips brushing the top of my head, sending a shiver through me.

I snuggled in a little deeper. "So good."

"Good," he responded. This time his lips touched down on the top of my head, and I smiled before allowing my eyes to close.

I don't know how long we sat like that—probably a couple hours at least—but my eyes flew open, and my head snapped up when the door opened. In strolled Dr. Davis with my chart and printed scans.

It would appear that having Jensen around might be good for more than just the obvious reasons. His mom had major pull at the hospital. *Score.* I rolled my eyes at my high self as Jensen's mom slid the scans onto the board and turned the backlight on.

Jensen offered me a comforting smile, and I shifted my body to sit up straight. I hissed in pain when I realized the morphine was starting to wear off.

"You okay?" Jensen asked, his left hand resting against the small of my back.

"It hurts again, is all," I said quietly, trying not to make it sound as bad as it was.

Dr. Davis turned to me. "The morphine is likely wearing

off. I can give you another shot to tide you over until you can pick up your prescription." She turned back to my scans and started pointing at them. "Well, it appears as though everything is going to be fine. There are small cracks in two of your floating ribs. They'll probably take three to six weeks to heal correctly. However, there are a few things you can do to help the process along."

"Yeah, anything," I interjected.

"Well, the first thing is to get plenty of rest. Which means no riding or physical labor at all. Move as minimally as possible." Jensen shot me a sideways smirk, and I glared evilly at him. "Heat therapy is also known to help. Do you have a heating pad?" I shook my head.

"We'll stop and pick one up," Jensen said, resting his hand on my thigh briefly.

His mom nodded. "Good, good. Also, eating a well balanced diet can help."

"Okay, yeah. I'll do all of those things."

"Good to hear. Now, I'm going to prescribe something for pain management. Vicodin and Oxycontin have the highest success rates for managing this level of pain," she continued to explain.

"Aren't ..." I turned to look at Jensen before returning my eyes to Dr. Davis. "Aren't they addictive?"

"They can be. If you're not careful; but with the level of pain you're experiencing you'd be best to consider them."

"Okay," I said quietly. After Dr. Davis gave me another shot of morphine and handed me my prescription for Oxycontin, Jensen assisted me down off the table and allowed me to use him to lean on as we made our way for the exit.

"So," Dr. Davis said as she walked with Jensen and me to the front door. "Take the painkillers I prescribed no more than three times a day. Call if you need anything."

I didn't get a chance to agree, or even argue, for that matter, because Jensen jumped in. "I'll make sure of it. Thanks again, Mom."

"Yes, thank you, Dr. Davis." It wasn't until I went to shake her hand that I realized Jensen was holding mine again. In fact, the only time he released it was when I was having my x-rays done — I didn't even realize he'd taken it again. It felt so natural.

After hitting the pharmacy to fill my prescription and pick up my new heating pad, Jensen and I headed back to the ranch. The morphine hit me harder than the first time, and I started slurring my speech when I was on the phone with Dad.

Jensen swept the phone from my hand. I let my head loll back on the seat as the trees outside whirred by. I couldn't make out much of what they were saying other than a few select words.

"Blah blah blah, cracked ribs," Jensen said. There was a short pause before he continued. "Blah blah, morphine, blah blah, prescription filled. Blah blah, needs to rest."

I was instantly bored with what he was saying, but liked the way he looked as he spoke. The way his strong jaw moved. There was also the way his eyes lit up when he turned to look at me. I shifted in my seat until I was almost directly facing him — not an easy task while buckled. I did try to remedy that, but Jensen quickly hung up the phone and snapped his hand over mine to stop me from releasing my seat belt.

"That's not a good idea, Landry."

"Boo," I pouted, jutting my bottom lip out. "You're too safe."

Jensen chuckled, his eyes sparkling as his smile reached them. Not literally — at least I hoped not. *Man, I'm so high.*

"I guess that's one of the reasons I'm still in one piece," Jensen teased, pulling the truck to a stop outside the house.

"Feeling better?"

"Mmm hmmm," I hummed, my head falling to the left to look at him. Even through the haze the painkillers caused, I noticed that he was gorgeous. "Mmm, you're pretty, huh?"

A short, loud laugh escaped him, and he opened his door before coming around to help me. "You're high." He slipped his arm around my waist, and I felt his hand brush against the skin of my lower back, igniting sparks in my belly that set my entire body on fire.

"But I don't hurt, and tha's gooood." As soon as my feet hit the ground, I lost my balance and fell against Jensen's solid frame. My hands started caressing his chest, and I wasn't sure if it was the drugs, but I swear I felt his heartbeat quicken. "I think my feet are broke." My voice was small as I looked up at him through my long eyelashes, my fingers tugging at the loose fabric of his shirt.

Jensen smiled before swooping down and lifting me into his arms carefully. My right hand rested on the back of his shoulder as he carried me bridal style. Meanwhile, my left moved against his strong chest, moving up his neck until they ran over his stubbly jaw. It had a mind of its own. I rested my head on his shoulder and pressed my face into the crook of his neck, inhaling deeply. *God, he smells good.*

"Thanks," he whispered into the top of my head before— I think—his lips brushed my forehead. It was the second time he'd kissed me like that, which helped ease my embarrassment at having vocalized a private thought. Well, the drugs helped, too.

While I figured the kiss to be completely innocent, I couldn't help but think that just maybe it meant more. My left hand slid from his jaw and rested on his chest over his heart, while the fingers of my right twisted and teased the short hairs at the nape of his neck. The butterflies I thought I had tamed—or doped up with pain meds—started fluttering wildly again, and I found myself becoming terribly ... needy. "Do you want me to take you to bed?"

My body quivered as his words hit any consciousness I had left. "I ... um ..."

"Relax," he crooned in my ear, his warm breath washing over my skin, and his soft lips grazing my ear lobe. "I have to get back to work, and you need to rest."

Of course. I found myself mildly disappointed that I had misinterpreted him, and my body fell slack in his arms. Jensen walked us through the house and laid me on my bed. He stood up straight and looked down at me nervously as I started to maneuver myself until I was comfortable.

"Ugh," I grunted as my jeans dug in at all the wrong places.

"What is it?" he asked frantically, leaning close to me and feeling my forehead.

"I can't sleep in jeans." He instantly straightened up, his posture hard and rigid. "Can you help me?"

"Um ..." He was unsure. It was kind of cute, but after the day I saw him naked and then stripped for him, not to mention waking up in such an intimate position, it was unnecessary.

"Please, I'm so uncomfortable. You've seen my panties before." Jensen swallowed thickly before tentatively reaching for the button on my pants and slowly undoing them. I lifted my hips so he could gently work them down my legs. Through hazy eyes, I watched as he folded them and placed them on the end of my bed before grabbing the fleece blanket from the rocking chair in the corner and placing it over me.

"I'm going to go and grab you some water and the phone. I'll leave my number on your night table so you can call if you need anything."

"Don't be ridiculous. I'll call Daddy. You jus' work. I'll be okay ..." I said groggily, my eyes heavy as sleep courted me.

My eyes were closed, but I felt Jensen's hand on my shoulder. "It's not ridiculous. Call if you need anything."

As I started drifting off, I was only vaguely aware of Jensen setting a glass on my night table before going back to work. And then there was silence.

JENSEN'S ORDERS

Pain shot through my torso as I rolled over, and I awoke in an instant. Instinctively, I wrapped my right arm around myself, holding my ribs gently and pushing myself up with the left. It was dark in my room, which could only mean I'd been asleep for several hours.

"Are you okay?" a gentle voice asked from across my room. When I raised my eyes, I saw Jensen sitting in the rocking chair I kept by the window. The sky outside was lightening as dawn broke over the horizon.

"How long have you been there?" I asked in a raspy voice as I moved to get off the bed.

Jensen was off the chair and at my side in a flash, helping me stand so I didn't over-exert myself. "Since about eleven?"

"And you were just watching me sleep ..." I looked at my alarm clock and realized it was almost five a.m. "... for six hours?"

He shrugged. "Well, not the whole time. I slept."

"In that chair? That couldn't have been very comfortable," I said, stating the obvious.

"I just wanted to be close. In case you needed anything." Even in the dim lighting in my room, I could make out the blue of his eyes and the strong cut of his jaw. "Do you?"

The silkiness of his voice left me breathless and void of thought. "Do I, what?"

He smiled, the right corner of his mouth curling up. "Need anything?"

I felt like slapping my forehead. How was it that every time he was within a three-inch radius, all brain activity seemed minimal? "Um, yes."

There was silence, and he cocked an eyebrow while he waited. His left hand was still on my waist. "Yes?" he inquired.

I couldn't find it in myself to turn away from his intense gaze. The electricity between our bodies hummed, and I found myself not wanting him to stop touching me. "M-my pills?" I hadn't meant for it to come out in a questioning tone, but having him so close and staring like he was made me nervous.

"Of course. Did you want to lie back down and sleep some more?"

I shook my head as I started to slowly get up, deciding I wasn't going to even attempt to make my bed today. "No, I'm not really that tired right now. I think I want to go and sit on the couch."

"Okay, but first," Jensen started to say before looking down. I followed his gaze and became instantly flustered.

"Holy shit!" I cried. "Where the hell are my pants?"

"You don't remember?" he asked softly.

I racked my brain, trying to remember taking my pants off. My eyes darted around the room for them and finally landed on them neatly folded on the end of my bed. That's when I vaguely remembered Jensen's hands on my stomach as he carefully unfastened them and shimmied them down my legs before covering me up with a blanket.

"Y-you took them off?"

He seemed a little afraid that I was about to lose my shit,

because his eyes went wide and he rushed to elaborate. "Only because you asked me to. Madi, you were so doped up on morphine that I couldn't just leave you unless I knew you were comfortable."

"Oh yeah," I whispered. "I kind of remember. It's all a little hazy, but it's there. It's okay." I dropped my face, but kept my eyes on him through my lashes. "Right?"

"Yeah ... as long as *you* think it's okay." I nodded my response, which seemed to put him at ease. "Okay, tell me where I can find you some comfortable pants."

"Um, I have yoga pants in the dresser drawer, second from the top."

Jensen went to my large dresser and opened the drawer. He pulled out the pair of basic black ones and came back to me. "Do you need help?"

I swallowed thickly, suddenly full of nerves as he offered to help me get dressed. While I wanted to believe I could get dressed myself, the simple fact that I could barely move my arms told me otherwise. "Please? If you don't mind."

"Wouldn't have offered if I did," he assured me sweetly. Easing me down onto the bed, Jensen knelt in front of me. Our eyes never strayed from each other's as he lifted my right leg and slipped it into my pants before doing the same to the left. He helped me back to my feet while remaining on his knees, and I held onto his shoulders as he pulled my pants the rest of the way up. His hands touched the outsides of my legs the entire time they moved upward, electrifying my skin.

My pulse quickened, and I took a shuddering breath as I tried to will the sudden ache between my legs to disappear. This man had far too much power over me, and I knew that if I wasn't careful I would give in to every desire I had.

He pushed himself to his feet slowly. With our bodies within inches of one another's, I could feel the heat that radiated off of him. I inhaled lightly, my eyes closing halfway as I took in his intoxicating blend of aromas. I could smell the shampoo and soap he had used to wash himself with the day before. That only caused me to remember walking in on him naked, and I felt more warmth spread throughout my body. I also picked up the faint scent of the laundry soap he used to wash the T-shirt he currently wore, and the heavenly smell that was just pure Jensen. The way my feelings had grown for this man after only a few days was so foreign—so wrong. Falling for someone I worked with was something I thought I'd never do again. Not after the way Dane had treated me. It wasn't worth it.

Or, was it? For the right guy.

Jensen cleared his throat as he looked down into my eyes, his own darkened by desire. "What about your shirt? It's ... still covered in dirt from your fall." As he spoke, his voice grew low and gravelly. The way it registered in my mind caused my knees to tremble. Jensen noticed this and caught me around the waist, careful not to hurt me any more than I was.

My hands gripped his shoulders as I found my footing again. I nodded slowly, telling him I wanted a fresh shirt as well. My grip on him tightened, my fingers clawing at his shirt when he tried to move away from me. He gave me a gentle squeeze before he tugged at the bottom of my T-shirt. His eyes held mine, silently asking permission to undress me. I swallowed thickly.

Slowly, I raised my arms over my head, drawing in a shallow breath as my left side protested the action, and Jensen removed my shirt. His fingers lightly trailed down both of my arms after he pulled my shirt from them, goose bumps erupting in their wake, and in that moment I wanted him to kiss me. I wanted him to forget everything I said to him two nights ago and just kiss me.

He didn't, though. No, instead, he cleared his throat and

backed up a few steps. "Where can I find you a shirt?" He averted his eyes from me, and I instantly felt rejected. Yes, while I realized I was the one who told him we would never happen, it still stung.

I wrapped my arms around my almost-naked upper body, shielding as much of myself as I could from him should he look. "Same drawer," I whispered hoarsely, my eyes stinging with tears. The tears weren't just from the situation, but from the stress the past day's events had caused on my system. I had no right to cry about Jensen not kissing me; he was only doing as we'd agreed.

After opening the drawer, I watched as he rifled through it in search of a top for me before furrowing his brow. "Um, there are no shirts in here. Where else?"

I slapped my right hand to my forehead in realization. "Ugh! I put them in the laundry the other night and completely forgot about them."

"So, dryer?" he inquired.

I shook my head. "Nope. Washer. That's okay," I said, trying to bend down to pick up yesterday's shirt from my floor where Jensen had dropped it. Jensen rushed to me and snatched my dirty shirt out of my grasp and wrinkled his nose.

"Forget it."

My eyes went wide. "Forget my shirt?"

With a chuckle, he left my room. Was he seriously going to make me walk around in my bra and yoga pants? I mean, yeah, I wouldn't be going anywhere. I was pretty much housebound due to my injuries, but I didn't want to be stuck in my bra all day. What if my dad stopped by to check on me? I moved toward my door just as Jensen reappeared holding a light blue shirt out.

"Here, you can borrow this. Borrow. Not keep. We clear?" He held out the T-shirt for me, and I took it hesitantly, unfolding it to see what the big deal was.

There, written right across the chest were the words, "I'm Giving Her All She's Got!" My eyes widened as I realized *exactly* what I was holding. Jensen Davis was a closet Trekkie. The quote on the T-shirt was a famous line of Scotty's. Yeah, the same Scotty who I wanted to beam me up the night I saw Jensen naked.

Deep like status just increased a few more points as I discovered this hidden gem about Jensen—because, yes, I was also a fan. I mean, I didn't go around speaking Klingon or going to conventions, but I appreciated the show. Or, I did until the third or fourth spin off. Give me some old school Kirk or Picard any day—though, Chris Pine from the new movie was pretty damn lickable, too.

"Well?" Jensen said, breaking the silence as I continued to stare at the awesome T-shirt I held in my hands. "Aren't you going to put it on?"

My entire body was vibrating. Not only was I going to be wearing a shirt that belonged to—and smelled like—Jensen, it was a Star Trek T-shirt to boot. There was no way he was going to get this shirt back. He'd have to strip it off my cold, hard body before that was going to happen. Of course, that could be all sorts of kinky fun, as well.

I held the shirt out to Jensen, and he looked at me strangely. "You don't want to wear it? Look, I know it's kind of geeky, but just think of it as dirty and not a Star Trek thing."

"Sooo ... You want me to pretend that I'm 'giving her all she's got'?" I inquired in my best Scottish accent, cocking my right eyebrow.

Jensen smirked, his eyes dropping to my chest briefly before catching my gaze again. "Hmm," he pondered for a moment. "I think I'd definitely prefer you to think of it as dirty."

I laughed and looked back down at the shirt, feeling better about what happened earlier. Sure, everything with Jensen was still complicated ...

But maybe it didn't have to be. Maybe we could just ... have fun. Lord knew I wasn't ready for a relationship yet, and Jensen said he was still trying to get back on his feet. Maybe he didn't want anything serious, either.

"Could you help me put it on?" I asked quietly, still holding the shirt out to him. When he took it, he turned it around and my mouth dropped open when I realized there was *more* written on the back!

"Oh my God! It *is* a dirty Trekkie T-shirt!" I cried as I read the words, *She can't take much more of this, Captain!* In my head.

Jensen shook his head. "Pervert," he accused teasingly with a wink. "Let's get you dressed so we can go dope you up again."

Carefully, Jensen slipped the shirt over my head, and I placed my arms in their openings one at a time. Jensen pulled the shirt down the rest of the way. It was big on me, but I didn't care; it smelled just like him. I was going to be wearing a shirt that smelled like Jensen. All day. Aside from the cracked ribs, I'd have to rate this day at a ten-point-oh so far. Best. Day. Ever.

"Thanks for the shirt. It's awesome," I told him sincerely, looking down at it again. I gasped when I noticed something black on the sleeve, and I almost passed out when I realized what it was. "Holy shit! Is this James Doohan's signature? Where the hell did you get this?"

Jensen seemed taken aback by my outburst. "You know who James Doohan is?"

"Uh, yeah!" I exclaimed, channeling my inner Valley-Girl. "But that's not the point! Where did you get this?"

"A convention back in 2001," he explained with a goofy

grin on his face as he scratched the back of his head. He seemed almost nervous. It was sweet. That smile was soon replaced with a serious look. "I wasn't kidding, Madison. I want it *back*."

I hugged the shirt gently — which essentially meant I was hugging myself. "We shall see," I said in a sing-song voice.

"You're lucky you're injured," he informed me, shaking his head. "Come on, I'll get you fed before I have to go. But don't think this conversation is over." Oh, yeah. I was about to score me an autographed-by-Jimmy-Doohan T-shirt. I repeat: Best. Day. Ever. Times a million.

As we walked out to the living room, Jensen stayed close to me, even helped lower me onto the couch before running back to my room to retrieve my fleece blanket. He wrapped it up around me, handed me the TV remote and disappeared into the kitchen to grab me my painkillers and some water. I'd be lying if I said I didn't enjoy his doting on me; it felt nice to have someone care enough to do this for me. Dane never would have.

Smiling, I turned on the TV and started looking through my recorded programs list for something to watch while I vegged out on the couch for the day.

"Here you go," Jensen announced as he returned with my pills in one hand and a glass of water in the other. I took the pills under Jensen's watchful eye, and then he was gone again, making an awful lot of racket in the kitchen as he whipped me up something I knew would be delicious.

The painkillers Dr. Davis prescribed were pretty good. Within the first thirty minutes, I was feeling pretty dazed, but not completely high. I definitely shouldn't have been operating heavy machinery, but I was lucid enough to have a conversation. They helped ease the pain in my ribs immensely.

I heard a knock at the front door before it creaked open, and Dad could be heard entering. "Good morning, Jensen.

How is she this morning?"

"She's good. She's awake and watching TV if you wanted to go and say hi. I'm just finishing her breakfast before I come out to the barn," he responded, and I swooned again. I was really getting the hang of that whole *swooning* thing.

"You're a good man, Jensen Davis."

I smiled, a soft blush warming my cheeks as I thought about just how good a man Jensen really was. I couldn't believe I misjudged him so hastily. Ultimately, he was the entire package. A package I shouldn't want, but did. Even if just for a rebound.

Dad appeared in the living room, walking over to me and kissing the top of my head before sitting next to me. "You scared the hell out of me, Madison."

"I know. I'm sorry. I thought I'd be okay on Glory. I really did. I guess my side was bothering me more than I thought." I felt horrible that I frightened him. As accident-prone as I was, this was the first major injury I'd ever sustained on horseback. I hoped it would also be the last.

"Nice shirt," Dad said with a smile as he read it.

"Thanks!" I said excitedly. "Jensen gave it to me."

"No, he didn't," Jensen corrected as he walked in just then, balancing not two, but three plates and handing one off to Dad before he handed me mine. "Jensen let you *borrow* it."

"You know," I began, smirking at him as he sat next to me on the arm of the couch since Dad had taken the seat next to me, "you should really stop talking about yourself in the third person. People might think you're crazy."

Jensen chuckled at my teasing and took a bite of his breakfast. I followed suit and enjoyed the first bite. I don't know what the heck he did to those eggs, but I swear they were the best eggs I'd ever eaten. Jensen was a great cook. His stock just kept rising as I made all these tiny discoveries.

While we ate, Dad and Jensen talked shop about what all

had to be done around the ranch, and it made me a little sad that I wasn't going to be out there helping. I was just supposed to stay in the house, sit on my ass and do nothing. Jensen and Dad also forbade me from doing anything slightly physical. I tried to remind Jensen I had laundry that needed to be rewashed, but he assured me he'd worry about it when he got home from work.

When his breakfast was gone, Dad stood up and kissed the top of my head. "Remember, take it easy. I need you back in one piece sooner rather than later, kid." He made his way to the kitchen to put his dish in the dishwasher. "I'll see you out there, Jensen?" he called from the front door.

"You bet. Just let me make sure Madison's all right and I'll head right out." Jensen stood, taking both of our plates and leaving me alone with my television. I still hadn't really decided on anything to watch. I was so bored already, and I had *weeks* of this.

Jensen finally reappeared with the phone in one hand and another glass of water in the other. "Okay, here's the phone. Your dad and I will have our cell phones on in case you need any help. I just want you to take it easy, okay?"

"I'm bored already," I pouted, repeating my previous thoughts and jutting my bottom lip out.

"Then have a nap."

"I just woke up. I'm not tired," I argued, sounding more and more like a child as I refused to relent.

"Well, just wait for the Oxy to fully kick in. That'll knock you right on your ass."

"Oooh," I groaned, wrinkling my forehead. "I don't think that sounds like fun. My ass already hurts."

Jensen laughed, shaking his head. "Okay. Remember, call if you need anything. We'll all be eating lunch here. You won't be cooking though, so don't even think about it."

I released an exasperated huff. "Fine."

"Good," Jensen said, happy with my finally giving him what he wanted. "All right then, I'm heading out." He started to leave the living room before turning sharply and pointing at me. "You ... stay."

"Woof," I barked softly, causing him to chuckle as he left.

With Jensen gone, the house was too quiet. Yes, he had only been here a few days, but in that time I had become accustomed to once again having a roommate. And even before that, I was rarely home, so the quiet never bothered me. I guess the truth was I really just liked having him around.

"Bored, bored, bored!" I cried out, letting my head fall onto the back of the couch. How the hell was I going to pass the hours?

Unable to take much more of this, I stood up and decided I needed to do something. Anything. Yes, Jensen and Dad both told me not to, but I was going bat-shit crazy here. I went out to the kitchen, but Jensen had left it spotless. Deciding maybe I would turn on the washer and at least re-wash my laundry, I went into the laundry room to find the washer already on. Jensen beat me to it. Again. The man was two steps ahead of me.

So, that left my bedroom. I walked to my room, and upon entering, my jaw fell. "That jerk made my bed!" The question was, *when?* "When he grabbed my blanket," I whispered to myself as I turned from the room, because I had no one else to talk to.

With nothing to do around my house, I decided to go and lie back on the couch and watch TV until I fell into a drug-induced slumber. I carefully lowered myself onto the couch and laid on my right side in order to get comfy, turning on last weekend's episode of *Saturday Night Live*. I maybe made it fifteen minutes in before I passed right out with visions of a naked Jensen dancing in my head. Okay, well maybe he wasn't dancing … because dancing naked? Nah, it was never pretty … or maybe he could have made it pretty? Food for thought, I suppose.

There was a good possibility the drugs had kicked in.

Anyway, as the dream progressed, it found Jensen and I alone. I was unclear where we were—somewhere outside—but we were together and alone. That was all that mattered. Oh, and he was no longer naked. Dream Jensen (that's what I called him) wasn't like that all the time. His soft blue eyes looked down into mine and he smiled softly before cupping my face in his hands and lowering his lips to mine. I moaned as our lips moved together, allowing his tongue to trace my lower lip insistently.

"Oh, God, Jensen," I mumbled against his mouth as he continued to kiss me, his hands twisting delightfully into my hair as he pulled my face closer to his.

"Yes, Madi?" he whispered back as I moved my hands to his chest and clutched the awesome Star Trek shirt he was wearing—wait, when had he stolen it back? Shit. Of course, as our tongues slid against each other, I couldn't be bothered to think about a shirt.

I hummed softly

"What do you want?"

"You," I told him breathlessly between kisses. "Just you." I released my hold on his shirt and snaked my arms up around his neck, pulling our bodies impossibly closer to one another's. The way our bodies fit together was so unbelievably right.

"I'm here," he told me. "I'm here."

It wasn't until I realized his lips and tongue were too occupied with my own to allow him to speak that I realized something wasn't right.

PLAYING HOUSE

My eyes snapped open, and my hand shot out like a rocket, connecting with a solid wall of muscle. My gaze locked on Jensen. "Jensen?" I sighed, confused. Still slightly hazy from sleep and my meds, my hand clutched his shirt softly before drifting up to move along his rugged jaw.

"I'm here," he said, just like in my dream. *Wait ...*

"Um," I said in a strained voice, still trying to separate fantasy from reality. "H—how long have you been here?"

"Not very," he assured me. "I came to check on you and start lunch before everyone arrived. I heard you mumbling something in your sleep, so I came to see if maybe you needed anything."

I could feel the blood rush to my cheeks as I remembered my dream. "Oh. Oh!" I cried before narrowing my eyes at him. "You made my bed!"

Jensen laughed. "Yeah. I told you to *relax*."

"You know, that's gonna cost you," I informed him as I relaxed my head back onto the soft, pillowy arm of the couch.

"Is that so?" he asked. The inflection in his tone indicated he wanted me to continue and tell me exactly what it was going to cost him.

"Yup. It'll cost you one kickass Star Trek shirt." It was a

long shot, but who could blame me for trying?

"Dream on," he retorted. "This ..." he placed the tip of his forefinger to my sternum directly above my heart, pointing either at me or the shirt—I wasn't entirely sure "... belongs to *me*."

"Okay, come on, let me help you up. Everyone will be here soon. Are you hungry?" he asked, holding his hand out for me to take. I nodded.

Very carefully, he helped me to my feet. "Um, I'm going to go to the bathroom," I said quietly.

"Sure, you'll be all right?"

I cocked an eyebrow at him as he released his hold on my hand and waist. "Yes. I think I remember how to pee."

"Fair enough," he conceded with a laugh. "I'll be in the kitchen."

"Okay." We turned to go off in separate directions before I stopped and turned back around. "Jensen?"

He faced me with a look of curiosity. "Yes, Madison?"

"Thank you."

"I told you, you can borrow the shirt—"

I shook my head and cut him off. "No, not for the shirt. For being so nice and taking care of me. Sure, it's kind of annoying, but I get it. I just wanted you to know I appreciate everything you're doing—just in case I become a pain in the ass in the next few weeks."

His lips turned up into a smile. "It's what friends do."

"Yeah," I agreed softly as Jensen continued on to the kitchen. "Friends."

Closing myself in the bathroom, I took a moment to register Jensen's use of the word *friends*. It kind of put the kibosh on my rebound idea, but it was a little comforting to know where we stood with one another.

As soon as I heard Dad, Jeff, and Tom's loud voices, I ran a brush through my hair and brushed my teeth before heading out to join them. The pain in my left side was starting to return. I could feel it with every step I took. So, I held my left arm tight to my body and entered the kitchen.

"There she is!" Tom exclaimed. "How are ya feelin', Madison?"

"I've had better days," I replied, making my way to the fridge for something to drink. I was just reaching for the apple juice when I felt a warm hand on mine.

"Hey, go have a seat. I'll get you whatever you need," Jensen assured me, his voice too low for anyone else to hear. As our eyes locked, I swore I saw more than mere friendship reflecting back at me—felt it in the way he touched me, even. The look disappeared just as quickly.

"It's ok. I can grab a glass of juice." As I grabbed the carton, Jensen retrieved a glass from the cupboard for me.

"Are you in pain?" he asked, once again being sure to use a voice too low for anyone but me to hear.

"It's not so bad," I told him, pouring my juice before taking a small sip.

Jensen shook his head and reached for my pills. It had been almost eight hours since my last dose, so it seemed right that I'd be feeling this way already. Jensen dropped the pills in my hand, and I took them before he ushered me to the table and out of *his kitchen*.

I sat in my chair, sipping my juice as Tom and Dad talked about going fishing the next weekend. They tried to go fishing every weekend, but this summer had been so busy with the ranch's expansion that they hadn't had very many opportunities. So, they planned to go now that the new barn was complete. Which meant it would be Jensen and me alone on the ranch. Jeff was going to be spending time with his friends that weekend, and Jillian had no lessons because she was going on a girl's trip to Vegas. Yup, just the two of us.

Jensen arrived at the table with a plate of freshly cut vegetables, causing my dad to groan and carry on about "rabbit food." "Relax, Wayne," he simply said with a chuckle before looking over at me. "I'm making soup and sandwiches, too."

I reached across the table and grabbed a handful of broccoli and cauliflower to munch on until lunch was ready. I didn't have much to contribute to the conversation because talking about fish guts and worms wasn't really my thing. Why did fishing have to be so gross?

In an effort to get the new, disturbing thoughts of torturing worms out of my head, I looked over at Jensen. He stood behind the island, facing me, and was making sandwiches. Every once in a while, he'd look up and smile at me, which made my tummy do a little cartwheel and a back flip. I no longer tried to pretend I wasn't staring at him, because I was fairly certain I didn't want to hide my feelings from him anymore. Hide it from my father? Most definitely. From Jensen? Nah, I didn't think so—not that I was particularly good at lying to him, anyway.

A few more minutes passed before Jensen returned with a couple of bowls that he started placing in front of each of us. He sat next to me at the table, our knees forced to rest against one another due to the fact that my small, circular table wasn't meant for five people. Not that I was complaining. Every time he touched me—even in the most innocent of ways—I felt a spark of desire between us that I couldn't ignore any more.

I finished my vegetables before I started eating the soup and sandwiches.

"So, Tom," I said, breaking the silence. "Do you have someone to help you out with training? I know Jill would in her down time."

"Actually, Jensen's going to help me out while you're out of commission," Tom said, shocking me completely.

My head snapped toward Jensen as he made his way

back to the table with Dad's the sandwiches. "You are?"

Jensen sat in his seat, his knee rubbing mine again and making my stomach flip-flop all over like a fish out of water. "Yeah. Tom, your dad, and I were talking about it, and I offered to help out." I was just about to thank him again—he truly was going above and beyond for me—but he spoke again in a teasing tone. "Plus, those horses won't get worked if you can't manage to stay on."

I narrowed my eyes at him, really wanting to tell him my falling off the first two times was his fault, but I knew that would just go to his already swollen ego. Seriously, though, if he hadn't come onto my ranch and distracted me, none of this would have happened.

Then, as if his teasing words weren't enough, he winked. The asshole winked at me, his head turned just enough that no one else would see it but me.

Oh, it's on, like Donkey Kong …

I remained silent for a moment, dropping my eyes to my lunch as I waited for everyone around the table to start talking again. Seeing this as the perfect opportunity to get him back for his little smart-ass comment, I dropped my sandwich on my plate and leaned in to Jensen. Moving to cross my legs beneath the table, I was sure to run my foot up the length of his shin and watch as his eyes widened.

"You must think you're soooooo funny, don't cha, Davis? That's fine. Laugh it up. Your Mr. Perfect exterior will slip away soon enough, and you better believe I'll pounce when the opportunity is ripe," I threatened in a low tone. I watched triumphantly as he blinked rapidly before looking around the table to see if anyone else saw our little exchange.

"This …" I pointed at my chest in exactly the same place he had earlier "… will most definitely be mine."

"You're evil, Madison Landry," he told me in a low, gravelly voice before shaking his head with a laugh. Feeling content in my success, I turned back to my meal and giggled as he stood to take his plate to the sink. After finishing my own lunch, I got up to take my dishes over to him, as well.

"Hey," I said quietly. "Before you go back to work, can you grab me my bread maker from the top shelf of the pantry, please?" I knew him doing me any favors was probably a long shot after my little stunt at the table, but I could at least try.

Apparently there were no hard feelings — quite potentially other hard things, but not feelings. "Madison, you need to relax. Doctor's orders, remember?"

"I know. But this is just measuring and button pressing. No heavy lifting. I promise. I'm not the type of woman who spends hours making dough by hand." Pausing, I shrugged. "I just want to make you dinner. You know, to say thanks."

Jensen took one look toward the table, my eyes following only to see the guys were still caught up in their conversation. He took my hand before pulling me from the room, hiding us from view around the corner. "You said thanks. Right before lunch. The only thing I want from you is to get better."

"The only thing?" I questioned, allowing my face to fall and see that our hands were still connected, his thumb stroking just below my outer wrist. "We're ... *friends*?" My breath shuddered, and I looked back into his darkened eyes, licking my lips and taking a step forward.

Jensen's chest rose and fell with heavy breaths, and his gaze intensified as he met my stride with one of his own. His free hand came up to brush my hair from in front of my right eye before his palm rested on my cheek, coaxing it up to his. The world stopped moving around us as he dropped his face to meet mine, our lips only inches apart and our eyes focused on nothing but each other.

"Madison, I—"

I started to nod because I wanted this—needed it—more

than the air I was struggling to take in right now, but we were very rudely interrupted.

"Madi?" Dad called out, his footsteps indicating he was just around the corner. Jensen and I quickly parted before my dad rounded the corner to find us standing there. "What's going on?"

I felt my cheeks warm, and I hoped I wasn't blushing too noticeably. "Um, nothing, Daddy. Jensen and I were just … You see, I …" I was no good at lying, and improv was most definitely not my thing.

"I was asking about Ransom. Tom and I are going to be working with him first, and I just wanted to know what to expect." His voice was smooth and soft like satin; there was no way Dad wouldn't believe him.

Dad's right eyebrow rose skeptically as his eyes moved back and forth between Jensen and me. *Oh, he knows.*

I held my breath and waited for him to call our bluff. Yes, I was a grown woman, but that didn't make it any easier for him. Especially not after what Dane had done.

"Madison?"

I smiled wide and tried to give him those innocent doe-eyes I was told countless times could get me out of hot water. "Yes, Daddy?"

After glancing once more at Jensen, he shook his head and smiled. "Just wanted to say have a good afternoon. I have to get back out there because the inspectors are coming by to check out the barn."

"Oh, okay. Sounds good. I'll see you later." I kissed my dad on the cheek, choosing not to look at Jensen until Dad was long gone. It was probably safest that way.

"I should go clean up lunch. We'll talk later? Over dinner?" Jensen asked quietly.

Turning to him, I nodded and offered him an apologetic smile. "Yeah. I'm going to go soak in the tub. You'll tell Tom and Jeff I said goodbye?" I asked. He gave a curt nod and disappeared into the kitchen.

After locking myself in the bathroom and starting the tub, I slowly stripped my clothes from my body. I was thankful my painkillers had kicked in for the most part because it made taking my shirt off a little easier. As the tub continued to fill, I stepped in, clutching the edge to carefully lower myself into the steamy, bubble-filled water. The heat of the water eased any residual aches associated with my injuries, causing me to relax further, and I found my thoughts drifting back to my stolen moment with Jensen.

He had wanted to kiss me—I could see it in his eyes—add to that the face-cupping, lips-almost-touching, which I suppose were the more obvious signs. The thought of any of it made me simply giddy. After seeing the look in his eyes, there was simply no denying just how deep his desires went—possibly as deep as mine.

I remained in the tub for just under a half an hour when the porcelain started to aggravate my bruised backside, so I grabbed my towel and stepped out after releasing the plug. Before wrapping my towel around me, I decided to check out my bruises to see if, maybe, they were looking any better. They weren't. I should have known better. After my most recent fall yesterday, I had bruises on top of my old, fading bruises. They were ugly and black, fading to purple on the outer edges. The darker ones were around my cracked lower ribs. It wasn't good. I was a mess.

Unable to look at the dark marks on my skin anymore, I wrapped my big fluffy towel around my body, grabbed my discarded clothes, and opened the door. I was startled to find Jensen on the other side. His eyes quickly moved down to the exposed skin of my neck and upper chest, causing my skin to blush under his stare.

"Y-you're still here," I stammered.

"Yeah." His voice was low as he spoke. "I wanted to wait until you were done. To make sure you got out okay."

"Oh, right." We stood in the bathroom doorway, the awkward silence that had become somewhat normal between us lingering before I nodded my head to my room. "I should, um, get dressed."

Please ask if I need help – no, wait …

"Okay. I'll be home in a few hours. Call if you need anything. I took the bread maker down for you, but please, be careful," he said, repeating himself for the millionth time in the short time he'd been here.

"Thank you. I will. I'll see you around dinner, then?"

"Wouldn't miss it." With one last longing look – at least, I saw it as longing – Jensen turned and headed for the door while I went and found my white, strapless summer dress to slip on. I didn't want to worry about pulling a shirt over my head, or a bra aggravating the bruises on my side, so it worked great because it just slid up my body. No buttons or zippers.

After putting on my underwear, I pulled the dress up over my hips and positioned it over my breasts. Once I was dressed, I folded my yoga pants and put them at the end of my bed before folding Jensen's shirt. I was going to place it on my yoga pants, but then figured Jensen would find it, so I went and hid it in my underwear drawer in hopes he wouldn't look there. I wasn't kidding when I said he wasn't getting it back.

I had a little over four hours until Jensen returned to get a vegetarian pizza put together. I measured each ingredient out perfectly into the handy little machine and pushed the button to start the process. By the time I was finished cleaning up, I felt exhausted; doing even the smallest things seemed to wear me out. Maybe Jensen was right to be so concerned.

Since I had a couple hours before the dough was done, I

decided to rest. There was nothing worse than feeling completely helpless; I hated just sitting around. Having slept through the episode of *SNL* I'd put on earlier, I decided to give it another go. I skipped through the monologue, having seen it already, and was laughing well throughout the show. In fact, there were a few scenes that had me holding my side because I was laughing so hard—maybe comedy was a bad idea in my current condition.

The timer on the bread maker sounded, so I got up and went to prepare the pizza. I placed the pizza in the fridge so I could cook it closer to when Jensen would be back, and then decided maybe that wasn't enough. I looked through my cupboards and decided to make a simple soufflé for dessert. Okay, simple for some people. I had just finished mixing and dishing them in their own dishes when the front door opened. I wiped my hands on a tea towel and turned to welcome Jensen back.

"Hey," he greeted brightly. "Still in one piece, I see?" His eyes moved down my body and his brow furrowed slightly—almost disappointed. "You changed."

"Oh, yeah. I couldn't really work the shirt alone. This just slid right up." I paused for a moment before turning toward the fridge and pulling the pizza out and setting the oven temperature "Um, I made pizza for dinner."

Jensen stood behind me, the heat from his body blanketing me, and he watched over my shoulder as I fidgeted with the shredded cheese on the pizza. "Pizza, huh? Looks delicious."

"Thanks." I beamed proudly. "I made dessert, too. I'll put them in the oven after the pizza so they're warm when we're ready for them."

My eyes were trained on our dinner and nothing else out of sheer nervousness. His head must have shifted, though, because I felt his breath on my cheek. I shuddered.

"You do realize that you're quite a catch, don't you?"

I laughed, because my latest failed relationship would prove otherwise. If I was such a *catch*, Dane wouldn't have felt the need to treat me the way he did and look elsewhere.

"You have a successful business, your own home, you're funny, beautiful. You're not afraid to speak your mind ... Madi, you're every man's dream girl. Some men are just intimidated by that."

Even though he didn't mean anything by it, my heart still strained upon hearing his words. "Well, not every man's," I whispered. A lone tear escaped the inner corner of my eye. I caught it with the tip of my finger before Jensen could see.

"He was a fool." There was a brief pause as our eyes found one another's, and I heard the sincerity in his words. I contemplated moving to the tips of my toes and kissing Jensen in that moment to forget the pain that remembering Dane's betrayal and mistreatment had caused. I wanted to feel something other than sad and angry about Dane and how I'd fallen for his lies time and time again. Jensen spoke before I could follow through. "I'm going to go have a shower while dinner cooks. I'll be out soon."

With Jensen gone, the oven beeped, alerting me that it was pre-heated, and I slid the pizza onto the top rack before setting the timer for thirty minutes. Moments after the bathroom door closed, the shower started, and I finished putting the rest of my dessert ingredients away.

As I was just closing the pantry, there was a loud knock on my front door that startled me. There weren't many people who knocked. Dad always just walked in; sometimes he'd give a light knock as he opened the door, but not always. Jeff and Tom rarely came over unless Dad was already here, so knocking wasn't something they did either. And my best friend, Willow, well she lived with me before shacking up with her boyfriend, Brandon, in Memphis. This was her home first, so she didn't have to knock.

So, who the hell was knocking on my door at six p.m.? There was another knock as I washed my hands, so I grabbed the dish towel off the counter and dried them as I made my way for the door.

As soon as I opened it, I wanted to slam it shut again but was frozen in place.

UNINVITED GUESTS

"Hey," Dane said, his honey-brown eyes appearing hopeful.

"Wh—what are you doing here?" I stammered, still shocked to see him here.

"Can I come in?" He took a step forward before I could answer, so I moved to close the door.

"No," I replied through a dry laugh. "Definitely not."

"I think I forgot my cell phone charger. Can I at least look for it?" he asked quietly, his eyes silently begging. It was the polar opposite to how he acted the last time I saw him. My dad made me leave the ranch when Dane came to pack his things, because he didn't want me in harm's way should Dane lose his cool again.

With an exasperated sigh, I stepped aside and allowed him through the front door, closing it behind him and following him to the kitchen. I didn't want him here; I hated even being around him. Just seeing him again reminded me of the look on his face when he shoved me against the wall and punched a hole through it just outside my bedroom.

I leaned against the stove and watched as he began rifling through the drawer of the island before looking over his shoulder at me. "You wouldn't take my calls."

"I had nothing to say to you. Still don't, actually." My annoyance and anger were slowly flaring up, pushing away the gut-wrenching hurt and disgust that seeing his face brought up.

"Well, I have plenty to say. I'm so sorry, Madison." Funny. He didn't sound sorry. No, he sounded like a guy who thought I was naïve enough to take him back. I'd be willing to bet the girl he'd been screwing might have caught a glimpse of his true nature and wanted nothing to do with him either, so he came crawling back to the moron who didn't see his cheating ways for months.

"You find it yet?" I asked, trying to hurry this process along before Jensen got out of the shower. That plan wasn't in the cards, though, because as soon as I spoke I heard the water turn off.

Dane perked right up, hearing it also. "Is there someone here?" he asked, completely astonished. "Are you fucking somebody else?"

My jaw actually dropped. Not quite to the floor, but it had to have been pretty damn close as I stood there while he asked if I was "fucking somebody else."

"Are you?" he demanded, slamming the drawer shut before completely turning around to face me. I jumped as the contents clattered, but then fought the fear that was clawing its way up my body and confronted him.

"Are you seriously asking me this, Dane?" The look in his eyes told me that he most definitely expected an answer. "What would it matter if I was? It's not like I would be cheating on anyone." I narrowed my eyes accusingly at him as I spat out my venom-laced words. "Look, have you found the damn charger yet? I need you to leave before—"

Before I could get another word out, he interrupted me, taking another step and getting in my face. At five-ten, Dane had to look down at me. "What? Before your new fuck-toy comes out and sees me here? No, I think I want to meet him," he snarled as he walked angrily over to the table and plopped down in Jensen's chair. Dane was pissed, and I felt really, *really* happy about that. Even just the thought that I had moved on seemed to get under his skin.

I only rolled my eyes and turned away from him to move the vegetables from the fridge to the island so I could make a salad to go along with dinner. "Dane, just leave. Anything that goes on in my life doesn't concern you anymore." He didn't budge, though. Instead he sat there, with his arms folded over his chest and waited — not for long, however.

"Smells good out here, love," Jensen called out as he approached the kitchen.

"Thank y— Wait, what?" Clearly I was hearing things. Before I could question him further on this whole "love" nickname, I gasped when I saw him enter the kitchen with nothing more than a towel wrapped around his waist. "Jensen ... we have com—" I wasn't given the chance to finish my sentence before he wrapped his arms around my waist, being careful when he pulled my body flush to his.

The look in his eyes was the same one he had given me earlier at lunch and the first time we had almost kissed. They were dark and stormy, his lids hooded with lust as he closed the gap between us. There was no time to protest his actions as his lips connected with mine, setting fireworks off all around me. My central nervous system was lighting up like the Fourth of July.

I had imagined this moment multiple times, but never had I expected his lips to be this soft. Soon, nothing mattered other than the way my body softened in his arms, and I gave in to whatever he wanted.

My hands moved up his arms until they were finally — yes, finally — locked into the hair at the nape of his neck, pulling his face closer to mine. His stubble scratched my chin, but in a good way that only added to the tingles that currently shot through me. The dull ache in my left side didn't even matter as Jensen's hold on me tightened, his left hand moving up my right side toward my breast. My breath hitched when he stopped just below it and his thumb lightly grazed it over the thin fabric of my dress. My nipples began to harden instantly, and I shifted my body slightly into his now-obvious arousal. Shockwaves moved like lightning through my body until they stopped between my legs, and I sighed softly into his mouth.

Everything about Jensen was intoxicating, especially how he was constantly aware of my injuries, even as we finally lost ourselves to our urges. I released my hold on his hair and allowed my hands to move down over the sculpted muscles of his back until they rested low on his naked hips. That was when my eyes snapped open. I pulled back from our kiss, licked my lips, and looked down between us. At some point in our impromptu make-out session, Jensen's towel had fallen to the floor, and I was now being treated to the sight of a very naked, very *hard* Jensen Davis. "Glorious" no longer defined him. He bordered on otherworldly.

Dane cleared his throat, and both of our heads snapped toward him as he stood from his seat. I was thankful for the large island in the middle of the kitchen that kept Jensen's naked body hidden from view. I bent down, trying to avoid eye contact with Jensen's junk in the process, and grabbed the towel from the floor before handing it to him. Even wrapping it around his waist didn't help conceal his huge problem. Not that I really expected it to.

"Oh, why didn't you tell me we had company, baby?" he asked, and that's when I heard a slight lilt in his voice that indicated he already knew.

"Well, *baby*," I said, playing my part. "It's a little difficult to talk with your tongue in my mouth."

Winking, Jensen walked around the corner, his erection still straining against the blue terrycloth of his towel. He held out a hand to Dane — whose eyes went wide as they focused on Jensen's lower half. "Hey man, I'm Jensen."

Dane blinked a few times before looking back up at Jensen's face. "Uh, Dane." He took Jensen's hand and shook it once before glancing back at me.

Jensen looked over his shoulder at me and smirked, then returned his eyes to my ex. "Dane? Oh! You're here to fix that hole in the wall, right?"

Looking irritated, Dane huffed, his nostrils flaring with anger. "I should probably go. Sorry to intrude."

After making a hasty retreat from the house, I heard Dane's car peel down the driveway quickly, kicking up gravel in his haste to get out of here. I turned to Jensen, who was now sitting on the island in just his towel, picking at the cherry tomatoes I was going to put in the salad.

"So, that was him, huh? He seemed to take the hint." He looked so smug up there, popping the tiny tomatoes in his swollen and kiss-reddened lips.

"And, what hint was that, exactly?" I inquired, my cheeks sore from the smile I hadn't realized was plastered on my face. *Jensen Davis just kissed me.*

"Indeed he did," he whispered with another quick wink in my direction. That sure as hell got the smile off my face. I really needed to check my brain wiring before I thought … or spoke … or did, well, anything.

"Ummm …" What was I supposed to say? Thanks? Was it good for you? No, that was dumb, clearly it was good for him. My eyes fell to his lap again to see his terrycloth poptent was still very much erect. An entire group of Boy Scouts could have camped out in there. Not that I'd recommend such things. That would be inappropriate.

"Madison, you're turning blue. Breathe," he instructed,

popping another tomato between his luscious lips. Lips that I felt on mine. *So soft …*

Listening to what he said, I took a breath and locked eyes with him. I was just about to ask him what the hell was with that kiss, but was interrupted by the timer on the stove. I went over, removed the pizza from the oven and placed it on top of the stove. "Dinner's ready. You should go and get dressed."

He hopped down from the counter.

"Madison, I haven't been in a relationship in a very long time," he said. "I …" He sighed. "I feel like there's something between us, but if I'm being honest, I'm not ready for anything too serious." His eyes held mine. "And I don't think you are either. Am I wrong?"

My heart fluttered like a hummingbird's wings as he reached out to push a tendril of hair behind my ear. There was no use denying it anymore. There was definitely something happening between us.

"You're not."

Jensen smiled, his gaze wandering over my face. "What are you scared of?"

I didn't even have to think about it. "Of putting myself in a position to be hurt again."

Jensen's brows furrowed contemplatively. Then he nodded, understanding. "Maybe we keep things light and casual. Fun."

His offer was tempting, but it also had the potential to get messy if feelings got involved. However, we were both adults. Surely we could figure out how to make it work.

Pulling my lower lip between my teeth, my gaze holding his, I thought about his proposal. Something about the way he looked at me convinced me to throw caution to the wind, so I slowly stepped into him, placed a hand on the side of his face, and pressed my lips to his.

PAST MEETS PRESENT

"Hey, you up?" I asked, poking my head in Jensen's room.

He was lying on his stomach with his arms tucked up under his pillow. The contrast of his messy brown hair against his white pillow was almost shocking. Until I looked down a little. The smooth, solid lines of his bare back were visible, and my eyes trailed down the contours of his body until it ended at the white sheet that was *just* barely covering his ass.

Lifting his head and turning it toward me, he smirked. "I don't know. You want to come over here and check?"

My mouth dropped open, but I couldn't help smiling at the same time as I went into his room and tore his pillow from under his head before beating him with it. "You're incorrigible!" I cried out with a laugh, forgetting all about what I originally came in here to do.

Jensen snatched the pillow from my hands and tossed it to the floor before gripping my wrist and pulling me down beside him. Yes, into his bed. He didn't pull me down hard; he was always so gentle with me because of my side—which actually was feeling a little better. I still took my Oxy three times a day, but the pain between doses was less and less. I was hoping that I was going to be on the lower end of the recovery time scale.

It had been three days since Dane had stopped by. Three days since Jensen and I confessed our attraction to one another. And three days of hot-and-heavy make-out sessions that left us both frustrated and unsatisfied. My injuries always put a damper on our pleasure, my side screaming out in protest just as soon as things started to heat up. It got old, fast.

While initially I was afraid to get involved with Jensen, even in a casual capacity, I couldn't deny the way I felt anymore. When I found out he felt the same way, I was thrilled. Relieved. Excited. But also nervous and cautious.

I had some serious trust issues because of Dane's infidelity and violent outbursts, and I couldn't just let someone else in so damn quickly. I wanted to; I just couldn't.

There seemed to be something Jensen was holding back from me, but I wasn't going to push. I wasn't his girlfriend. It wasn't my place. Based on what my dad had told me when Jensen first joined the ranch, he'd had a hard few years. How hard? I wasn't sure. What I did know was that having someone press you for the details of a difficult past only made you want to hide it even more.

"How are you feeling?" Jensen's fingers lightly brushed the hem of my (his) shirt, tickling the exposed sliver of flesh below where it had ridden up. My breathing was shaky as I inhaled slowly, my skin trembling beneath the heat of his touch. He looped one finger in at my left hip and started to inch it upward, his face moving toward mine until his nose was nuzzling my neck. The scruff of his jaw tickled my shoulder as he inhaled deeply, and a familiar tingle gradually worked its way down my body until it rested between my legs.

In the three days since we agreed to … whatever it was we agreed to, we haven't had sex. It wasn't because neither of us wanted to, but because my injuries hindered us from getting too physical. Jensen was afraid of exacerbating the issue.

This meant we didn't get much further than a few fully-clothed make-out sessions, dirty-talking, and stolen glances. We were both desperate for my side to heal.

I sighed as his fingers continued to pull my shirt up my torso, stopping just below my breasts. Yeah. This wasn't sexual at all—well, not entirely. *Tease.* "I feel fine," I told him as he pushed himself up onto his right arm, his face leaving the crook of my neck. "How does it look?"

His hand pressed against my hipbone; it hurt a little, but it wasn't excruciating, so that was good. Slowly, he inched his hand up, adding pressure every so often. "You'll let me know if it hurts?" I nodded, my eyes locking on his before he looked back down. "They're fading fast. Except around here." He ghosted his fingers over my two broken ribs, knowing that if he added any pressure there I'd be kicking his ass into next week. "If I had to guess, I'd say you'll make a full recovery in less than the full six weeks. Less if you continue to listen to me and take it easy."

"Yeah? You think?"

Jensen nodded. "Yeah, you're lucky. The bruises around the break made it look so much worse. I'm not going to lie; from the way they looked, I was terrified that maybe you had internal bleeding."

As I listened to Jensen, I suddenly remembered something he had said the morning after he moved in. "Hey, can I ask you something?"

Jensen slid my shirt back down into its place, smiling at me as his sparkling blue eyes found mine again. They were mesmerizing. "Of course."

"Remember when we first met?"

He smirked at me slyly. "It's been a week, Madi. Of course I remember."

"Not what I meant. I was just remembering how you said that you'd seen this kind of thing before …?" As I let my question trail off, I noticed that his eyes faded from bright to dull in a matter of seconds. "Well, I was just wondering what you meant by that?"

Jensen sighed, sitting up and running his hand through his hair. I remained on my back, staring at him curiously, my eyes moving down his solid back until I caught a glimpse of the top of his ass. His *naked* ass. Apparently, Jensen slept in the nude. *Awesome.* I couldn't focus on that delicious little factoid for long, however, because I could feel the tension rolling off of him in waves. It worried me. I had just started to push myself up to sit next to him when he spoke.

"About four years ago, I found my sister in her apartment." He paused, inhaling an unsteady breath and fisting his hair with his right hand again as he rested his elbow on his bent knee. Refusing to look at me, he continued. "She was living in Chicago at the time, and I had gone to visit her and her fiancé for the weekend. Robert." He cursed under his breath after that. "We were friends. She met him because of me."

This seemed to be affecting him on a much deeper level than I ever expected, and I didn't know what to do. Stop him? Let him go on? Apologize? I had a feeling I screwed up. Not knowing what else to do, I pushed myself up completely and laid a hand on his bare back, silently letting him know I was there for him. That he could tell me anything.

"I knocked for a few minutes, but no one answered the door. It wasn't like they weren't expecting me; Lilah knew when my flight was getting in." He shuddered beneath my touch before continuing. "Then—and I don't know why it hadn't occurred to me sooner—I tried the door and found it unlocked." Jensen let out a dry, humorless laugh. "The place looked as though it had been ransacked. Shattered glass, holes in walls. As I made my way through the house, it didn't appear that anything was missing, just broken. I wondered if maybe she and Robert had fought. It wouldn't have been the first time, unfortunately." He paused again as if trying to re-member the details of what had happened — not that I needed them; maybe he just found this therapeutic. "That's when I found my sister's broken and bleeding body on the kitchen floor."

I gasped sharply, and Jensen turned to face me. Tears had begun to form in the corners of my eyes as I envisioned what he must have seen. "She's okay *now*," he assured me.

"W-what happened?" I asked softly.

"Initially, we all thought she had walked in on someone robbing her and Robert. Lilah is quite scrappy, if that was the case she wouldn't have gone down without a fight. I tried calling Robert while I was waiting for the ambulance to show up to take her to the hospital, but he wouldn't answer. No one thought anything of it."

The way his lip curled up into a sneer every time he talked about this *Robert* person was all I needed to fully un-derstand what had happened. "*He* did it?"

He nodded once, breaking eye contact with me again to crack his knuckles. The pain he felt as he relived this part of his life broke my heart, and I immediately regretted prying. I really needed to learn to mind my own business.

"She had four broken ribs, a punctured lung and her right cheekbone had to be reconstructed," he continued. Jen-sen was clenching his fists in his lap while the rest of his body had gone rigid as he recalled that day. When I slipped my hand over his balled-up fists, he seemed to relax. A little. "I had known him for *years*, Madison. And he almost killed my baby sister."

"That's not your fault," I told him, taking my hands and cupping his strong jaw until his eyes locked on mine again. He looked as though he was about to cry, his eyes red-rimmed and glassy. Before I could even think about it, I moved toward him and straddled his lap. I wanted to kiss him. To take away any hurt or guilt that he must have been feeling. Was it wrong to want that? To want him? Now? Like this?

His strong arms encircled my waist lightly as I slowly pressed my lips to his. "Not your fault," I told him over and over again between chaste kisses, my voice soft and breathless. I needed to comfort Jensen in any way I could. This kiss was nowhere near one of passion and desire; it was solace, plain and simple.

Inhaling a steady breath, Jensen removed his lips from mine. There was shame in his eyes, and I couldn't figure out why. "I know," he assured me, keeping his hold around me firm, yet gentle. "Robert was found and charged. Being in jail did little to reassure Lilah that he wouldn't eventually get out and come after her, though. So, after she was released from the hospital, she came to live with me in Houston. That's where she met her fiancé, Kyle. They started out as friends, as she was in no way ready for a relationship so soon, but eventually they fell in love and are now getting married. Accepting him wasn't easy for me. I'm ridiculously over-protective."

Hoping to get him to smile, I offered him a small smirk, running my hand over his stubbly jaw. "Hmmm. I hadn't noticed."

He didn't smile, though, instead he closed his eyes and turned his head to the right.

"Hey," I said softly, placing my hands on his jaw, my thumbs stroking his morning scruff. "What is it?" He seemed reluctant to open up, and I know I said I wasn't going to push him, but I couldn't help myself. Something was gnawing at him, and I wanted him to know I'd be there for him. No matter what, and in whatever way he needed me.

Another minute passed by, and I was just about to leave it alone; if he wasn't ready, he wasn't ready. Who was I to push him beyond that point? But, with a heavy sigh, he shook his head. "What I'm about to tell you is ... well, it's not something I'm proud of, and I don't want you to think any less of me."

"Less of you? Jensen, I—"

"I went to prison." His blue eyes snapped to mine, gauging my reaction.

The blood in my veins ran cold.

Before I could say anything, Jensen tried to explain further. "I flew out to Chicago one weekend—I told my family I was flying to New York for business. I tracked Robert down at a bar. He was there celebrating his acquittal with a group of friends and his scumbag of a lawyer."

My mouth fell open, but no sound came out; I knew exactly where this story was headed.

"I watched him from a dark corner like some kind of predator waiting to attack. I watched as he laughed and drank his legal troubles away while my baby sister was suffering emotionally back home." There was a brief pause. "I followed him into the restroom, waited until the one other guy who was in there left, and then I let him know I was there."

I slid off Jensen's lap, my right leg still casually draped over his thighs. His gaze followed me. "I didn't kill him—though I would be lying if I told you the thought hadn't crossed my mind."

"Wh-what happened?"

"I did to him what he did to Lilah," he told me, his voice even. "Unlike him, I didn't have a barracuda for a lawyer, and I wound up serving three years for assault and battery."

"Three years?"

Jensen released a dry laugh. "I got off lucky, likely due to my sister's own recent assault at Robert's hands. I could have been in there for twenty-five." Looking down at my bare leg,

Jensen placed a hand on my calf. I jumped, not because I was afraid of him, but because I wasn't expecting it.

He didn't see my reaction that way and slid his legs from under me until he was facing away, his feet firmly on the ground. "Right. That's pretty much the reaction I should have expected," he said with a light laugh that broke my heart. "No one outside our family, her doctors, or the authorities know. Lilah didn't want everyone to look at her with sympathy when she moved back to Tennessee. You're the first person I've told. Your dad knows, too—but only because I was having a hard time finding work and my parents inquired on my behalf. He didn't even bat an eye."

"Of course he didn't," I said, shaking my head; it didn't surprise me that my father would do something like that. Focusing all of my attention back on Jensen, I crawled across the space between us and sat on my knees behind him. I wrapped my arms around him and rested my chin on his shoulder. He breathed a sigh of relief and brought a hand up and gripped my wrist. "You're a good man, Jensen. It's important you know that."

Turning his head, he leaned his forehead against mine, and I offered him a smile. "Thank you."

There was an instant shift between us now that he'd told me more about his past, and while I was glad for it, I could still sense he was nervous. "I like you, Madi. More than I should, but I'm in no place to give you more."

I released my hold on him and sat up so he could turn to face me again. "Neither am I," I assured him. "This is enough."

Jensen's blue eyes drifted down to my lips, and he reached out to cradle my face. I inhaled, my breath shaky, as he moved his face closer. "You'll let me know if it gets to be too much for you?" When he lifted his gaze to mine, I nodded, and he closed the gap entirely.

His lips were warm and gentle against mine, but it didn't take long for the desire we shared to burst forward. With an explosion of lust, Jensen moaned against my lips, and I took that as an invitation to deepen our kiss. His fingers tangled into my hair, and my hands moved down his chest, but before they reached his waist, he pulled back with a chuckle.

We were both breathing heavily as I pressed my forehead to his, and he closed his eyes, most likely in an attempt to collect his thoughts. "I'm sorry," he mumbled. "You have this way of making me lose control."

Smirking, I shrugged. "Sometimes letting go can be good." His hands moved down my back, his fingers curling into the fabric of my shirt just above my ass.

Jensen pressed a kiss to my lips before wrapping his arms around me. He started nuzzling my neck again, his warm breath tickling me. I giggled. He hummed, the slight vibration working its way beneath my skin and down my body. "You smell delicious. What is that? Cinnamon? Why do you smell like cinnamon?"

It was almost impossible to focus on his words as they left his mouth—his mouth that was peppering feather-like kisses on my shoulder. When his question finally reached my brain, I pushed him away, scrambling to get off his lap. His eyes were wide and apologetic, almost as though he thought he had crossed some kind of boundary he hadn't meant to.

"I made a French toast casserole!" I exclaimed, suddenly realizing that it was still in the oven and probably on the verge of burning.

"You made a what?" he asked as I moved for the door.

I watched as he turned and stood up. My cheeks filled with a deep blush when I caught a glimpse of his ass before I had the common courtesy to turn away. I'd completely forgotten that he was naked during that whole conversation. "Um, a French toast casserole. It's basically French toast, just cut into cubes with chunks of apple. Then you bake it until its golden brown and top with whatever you want. I made whipped cream and sliced some strawberries. I'm going to go take it out of the oven before it burns."

I rushed down the hall as quickly as I could without overexerting myself, screeching to a halt when I saw my dad sitting at the kitchen table. A long string of expletives lay on the tip of my tongue as our eyes met.

A HAPPY SURPRISE

"Dad. What are you doing here?"

"I came to check on you. Smelled your famous French toast casserole baking and invited myself to breakfast," he told me, his face showing no sign of happiness. He looked intense. He knew something was up; I could feel it.

"H—have you been here long?" My heart started thumping hard in my chest and I was afraid his super-dad ears would hear it.

"A little while."

What the hell does that mean?

I heard Jensen hum as he approached the kitchen. "Madi, that smells amazing. Almost as good as y—" Yup, he rounded that corner to see Dad sitting there. My head snapped toward Jensen as he entered the room, and when his eyes found our unexpected company, they almost popped out of his head. "Wayne, hey." Frantically, he looked to me and then back at my very stern-looking father.

"Go on. I'm curious to know what smells better." Dad inquired, leaning back in his seat and crossing his arms.

I had the sudden urge to use the bathroom, but I was also curious to see how he'd get himself out of this.

"I was going to say it smells almost as good as your waffles," Jensen said, directing his attention back to me, his voice steady and smooth. Not bad.

Feeling confident that our asses were saved for the moment, I turned to take the casserole out of the oven before going to the fridge to grab the strawberries and whipped cream. "Big day today, Dad?"

"Not really. I actually wanted to let Jensen know that if he wanted to take the morning off, that would be fine. Tom and I won't be too busy. Tom just said he'd need someone to ride Ransom this afternoon," Dad explained.

Jensen grabbed a few coffee mugs and set them on the counter, filling two before turning to Dad. "Coffee, sir?" Dad nodded his reply as I turned back to grab the casserole.

"How are your ribs feeling, Madi?" my dad asked as I placed the casserole on the table. "You look like you're doing better."

I pulled my chair out and took a seat as Jensen carried our coffees over and set them in front of us before going back for his own. "I feel good. The bruises are fading. My ribs still hurt, but I think I'll be okay sooner rather than later."

The look Dad gave me as I sipped my coffee wasn't missed. "What?" I inquired curiously.

"No cream and sugar?" he asked.

I looked down and noticed that my coffee looked fine, light as ever, making Dad's question strange. "No, it's in there."

"He knows how you take your coffee?" I arched an eyebrow at my dad as he smirked and took a sip of his own black coffee. "Sorry, it's just ... I don't think Dane even knew that about you."

"Shocking," I replied, rolling my eyes.

Jensen joined us at the table just then with another quick save—I'd have to remember to ask him how he did that. "I don't know if you've noticed, Wayne," he began. "But Madi's pretty insufferable if she hasn't had her morning coffee. I learned pretty damn quick how she takes it."

Any way you'll give it to me, I thought, staring a little too dreamily at him. Suddenly aware that my brain-to-mouth wiring wasn't always super sharp, I looked between Dad and Jensen to make sure that my dirty little thought was in fact just that: a thought.

They were both staring at me funny, which scared the shit out of me, and I had just opened my mouth to explain my freaky little outburst when Jensen held out his hand.

"Do you want me to take the serving spoon before you snap it in half with your death grip?" The tone in his voice indicated that he wanted to wink, but my father was within castration distance. And he knew where I kept the good knives.

"Oh, yeah. Sorry. My meds make me feel a little hazy." I handed the spoon to Jensen and watched as he scooped some of the breakfast onto his own plate before offering it to Dad, who then returned it to me.

Tension hung in the room — of course, it could have just been mine, because both Jensen and Dad were eating, laughing and talking as if they were long-time pals. *Bet he wouldn't be so chummy with Jensen if he knew what was going on between us.*

"What's going on?" Dad asked, causing me to gasp sharply and gaining me a very concerned look from both men.

"W — what?" I asked, my entire body feeling as though it was on fire. "Nothing's going on. Why would you think something's going on?" Jensen shook his head — or at least I thought he did. It all happened very fast.

Dad set his fork down before leaning forward to look at me a little more closely. "Madi, honey? You okay?"

"Uhhhh ..."

Say something, idiot!

"Uhhhh ..."

No! Not that!

"Well, I was going to go help out in the barn, but since you gave me the morning off, I don't have anything planned. I don't know what Madi wanted to do." Jensen looked at me as he slipped his fork into his mouth, nudging my foot below the table to bring me out of my panicked state.

"Willow." Jensen sputtered and choked on the bite he was working on, getting up from the table to grab a glass of water to clear his throat. "Um, I was going to call Willow and see if she wanted to come and hang out this afternoon. It's been a while, and I miss her. She's always looking for an excuse to come stay here."

Dad smiled wide. "Good! Make sure she comes out to say hi before you keep her cooped up in here. I haven't seen her in ages."

"Actually, I was hoping to come out to the barn today —"

"Absolutely not!" both Dad and Jensen cried out in unison from opposite sides of the kitchen; it was like High-Def, Dolby Digital surround sound.

Being treated like a child was starting to piss me off. "Look, I walk around the house all damn day; I can walk the grounds without falling down."

"Ha!" Jensen snorted as he took his seat beside me. "I've seen you 'walk the grounds', b — er, Madi." My eyes widened as he almost called me one of the nicknames we had yet to discuss."

"Don't make me cuss you out in front of my father, Davis," I warned low and menacingly.

"You'll do nothing of the sort, Madison. He's right," Dad said, taking Jensen's side. He took a bite of his breakfast as I continued to glare daggers at him. Sharp, pointy, little daggers.

I huffed in annoyance and slammed my fork on the table before crossing my arms childishly across my body. Of course, I was a little too rough and I felt the repercussions of my tantrum in my ribs. I didn't vocalize my pain, but you better believe Jensen saw my face contort in discomfort.

"Madi?"

"I'm fine," I said through clenched teeth. "I'm also twenty-five years old, dammit. And if I want to walk the grounds, you better believe I'll do just that."

"You're so stubborn," my father told me, looking up at me as he took the last bite off his plate. "Fine. But you don't go alone. Wait for Willow to get here."

"Deal," I said quickly, my lips forming a smile before I looked at Jensen smugly. He didn't seem too impressed that Dad had given in so easily.

"Okay. Jensen, enjoy your morning off. I'll see you around this afternoon." Dad got up, putting his plate in the sink before leaving us alone.

The room was silent for a while as both Jensen and I focused on our breakfast—or ignored his annoyance—could have been either one, really. Unable to take the awkwardness anymore, I finally spoke. "I think he knows there's something going on."

That got Jensen smiling ... kind of. It wasn't the smile I was used to, but it was better than the scowl he wore on his face. "He'd be blind not to." He didn't say anything else.

"A-are you mad?"

With a sigh, Jensen set his fork down on his plate. "I just don't understand why you can't stay put until you're feeling better."

"But I *am*," I assured him, setting my own fork down again. "I can't stay cooped up inside. I'm going crazy. And it's only been four days. It's a walk." No response. "You said yourself I was doing better. Please, I need you to be okay with this."

His next words came out snarky. "Why? Your father's already given his consent." *Wow, I've really pissed him off.*

"Don't be like that." I turned to him and took his hand in mine. That seemed to relax him, thankfully.

"You're right. I'm sorry." He offered me a genuine smile and it immediately made me feel better. "So, what do you want to do this morn—" he started to say before being interrupted by the shrill ring of our telephone.

"Sorry. Hold that thought," I said as I got up to grab the phone. The minute the handheld was in my hand, I laughed as I put it to my ear. "Willow! How on Earth do you do that?"

"Do what?" she replied, her voice full of energy.

"Know when I'm about to call you, therefore beating me to it time and time again?"

"It must be a gift," she trilled with a laugh. "What are you doing today? And before you answer that, know that the correct answer is 'hanging out with you all damn day because we haven't seen each other in over a month.' Okay. Go."

I laughed hard, causing a dull ache in my left side and Jensen's eyes to widen in concern. I shook my head dismissively at him, mouthing the words "I'm fine" before returning to my phone call. "I'm hanging out with you all damn day because we haven't seen each other in over a month," I told her, repeating her word-for-word. "Are you only in town for the day?"

"Well that depends on how long you'll have me. Brandon is in Colorado for a few days, so I could stay a while."

"Of course you can stay for a few days ... though, your old room has been claimed."

"You let someone take my room?" she asked, feigning hurt. "Male or female?"

"The first." I had to be cryptic so as not to alert Jensen to our conversation.

"Be nice, Landry," he teased, somehow knowing we were talking about him. I guessed it was when I brought up Willow's room being occupied.

"Oooh!" Willow said into the phone excitedly. "Was that him? He sounds sexy. Is he sexy? I bet he's sexy."

As I listened to her, Jensen turned in his seat and arched an eyebrow at me as if he could hear her and was curious to know the answer too. It was ridiculous ... Right? "Yes," I told Willow. "Definitely yes. So, when are you going to be here?"

Before she could answer, there was a knock on the door, causing both Jensen and me to glance toward it. "No way," I said under my breath as I made my way for it. It shouldn't have surprised me when I yanked the door open to find one Willow Martin standing on my front step.

Standing at just over five feet tall, she was dressed to the nines in designer jeans and a T-shirt that probably cost more than my entire wardrobe. Yes, a T-shirt. She had a sickness when it came to buying expensive clothes, but I loved her. Her long black hair was styled sleekly, hanging down to her waist, and the light blue color of her eyes really popped in contrast with it.

I hung up the phone, tossing it on the bench next to the door and pulled Willow to me, instantly regretting it as my side exploded in pain. "Oh, shit!"

Willow stepped back, completely horrified as I held my left arm to my side and folded in on myself. Tears sprung to my eyes as I tried to focus on something other than the blinding pain. "I didn't even hug you that hard. I'm sorry."

"No, no," I assured her. "It wasn't you. I fell off Glory and cracked a couple of ribs."

Chair legs scraped across the kitchen's tile floor before hurried footsteps were heard approaching. "Madison?" Jensen called, his voice loud as he came rushing into the room to see me now gripping my ribs with my right hand.

"I'm okay. Just a little forgetful in all the excitement." I looked at him to see he wasn't entirely convinced on the *okay* part of my explanation. "Jensen Davis, this is Willow Martin. My best friend since we were kids."

Willow gave Jensen the once over before looking back at me and smiling; she was giving me her approval. "Nice to meet you, Jensen. So, how long have you two been shacking up?"

"Wow! Getting right down to it, are we, Willow? How about I show you to your room," I said, taking her by the hand and pulling her away from Jensen before she said something that would embarrass me completely.

"Don't be silly, Madi. I know my way around the house. I'm interested in how the two of you are getting along. If I had to hazard a guess, I'd say, pretty well?" Willow sure knew how to read a situation.

"Well, it was hard at first," I started to say before Willow's eyes went wide and Jensen's lips curled up into a smirk. I was ashamed to admit that it took me a few seconds to catch up. "Oh ... OH! You two are horrible! You know what? You two go ahead and talk it out. I'm going to go and drug myself into a coma."

"Madi!" Willow called after me with a laugh as I stalked back to the kitchen. "I was only teasing! You're too sensitive!" I pretended to ignore her as I cleared the table and loaded the dishes into the dishwasher. "Come on. Don't be mad. I came all this way," she pouted.

Sighing, I turned to her. "Fine. I forgive you."

Willow clapped excitedly, her smile so wide it made her eyes sparkle. "Sweet!" She hopped up onto the counter effortlessly and looked me over as I loaded the last dish into the top rack and closed it. "By the way, what the hell are you wearing?" she asked, wrinkling her nose.

I looked down at my yoga pants and Jensen's shirt that I

had washed the day before only to wear again that night. Oh yeah, he wasn't pleased. The only thing that kept him from tearing it from my back was my injuries. *Stupid injuries.*

"Um, my shirt and pants?"

Jensen cleared his throat loudly, forcing me to jump and offer him a sheepish smile.

Willow's giggling drew my attention right back to her. "Mmm hmm. That's what I thought."

"You zip it," I threatened, pointing my finger at her.

"Fine. But please tell me we're going to do something today. I don't know that I can stay cooped up in here. I want to ride," Willow told me.

I looked at Jensen, and I knew from his expression that he thought I was going to try and sneak in a ride. "Um, I can't ride, actually. Because of my ribs. But you should totally go. I'm sure Tom would love your help, too. Plus, Halley hasn't been ridden since earlier this week."

"She's better? Why don't you call and tell me these things?" Willow demanded. "I will absolutely ride her."

I was suddenly jealous. It had been ages since Willow and I rode together, and I wasn't going to be able to while she was here. It sucked. Hard. "Cool," I said, my tone clearly indicating how sad I was by it.

Willow hopped down from the counter, her mood suddenly mirroring my own. "You know what? Never mind. I'd rather hang out with you. Forget I said anything."

"Nah," I said, waving my hand at her. "It's fine. You should ride. It's not often you're here. I'll find something to do." Jensen shot me a look. "Something *boring.*"

"You're sure?" she asked; it was evident just how much she wanted to ride while she was here, and I didn't want to disappoint her. She so rarely got to ride, and I knew how much she loved it, having practically grown up here with me.

I nodded. "Yup. Come on; let's take your things to your

room."

I took Willow down the hall and set her up in the other bedroom on the main floor. It was ridiculous because I knew she'd likely just pass out in my bed after we stayed up late, catching up.

It took Willow an hour to unpack her bag. It shocked me just how much she had brought with her for only a few days. The girl was insane—though, she preferred to be called "eccentric."

"So, what's his story?" Willow asked, hopping onto her bed beside me. "He's cute. You like him, right? I mean, it seems like you like him. Plus, you're wearing his shirt. That's his, right?"

So many questions came flying out of her mouth at once. I had almost forgotten how quickly she spoke when she was excited. "Uhhhh," I said, still trying to think of what to answer first. "Yes?"

"That's all I get? *Yes*? What the hell is that?" she screeched, louder than I'd have liked.

"Willow—"

"Oh, don't you 'Willow' me, missy. I saw the way you looked at him. The way *he* looked at you. Have you boned him yet?"

"Willow!" I was mortified. "Do you kiss your mother with that mouth?"

A sly smirk played at the corners of her mouth. "No, but I could tell you a few things that I—"

"I'll pay you to stop," I interrupted with a laugh, not interested in hearing what she did with her mouth. "Fine! Yes, I like him. Happy, now?" She shook her head, and I rolled my eyes. "No, we haven't slept together, yet ... well, actually we have—slept, that is. On the couch. But we haven't—you know. Naked—no, wait, there was naked, too ..." Willow's eyes continued to widen as I rambled like a fool. "Ugh! See what you've done? It's like verbal diarrhea."

"So, *you* naked, or *he* naked?" she inquired in a language all her own, eyebrows waggling suggestively.

"Him. Oh God, him," I said, sighing my words as I remembered the first and second times I had caught a glimpse of Jensen in the buff. "Twice."

"Twice?" she squealed, giggling manically. "Tell. Me. Everything! Oh, wait. First, I have to pee." She hopped off the bed and ran to ensuite bathroom.

"Hey, Willow?" I called out, hoping she could hear me through the door. "I'm going to go and grab a glass of water. You want anything?"

"Sure! Water would be great," she responded.

I climbed down off her bed and jumped in shock when I opened her door to see Jensen in the hall. "Are you eavesdropping?"

He took my hand and pulled me toward his room before wrapping his arms around me. "Is it my fault your friend's voice carries?" he asked, his lips finding that sweet spot on my neck that made me weak in the knees. "I'm going to head out. You should spend some time with your friend."

I moaned as his lips trailed up, kissing the shell of my ear before peppering light kisses along my jaw, finally landing one super-soft one on my lips. I'd have traded my soul to deepen that kiss, but he pulled away before I could follow through.

"Breakfast was delicious. Thank you. Come find me later while Willow's riding. I'll try to sneak away and keep you company," he offered.

"Yeah? What if my dad finds out?"

"We're two consenting adults just ... having a good time, Madi. There's not much he can do," Jensen responded confidently.

I laughed. "You mean besides fire you, or worse, shoot

you and bury you out back."

He contemplated what I'd said, even though it was meant as a joke. "Hmmm, you make a compelling argument, Miss Landry. I guess we just sneak around a while longer. What do you say?"

"Sounds deeply dangerous. But it's your only chance for survival," I teased.

"Madi?" Willow called from her room.

Jensen kissed the tip of my nose before releasing his hold on me. "Okay, go, have fun. I'll see you later. Be safe."

"Always am," I told him with a wink, tripping on my feet as I backed out of his room. Jensen moved fast, catching my right arm in his hand before I toppled over. "Errr, pretend that didn't happen?"

"You're going to be the death of me," he told me as he slowly released me, making sure I wasn't going to fall over again. "No more walking backwards, okay?"

"You really suck the fun out of everything. Live a little."

Jensen chuckled as he followed me down the hall. He veered off toward the front door while I headed to the kitchen to grab water for Willow and myself. The front door closed, and I watched Jensen through the kitchen window as he sauntered off toward the barn.

LETTING GO

As we sat around the table, I told Willow about the day I walked in on Jensen in the bathroom as he was getting out of the shower. Her mouth dropped open in shock, but soon she was face down and pounding her fist into the wooden table top as I told her the rest of the fiasco. "Classic, Madison. Classic!"

"Huh," I grunted with realization. "I guess it was three times."

"*Three*? Oh my God! Tell me! Tell me! Tell me!" Her excitement was contagious, and soon I found my own enthusiasm rising as I told her about Dane stopping by.

"Bastard," Willow grumbled.

"Well, he heard the shower shut off and was immediately pissed that there was another man here. Claimed I was 'fucking someone else.'"

"Hah! Coming from him, that's rich. Asshole," Willow muttered.

"Right?" I agreed. "Well, Jensen came out into the kitchen in a towel. At first I didn't think anything of it, I mean, I'd already seen him naked, so a towel was nothing to sneeze at." Willow nodded her head, listening intently. "Until he kissed me." I could feel the goofy grin return to my face as I remembered how amazing it felt when Jensen's lips were pressed against mine that day.

"He kissed you?"

I nodded, my entire body starting to warm as I remembered his hands on me, running up along my right side until his thumb grazed the swell of my breast. "At first, I figured maybe he just couldn't take the tension between us — we had been teasing each other a lot over the first few days. God, Willow, I have never felt anything like that before. I just felt so safe in his arms, like we were the only two people in the world."

"At first?" she questioned, placing her chin in her palm, her elbow resting on the tabletop.

"Yeah, in reality, he had heard Dane say he wasn't going anywhere and wanted to show him there was nothing here for him anymore."

"Hot," Willow said, nodding her head in approval. "So, when do we get to the naked part?"

I blushed again. "Well, as we were kissing, I got so wrapped up in it that my hands started moving all over his body until they rested at his waist — "

"You totally de-toweled him, you little hussy!" she exclaimed, eyes shining with excitement.

I shook my head. "Not intentionally. But his towel *did* fall off all on its own." Willow's eyes continued to widen as I, embarrassingly, told her how turned on Jensen was — how turned on we both were.

"But ..." Willow's ears perked at that, her eyebrows pulling together in confusion.. "He's not ready for a relationship. And to be honest, neither am I. I need, I don't know, some time after Dane. I need to figure my shit out before I just hand my heart over to another man."

"So, you're just messing around?" I waited for her to judge me, but she just shrugged. "He seems like a good guy,

Madison."

I nodded, but shrugged at the same time; I knew he was, but it still didn't stop the fear that Dane had left in his wake. After Dane, I had put up these walls to protect myself, and I wasn't ready for them to come down—for anyone. "Even though we've agreed on what this is, I guess I'm still a little apprehensive about the whole thing. I mean, he's been great. Taking care of me and being so protective, but—"

"But what? Madison, he's *not* Dane."

"I know that." I started to pick at my fingernails, avoiding Willow's eyes completely. "Jensen has been great, and I've learned just how much he cares about his family, which is admirable, but what Dane did—how he always apologized for his behavior while telling me that I shouldn't get him worked up like that—it's so burned into my memory that I sometimes wonder if he was right. Maybe it is me that brings it out in people."

"I need to kick Dane in the balls," Willow announced, shaking her head dramatically. "Madi, what Dane did to you—how he treated you—was not your fault. The bastard was gas-lighting you in order to maintain the power in your relationship by stripping your self-confidence. I mean, you're gorgeous and have legs for days—"

"I'm only a few inches taller than you," I said, smirking at her as she tried to validate me.

"All of which is leg. Just shut up, okay?" Doing as she asked, I listened instead. "You're funny and smart. And I'd guess an animal in the sack considering the mouth on you at times." I blushed again as she winked and giggled. "Try to see what I see in you. What Jensen and so many others see in you. You're amazing and strong, and you're so much happier with him gone."

With a roll of my eyes, I stood up to get another glass of water. "You're only saying this because you're my friend."

Willow's laugh carried through the kitchen. "I guess now's a good time to tell you I never really liked you then, huh?" she teased, and I retaliated by tossing a dishtowel at her face across the kitchen. "All I'm saying is: live a little. Have some fun. He's not asking you to marry him ... yet."

"Thanks. No pressure, or anything, right?" I asked sarcastically, glancing at the clock and frowning when I realized it was half-past one and the guys hadn't stopped by for lunch.

"What's wrong?" Willow asked.

"The guys aren't here for lunch. We usually eat at one," I pouted. I knew Dad wanted to see Willow, so it was strange that they weren't here.

Willow shrugged it off. "Maybe they got busy. I've seen this place in the summer. It can get pretty crazy."

"Maybe," I said, reaching for the phone so I could call Jensen. "I'm going to call and see what's up, though."

After dialing Jensen's cell phone number, I waited for him to answer; it only rang once. "What's wrong?" he answered frantically, causing me to laugh.

"You're so paranoid," I told him. "Nothing's wrong. Well, except you guys aren't here. Did you get busy or something?"

"Oh, uh," Jensen said nervously, and I could hear a chair shift on his end before the background noise suddenly quieted. "We're eating at your dad's. We thought you guys would want a little girl time. Sorry."

"No, it's okay," I said, the pout in my voice audible.

"Have you eaten yet?" he inquired.

I shook my head and spoke simultaneously. "Not yet. I'll make something for us now, though. I'll, uh, see you in a bit?"

"You bet." He paused for a minute, and I heard my dad calling for him. "I should go. See you soon."

We hung up, and when I turned back to Willow, she was standing on the other side of the island, elbows on the countertop, face-in-hands and smiling a smile that rivaled my own dorky grin. "You may be *having fun*, but you're going to fall hard, Madison Landry," she stated, her voice melodious as she almost sang the words. "You're not exactly the casual sex kind of girl."

"What do you want for lunch?" I asked, trying to ignore her, because, deep down, I knew she was right.

Willow shrugged. "What do you have?"

"Well, I could make soup, or sandwiches, or both?" I paused to look in my pantry. "Tomato and grilled cheese?" It was Willow's favorite.

Not moving from her spot at the counter, Willow made yummy noises as I started lunch. Within fifteen minutes we were back at the table and eating. "I swear, Madi, you make the world's best grilled cheese sandwich. If I weren't straight — or in a relationship — I'd marry you."

"Over grilled cheese? Brandon hasn't mastered this sandwich yet? Does he not know you at all?" I joked.

"He's got his talents, none of which are in the kitchen — well ..." she paused to contemplate something before I recognized the filthy glint in her eyes "... sometimes he's talented in the kitchen."

"You two are never allowed to be alone in *my* kitchen," I warned, taking the last bite of my sandwich.

Willow smirked, avoiding my eyes, and I knew what she was going to say before she opened her mouth. "You mean, again, right?"

Speechless. Willow had rendered me completely speechless. My mouth opened and closed as I tried to think of something to say. Finally, I just laughed. "Willow!"

"You weren't home," she said with a shrug as she stood up and cleared the table for me.

After Willow cleaned up lunch, she pulled me from the table and dragged me to my room. "What are you doing?"

"Getting you into something a little less frumpy," she told me. "You're going to rock those jeans I bought you a few months ago."

I groaned. I knew girl-time would quickly turn into dress-up. "Will, I can't wear those on the ranch. I'll ruin them."

"You're not riding in them. Plus, when Jensen sees how sweet your ass looks in them, he won't be able to take his hands off of you." I swear I saw her sprout devil horns and a tail as she deviously plotted some master hook-up plan in her little matchmaker brain.

Willow plopped me down on my bed before heading to my dresser and digging through it until she found the jeans she was talking about. They were great jeans, and I couldn't deny that they made my ass look spectacular. They just weren't practical for work. They were a dark wash denim, slightly faded on the thighs, and they had thick, blue stitching at all the seams. I loved them. I did. I just had nowhere to wear them.

"Okay," Willow said, tossing them next to me. "Strip. I'll go find you a shirt that will make Jensen fall over when he sees you."

I didn't get a chance to protest before she headed to my closet and disappeared inside. What was scary was that my closet wasn't a walk-in. I removed my yoga pants and slid my legs into the jeans pulling them up and fastening them before checking myself out in the mirror across the room.

"Perfect!" she exclaimed, her voice quiet and muffled from her hiding spot.

"No way!" I told her as she reemerged with a top that she had forced me to buy a year ago for a night out. "Willow, it's satin. We're not going clubbing."

"Fine," Willow huffed before disappearing again. "I'll find something casual, yet still wow-worthy."

"It's hot outside. Can't I just wear a tank top?" I inquired, carefully lifting Jensen's shirt over my head. As it passed by my face, I wished that I'd have given it back to him after washing it so he'd have worn it before I stole it back. I wanted it to smell like him. *I suppose I could go roll in his bed ... or is that creepy?*

"A tank top? Seriously?"

"Yeah, why not? They're tight, low cut, basic. Less is supposed to be more, right?" Man, I hoped I was wearing her down before she came out with another ridiculous bar shirt.

I could hear her giggle in my closet. "Actually, I never thought of it like that. Plus, you'll be showing a lot of skin." She contemplated it further. "Okay, I give you my blessing."

She rifled through my dresser again before bringing me a white, ribbed tank top. As I pulled it on over my head, cringing slightly as my left side strained, Willow went and changed into a pair of jeans that she could comfortably ride in. I stopped by the kitchen to take my afternoon painkillers before we headed for the door and put our shoes on so we could make our way to the barn.

The summer heat was no joke. Upon entering the barn, we saw that the stalls were all empty. Willow and I went and grabbed Halley's lead so we could go and catch her. I would leave that to Willow since I had promised Jensen I would do "boring" things while Willow had all the fun. On our way to Halley's paddock, a flash of movement in the outdoor arena caught my attention, and I stopped dead in my tracks when I realized what it was.

Jensen. On a horse.

Sweet Jesus. It may have been hotter than naked-Jensen. I shook my head. Okay. Not *hotter*, but it ran a pretty close second. Watching a man riding a horse with confidence and skill was basically porn to me. I couldn't help it.

He was atop Ransom, with Tom standing in the center of the arena watching. Ransom's lope was smooth, controlled, and Jensen looked so at home on him. His seat was deep in the saddle as Ransom moved, and his hands didn't budge an inch between strides. He'd said he could ride, but I figured maybe he was embellishing just how well. Turned out he wasdn't.

"Madison, you're drooling," Willow whispered, nudging me with her elbow as she tried to tear my eyes away from him. I couldn't, though. I was completely fixated on him. Ransom's gait was fluid, his neck rounded perfectly; Jensen made riding him look effortless.

"Okay, Jensen," I heard Tom say. "Ransom did well. You can cool him down for the day. Good session."

Once Ransom slowed to a walk, Jensen's eyes found mine, and he smiled and offered me a quick wink before Willow dragged me off to the pen. I raised a hand to wave at him before nodding in the direction of Halley's pen. It was hard to tear my eyes away from him as he sat on the massive Trakehner stallion, but Willow was having none of it.

"Ugh, don't make me blind you, woman! You'll see him soon enough."

As Willow slipped into the paddock that Halley and a few other mares shared, I stayed on the outside, knowing that, even though the horses were all pretty well behaved, it was a little too risky in my condition. If something went wrong, there was no way I'd be able to move fast enough.

Willow approached Halley, who huffed and snorted upon seeing the halter. With the halter in place, Willow led her to the exit, and I went to open it for her, running my hand along Hails as they passed. Sadness wormed its way back in because I couldn't ride her, but at the same time, I was happy that at least she was going to be getting some exercise.

"No jumps, okay? Dad said the vet okayed her for light ground work," I explained.

"Sounds good. Is your locker combination still the same?" she asked as she tethered Halley up outside to groom her.

"Sure is. If you need help, I'm sure Jeff's around here somewhere." I gave Halley one last pat before looking at Willow. "I actually wanted to go and talk to Jillian about seeing if she'd be interested in me teaching a couple of her lessons during the week. If you have any problems, come find me, okay?"

Willow nodded, blowing lightly on Halley's nose and laughing when Halley started nodding her head up and down. I left the two of them and headed back to the barn to see if Jill was able to talk. I still wanted to talk to her about maybe taking April on for some private training. As I walked back past the outdoor arena, I noticed it was empty, and it made me sad. I could have done with seeing Jensen on a horse again—even if it was doing unspeakable things to my libido.

Inside the barn, I saw Ransom tethered without his saddle, but no Jensen. I frowned, but figured maybe Tom or Dad needed his help with something. One look at the lesson board, told me that Jill was scheduled to be in a session, so instead of just going into the arena, I decided I'd go to the viewing gallery and watch until she was done.

As I walked to the gallery entrance that was through the locker room, I spotted Jeff. "Hey."

"Hey, Madi. How're you doing? Dad says you're feeling better."

Offering him a smile, I nodded. "Yeah. Feeling pretty good. Hey, Willow is here and she's going to take Halley for a ride. Can you grab my tack and run it out to her?"

"Sure thing, boss," he said, even tipping his head and saluting me.

Laughing, I carried on through the locker room. The gallery was empty as I entered, but the arena wasn't. Jillian was there and so was Jensen. They stood in the center of the arena, completely oblivious that I was there watching them. Jillian said something, smiling flirtatiously while she did, and Jensen laughed. I watched their exchange for a while before I felt my earlier fears seep back in.

I knew I had no right to be jealous. We were just messing around, after all. So why did I feel this way?

In an instant, my protective walls had built reinforcements, and just as I turned to leave the gallery, Jensen looked up and saw me. He offered me a smile, but I only shook my head and walked away.

"Madison, wait!" I heard Jensen call, opening the side door to the viewing gallery.

"It's okay, Jensen, really."

"What is?" he asked, catching up to me and wrapping a hand gently around my wrist to stop me before I could make it to the locker room.

I turned to him, my eyes connecting with and then quickly leaving his. "Whatever you and Jill have going on. I get it. She's great. Besides, we're just messing around, right?"

Jensen cocked an eyebrow at me. "What the hell are you talking about? There's nothing going on with us. She asked for my help as I was brushing down Ransom."

"Didn't look like help," I mumbled childishly, dropping my eyes to the floor as I toed it with my shoes. I didn't want to feel this way, all meek and insecure, but I couldn't help it.

Jensen placed his index finger under my chin to coax my eyes to his. "Madison," he said, his voice soft and enthralling. Our eyes locked, and soon I was lost in a sea of blue with little flecks of gray and green swimming around.

Before I could speak—whether to apologize or tell him

this was a bad idea, I didn't know — Jensen's mouth was on mine, frenzied and ravenous. It took a minute for my lips to catch up to his as my brain tried to process what was happening.

Melting into Jensen's hard, sweaty body, my eyes fluttered closed. My arms wound up around his neck as he pressed me into a hidden corner of the gallery, just outside the locker room. Our breathless moans filled the room as we completely gave in to the desire that flowed through our veins.

My hands fisted his hair — I really liked his hair — while his roamed over my body until they gripped my ass. Warmth spread throughout my body. My skin was on fire beneath my clothes as he continued to knead my ass. Our passion gained momentum as though it were on a downward slope, and before I knew what I was doing, I moved one hand down his neck and over his chest until I found the hem of his shirt. I slid it up the smooth skin of his body before trailing it back down toward his belt.

His abdomen quivered beneath my feather-light touches as I traced the waist of his jeans, and he removed his lips from mine. "Madison ..." he whispered breathlessly, resting his forehead to mine. "We can't. I could hurt you."

"I'm not asking you to fuck me, Jensen," I told him, his eyes widening at my profanity. "Just don't stop touching me."

With a groan, his eyes closed and his lips reclaimed mine, causing waves of lust to consume us wholly. Without another thought, Jensen tightened his grip on my backside and lifted me, my legs wrapping around him until he pressed his hips flush against mine. I could feel his erection through our jeans, and I desperately wanted to shed the layers between us and feel him completely. Flesh on flesh. I whimpered into his mouth — a little louder than expected — when he thrust his hips into mine, hitting me where I ached.

As our hips pushed against one another hastily, he used one hand on my ass to leverage me while the other trailed up my right side and groped my breast over my shirt. His touch was firm, yet gentle, and I yearned for more. "Touch me," I pleaded, removing my mouth from his as my breaths turned to pants.

"I am," he growled against my throat, squeezing my chest to remind me.

"N—no," I stammered. "Touch. Me." The fog that filled my head didn't allow for more clarification than that; I only hoped he'd get it.

"Fuck," he cursed under his breath as he removed his hand from my breast, moving it down my body and slipping it up under my shirt. I gasped as he shoved my bra out of the way and palmed my bare breast. "Madi ... we should ..."

I moaned, grinding my hips into his. "If you say stop ..."

I could feel he was about to protest, so I pressed my lips to his, sweeping my tongue over his bottom lip until he opened up and skimmed it with his own. Lost in the moment, all I could think of was how every inch of my body felt like a live wire, crackling and sparking and so dangerously close to exploding. The sounds of our climbing ecstasy was almost symphonic—four legs trembling, three hands exploring (because one was still holding my ass, remember), two tongues tangling and an orgasm building fast—it was like our own dirty, little Christmas carol.

"*No, I think I saw her head outside to get some fresh air.*" Willow's voice rang out behind the door to the locker room. Jensen and I stopped moving against each other, our mouths parting and chests heaving as we listened.

"*I was just outside, Willow, and I didn't see her anywhere.*" Dad.

"Fuck," Jensen and I said simultaneously, still trying to

catch our breath.

"You have a lot of land. I swear, I just saw her."

Jensen removed his hand from my chest and helped me to the ground as I repositioned my bra and shirt. Even though I was terrified that my father was just behind the door beside us, the smile that was on my face was so wide it was painful. Once my shirt was in place, I looked up at Jensen as he adjusted himself and felt bad for getting him so worked up. As a woman, I knew what it was like to be left sexually frustrated. It sucked, but it was manageable, and we could hide it easy enough. I couldn't imagine what he had to go through.

"I'm sorry," I whispered.

Raising his eyes to mine, I was left breathless when I took in the flushed skin of his cheeks and his red, swollen lips. I wanted to kiss them again. Dad's voice put the kibosh on that desire, though.

"Willow, you're in my way."

Jensen looked at me, panic in his eyes. "You stay," he told me, giving me a quick peck on the lips before bolting for the arena. "I'll meet up with you in a few."

I nodded, my mind still kind of hazy, and I watched Jensen run swiftly through the arena before escaping out the far door. While I realized it wasn't the time, I was curious as to how he ran in his current condition. I shook the thought from my mind, instantly propelled back into what was going on in the locker room. Running my fingers through my hair, I reached for the doorknob.

"Oh!" I cried, feigning shock — yeah, I should have gotten an Oscar for that little performance. "What are you guys doing out here?"

Dad dropped his eyes to Willow. "Outside, huh?" he said, cocking an eyebrow at her; he was really pulling out all the dad-looks lately.

Willow shrugged before smiling over her shoulder at me

skipping out of the locker room. *Eavesdropping little troll.* Regardless, I'd have to thank her for offering a distraction. With my heart thundering, I looked up at my dad and smiled. He didn't return it.

"Where were you?" he asked.

"Um, the gallery?" I said, pointing with my thumb over my shoulder to the still-open door.

"Doing?"

Jensen. "Watching Jillian's lesson—well, I was going to, but it was over by the time I got there. I was going to try and talk to her about seeing if I could help out by taking on some of her lessons for her." I hoped that by bringing up my desire to teach, he'd forget about his interrogation, therefore keeping me from having to lie—poorly.

"Oh." Yup, I marked a point down on my mental chalkboard for me. "I think I just saw her head out for the day. She might still be here if you wanted to catch up with her. Come find me when you're done, though?"

Damn. I then *erased* that point I'd just chalked up for myself. "Of course," I told him, forcing a smile as I tried to keep my guilt for sneaking around under wraps. At least I still had a bit before I had to face him—as long as I could find Jillian.

I had just exited the barn from the door near the locker room and headed out to see Jillian about to climb into her car. "Hey, Jill! You got a minute?"

She smiled. "Of course. What's up?"

My talk with Jillian lasted all of five minutes. While it was great that she was willing to share her workload with me, I was hoping to stall a little longer before I had to face my father. "Thanks, Jill. I appreciate it." I told her when she said she'd talk to April and her parents for me.

"Of course. I should head home, though. Tyler will wonder where I am."

My eyebrows rose curiously. "Tyler?"

"Yeah, a guy I've been seeing for a couple weeks. We were going to go to dinner and a movie tonight." While I felt relieved at hearing that Jill was in a relationship, I also felt like a total asshole. I had completely overreacted to what I thought was going on between her and Jensen. *Shocker.*

"Okay, well you go. Have fun tonight, and I'll see you sometime next week. I'll call if I have any questions about Monday's lessons," I assured her before she closed her car door and backed out of her spot.

I remained outside, watching until the dust behind her car settled and she was no longer in sight. I was stalling; facing my father about what I assumed he knew was something I wasn't looking forward to. I had just turned to head back inside when I heard something.

"Pssst." I looked toward the side of the barn and laughed when Jensen's head poked around the corner.

After looking around me, I headed in his direction, and as soon as I rounded the corner of the building, he crushed his lips to mine. "Mmmf, Jensen?" I mumbled against his mouth. It wasn't that I didn't want him to kiss me, but we had already almost gotten caught.

"Sorry," he said, smirking crookedly. "What did he say?"

I shook my head, looking up at him. "I don't know. I told him I needed to talk to Jillian before she left. He wants me to go find him."

"He's going to kill me."

"I'm an adult, Jensen." I paused, hoping I was able to harness my insane anxiety over my father finding out what was happening between us. At this point, I wasn't sure what would be worse: him thinking I was in another romance with an employee, or finding out I was having a casual fling with the new ranch hand. "Look, I should go see what he wants. I'll talk to you later?"

"Sure," he agreed, nodding nervously. "It'd probably be

best if we talked at home, though?"

"It's like you read my mind," I told him. He took one last look around before leaning in to kiss my forehead and taking off down the length of the building while I went in the opposite direction to find my father.

Even at twenty-five, I was terrified of disappointing him by repeating my mistakes.

CLOSE CALL

"Okay, Dad," I said as we walked out of his office in the barn together.

"You're sure you two can handle things next weekend? If you're still not ... um, *comfortable* with him, just tell me and I'll cancel my fishing trip." Dad hadn't wanted to talk to me about what he *had* to have suspected was going on between Jensen and me. No, he just wanted to remind me that next weekend he and Tom would be going fishing, and I breathed a huge sigh of relief upon hearing it.

"It's just, with you still being injured, I don't want to leave you short-handed. Jeff wanted to spend the weekend with his buddies, and Jillian actually has that weekend off to go to Vegas. She doesn't have any lessons, so it would be just the two of you."

I had to fight to keep the devious smirk off my face. An entire weekend alone with Jensen now that I'm feeling better? Oh, the possibilities.

"Madison?"

I shook my head, clearly having zoned out. "No, it's fine. We're getting along great. You should go. It's been forever since you guys have fished. Have fun. I can handle him ... *it*. I can handle it. The ranch! I can handle the ranch." Holy shit, if

I didn't calm the hell down I was going to definitely reveal my secret, and then Dad would never go away for the weekend. Ever.

Dad didn't say anything. He just cocked an eyebrow — making me nervous as hell — and mumbled an "Mmm hmm. I bet." Maybe he wouldn't be upset at finding out. I mean, he knew Jensen's family. Not to mention he let Jensen move in right away, especially knowing his past. That could only mean he already knew Jensen was a good guy.

"Okay, well I should head back out. You sticking around the grounds?" Dad asked as I followed him back down the barn aisle, completely ignoring my spaz-attack.

"Um," I said contemplatively. "I might go see how Willow and Hails are doing, but then I might go home and rest for a bit. I'm pretty wiped. Mostly from the painkillers, I think."

"Sounds good. Let me know if you need anything."

"Of course." After Dad left the barn, I headed for the opposite exit to go watch Willow riding in the outdoor arena. It was always kind of funny to see Willow's slight frame on my mare, but she handled her well. As Willow and Halley made their laps around the arena, I felt my jealousy growing. I would have given anything to be riding.

"Hey," Jensen's voice said from behind me. Excited at hearing his voice, I turned to him as he made his way over from the new barn, pieces of straw scattered in his dark hair and peppered all over his white T-shirt. Seeing him covered in straw gave me deliciously dirty thoughts of rolling in it with him as we made love — something that, after this afternoon, wasn't entirely out of the realm of possibilities. "I know I said we should wait until dinner to talk, but I don't think I can wait that long. What did he say?"

"Oh, he was just reminding me about his fishing trip next weekend. It's going to be just you and me here." I felt myself blush, certain he could see with perfect clarity the dirty thoughts my brain had been cooking up for when we were alone.

"So, I don't have to say my final good-byes to my family?" he joked.

"Mmm, not yet." I laughed. "I still think he knows, but I don't think he's upset about it. If he is upset about anything, maybe it's just that neither of us has come clean about— whatever this is," I confessed, indicating between the two of us with my hand.

"*Whatever this is?*" he inquired, raising his eyebrows and taking a slow, predatory step toward me.

I shrugged, pretending that the look in his eyes didn't set my entire body on fire with excitement. "Well yeah. We haven't exactly labeled it yet, right? I mean, are we together? Scratching each others' itches? Having fun? Completely casual?"

Jensen smirked as I continued to ramble on and on. "Is 'all of the above' one of my options? Can't we have fun, casually scratching each others' itches ... *together?*"

"I'm being serious!" I told him, reaching out to playfully swat him. "I'm quite content to let things play out naturally without getting too serious. But eventually, Dad is going to question it, and we should be prepared with an answer. To hear that we're casually dry humping in the viewing gallery isn't an image he's going to want of his little girl. I'm just sayin'."

Jensen's smiling mouth dropped open. "Did you just say dry hump?"

Not realizing I said it before it was already out there, I was embarrassed. However, I didn't want Jensen to use that against me, so I nodded. "Does that offend you?"

"Not at all. It's just hearing you say that—among other things you've said today—well, let's just say you shouldn't be surprised if we find ourselves in a very similar situation at some other point today." His words caused my cheeks to fill with color, and he smiled lazily. "I love when you do that?"

"What?" I snorted. Sexy, right? "Get embarrassed?"

He shook his head and took another step toward me and shrugged. "Sure. I've seen it a couple other times, though. It's not *only* when you're embarrassed, you know," he told me with a suggestive eyebrow waggle.

Now I was embarrassed. My entire face had to be flaming red as he alluded to the other times we were together that caused my skin to blush. *Fan-freaking-tastic.* Suddenly, another wave of fatigue washed over me, causing my knees to buckle and me to fall right into his arms.

"You okay?" he asked as he helped steady me.

Back on my feet for the moment, I ran my fingers through my hair. "Um, yeah. I'm just tired. I should go back to the house and lie down."

"I think the heat might be getting to you. Come on, I'll walk back with you." Jensen started turning me toward the house when I stopped him, placing my hand on his chest. His warm, hard chest.

"No, it's okay. You work. I'll be fine."

"I'm not going to let you walk alone, only to discover three hours from now that you've passed out on the way home from heat stroke," he told me, moving us forward and forcing my feet to move or be dragged behind us. As soon as we were out of sight of the barn, Jensen swept me up into his arms and carried me the rest of the way. I didn't protest—I could have, I just didn't. I enjoyed being in his arms.

Leaning my face into his neck, I inhaled deeply, taking in his intoxicating blend of aromas and deciding that, at some point, I was definitely going to go and roll in his bed with my (his) shirt on. Creepy or not, I was like a junkie looking to score her next hit.

Jensen shifted my weight slightly in his arms to free his right hand and open the front door so he could carry me through.

My limbs became heavy and my eyelids started to droop as Jensen kicked the door shut behind him. "Do you want me to put you on the couch or in your bed?" he whispered into the top of my head.

The feeling returned to my arms as my mind breeched consciousness for a split second. "Mmm," I mumbled, pressing my head closer into him and inhaling once more. "Can I ..." I yawned. "Can I sleep in your bed?"

"Sure," he said softly as he turned down the hall and took me to his room, being sure to tuck his comforter tightly around me. "Do you need your heating pad? How are your ribs?"

"Mmm. Yes please. They're sore," I told him, my eyes opening slightly as my exhaustion forced my words to slur together.

I was nearly asleep when Jensen returned and slid the heating pad beneath me before plugging it in and setting it to low. "There you go. Sleep. I'll let Willow know where you are so she doesn't worry."

I snuggled deeper into the comforter, breathing Jensen in all around me, and sighed in contentment. As I took one last deep breath, I felt all consciousness slip away until everything was dark and peaceful. *Smells so good ...* From somewhere far away, I heard a faint chuckle before warmth caressed my forehead.

"You're kind of crazy, but I love it."

"Ha! Yeah, that sounds about right!" I heard Jensen exclaim as my eyes fluttered open. It took me a moment to recognize my surroundings. With no one privy to my awakening, I smiled and pulled Jensen's blanket up around my head, holding it around me for just a little bit longer.

"Oh, you'd have laughed your ass off, Jensen!" Willow told him, grabbing my attention by the balls and forcing me to leave the warmth of Jensen's bed. Whenever Willow spoke to anyone and the words "you'd have laughed your ass off" were involved, you could almost guarantee she was spinning tall tales — or telling frightening truths — about me.

I flew down the hall, ignoring the blistering pain in my side and screeching to a halt when I reached the kitchen to see Willow perched on the island as Jensen stood at the stove stirring something in a saucepan.

"Hey, sleepyhead," Willow chimed, turning her face to mine.

"What are you guys talking about?" I asked in a panic, trying to catch my breath.

Jensen and Willow exchanged a look, secretive smirks on both of their faces. "I was telling Jensen about our senior year in high school."

No good could come out of any story regarding my senior year. My face scrunched, showing my displeasure with their choice of topic. Anything Willow had to say about me in high school would only cement what he was already suspecting about me: that I was a super-duper klutz. Yes, I had fallen off my horse, tripped several times, stubbed my toe and countless other things since he had arrived, but as far as he knew that wasn't the norm for me. Well, he didn't until Willow opened those pouty pink lips of hers. Whore. And I meant that with love.

"You can't believe a word she says, Jensen. Women can't be trusted. Trust me," I joked, trying to avoid knowing what they were talking about while saving face.

Willow smirked, her perfectly shaped eyebrows arching sinisterly. "So, you're telling me that during gym class ..."

Oh shit. Not this story. Please tell me she didn't tell Jensen. Please tell me she didn't tell –

"... when we were learning the Macarena that you didn't get all mixed up before bumping into Alan Tripp and take your entire row out like dominoes?"

Oh, she is so dead.

As soon as she finished talking, I felt my face heat and saw Jensen snickering over whatever he was stirring on the stove. Visions of me grabbing one of my brass pots off the rack that hung above the island and chasing Willow around the house ran rampant in my mind.

"Sleep with one eye open, shrimp." I stepped over to Jensen, who was still trying to keep his laughter controlled, and poked him in the side. "It's not that funny. I broke Alan's nose." He didn't seem to find that quite as tragic as I did and broke out into hysterics while Willow fell to her side on the island and slapped her palm against the counter as she remembered.

"That's right! How did I forget that part?" Willow exclaimed.

"Oh, come on, you guys!" I cried out, feeling my own laughter on the brink of escaping. "Please, stop!"

Jensen struggled to catch his breath, wiping tears of laughter from the corner of his eye. "It's a little funny, Madi." I shoved him lightly before sidling up to him and looking at what he was working on.

"It's roasted red pepper cream sauce. I'm going to serve it over penne," he told me before I got the chance to ask. As he spoke, my stomach growled and he laughed. "How was your sleep? You feeling okay?"

"It was good," I responded before laughing quietly.

"When I woke up I almost didn't recognize where I was. I forgot I'd asked."

Jensen smiled wide. "I'm glad you did. I quite enjoyed seeing you in my bed."

"Oh, you guys are sick," Willow complained, her tone teasing as she leafed through a tabloid magazine she had to have brought with her, because I didn't subscribe to that trash. "Get a room. And not the viewing gallery this time. I totally saved your asses earlier."

Rolling my eyes, I picked up the dishtowel and chucked it at her for the second time that day. "Yes, Willow. Thank you. I *owe* you."

"Damn right you do. And you know how I'm going to collect?" It took one look at each other to know that I was in for a long afternoon of shopping in the city with her. "Shopping, baby!"

"Aw, shit." I groaned, pressing my forehead into Jensen's bicep. "Tell her I have to stay home and relax. That shopping's not good for me. *Please.* I need you to be on my side."

Flipping the burner to low and pouring the dried pasta into the other pot of boiling water, he turned to me. "I wish I could. But, you seem to be feeling great. Plus, Willow is only here for a few days."

"Why do you hate me?" I asked, poking his arm as I turned to grab my bottle of painkillers.

Jensen smiled. "I don't hate you, Madison. Far from it, actually." Yeah, I was no longer upset with him—okay, so I was never *really* upset with him.

"All right, Willow. Tomorrow you and I will head into town and shop for the afternoon." Willow clapped with glee, practically vibrating on the island.

"Nope! I'm taking you to Memphis!"

I looked at Jensen, hoping he'd tell her it was too long a

drive, but he only winked at me. At least in Savannah shopping was limited. In Memphis, though? Shit, Willow could make me shop for weeks.

"Memphis?" I croaked.

"I already told Willow to make sure she watches you. She assures me she won't keep you out too late." They planned this. *Motherfu –*

"Willow, the pasta's almost done," Jensen announced. "Would you mind setting the table? Madison, you should go and have a seat."

With Willow hard at work, she told me about a few of the new stores in the mall since I'd been there last. I sat in my seat and waited for dinner to reach the table. Okay, so maybe I was a little excited to go into the city with Willow. It had been far too long since we'd had a girl's day out. Chances were we might even hit up Willow's spa for a deep tissue massage. That sounded pretty great, as long as they avoided my side.

"How was Ransom today?" I asked as Jensen set dinner in the middle of the table. He sat between Willow and me. Willow started dishing food onto her plate as Jensen and I talked about work.

"He was great. Tom says you've really made a lot of progress with him the last few months. It's noticeable in a stallion his age." Jensen paused before offering me the chance to dish up next. "He's a marvelous horse. I'd love to ride him more."

"Well," I said, covering my pasta with the delicious-smelling roasted pepper sauce. "Until I'm feeling better, he's all yours. And I suppose I could even share after that."

"How very gracious."

Dinner was – amazing would actually fall short of just how delicious it was. The conversation was good – which was to say no more embarrassing stories of my teenage years were told, and the food was to die for. Jensen's cooking continued to surprise me.

Willow and Jensen both had a couple of glasses of wine with dinner while I pouted that I wasn't allowed to have any while on my medication. I wasn't a heavy drinker, but every once in awhile, a glass of red wine with my dinner was a nice option to have.

"So," I said, standing up and gathering our three empty plates to clean up after they both made and set up for dinner. "What do you guys want to do now? I'm sure there's something good on TV. Or we could put a movie in."

"That sounds like fun!" Willow exclaimed as she and Jensen hopped up and helped clear the table for me as I filled the dishwasher.

Between the three of us, it didn't take long to clean the kitchen so we could make our way to the living room. Before Jensen or I could even reach the couch, Willow swooped in and sat in *my* spot. Probably to force Jensen and I to sit next to one another — not that I minded in the least, of course.

"Hmm," Jensen pondered. "Quite meddlesome, isn't she?"

I laughed, causing Willow to look up at me with a look of curiosity. "That would be an understatement."

"What?" Willow asked, that same devious sparkle in her eyes while being simultaneously oblivious.

Shaking my head, I moved to the shelf that housed my movie collection. "So, what did you guys want to watch?"

"As long as it's not *Star Trek*, I'm easy," Willow quipped, and I shot Jensen a look over my shoulder as he sat in his usual seat and nodded once. Willow didn't miss our silent exchange, and she groaned loudly. "Awww, come on!"

Shrugging, I grabbed the disc and popped it in the player before standing up and plopping down next to Jensen with a few inches between us. "Sorry, babe," I told her. "Two against one."

"Ugh, you Trekkies." Willow wiggled in her spot to get comfortable until her legs were twisted to the side and her feet were kicking into my thigh. Oh, she was a subtle creature.

Not really enjoying the feeling of her bony feet in my leg, I moved over until I was pressed against Jensen. Willow smirked in triumph. In an effort to get comfortable, Jensen moved his left arm from between us and draped it behind me on the back of the couch. As the movie played on, his arm relaxed until his long fingers brushed my shoulders, sending a shiver through my body.

"Cold?" he asked upon noticing, shifting as if to get up and retrieve a blanket for me.

I shook my head. "Nope. That just tickled."

Teasing, Willow gagged loudly. "Ugh. If you two start making out during this movie, I'm going to puke. How is this stuff even sex— Hello! Who is *that*?" Trust Willow's attention span to shorten at the sight of the baby blue eyes of Chris Pine.

"That's Captain Kirk," I told her. Had she never seen this movie? "Cute, right?"

Jensen looked down at me. "You think so?"

Sensing some kind of weird jealousy over a man I was never going to meet, I decided to play with Jensen a little. I shrugged. "Sure. He's got nice eyes, nice voice. His body's pretty decent."

"You sure you're talking about this Kurt guy?" Willow teased from beside me.

"*Kirk*," I corrected her, being sure to put heavy emphasis on the last "k."

She rolled her eyes. "Whatever. Let's call him 'Hotty-McSexy'. Anyway, like I was saying—"

Thankfully, Willow's iPhone took that moment to blare

out "*Touch me touch me touch me touch me, I want to get dir-ir-ty*" from the *Rocky Horror Picture Show*. Laughing, I shook my head. Willow just grinned and hopped up off the couch.

"Hey, babe!" she exclaimed. "I miss you." Her voice dropped to a whisper, and she eyed Jensen and me nervously before fleeing the room. "Um, nothing. What are you wearing?"

"Oh, I did *not* need to hear that!" I called out after her, only to have her giggle before her bedroom door closed.

"I'm in serious need of brain bleach," I whined, pulling my legs up onto the couch in front of me. Relaxed, I let my head fall back onto the couch—onto Jensen's arm—before turning to look at him. He was still facing me, staring intensely.

"Hi," I whispered, trying to control my now-racing heartbeat.

"Hi." Slowly, he lowered his face to mine and kissed me softly. Our lips moved together gently, and he cradled the side of my face with his right hand, his fingers twisting into my hair to deepen our kiss. I hadn't meant for our kiss to escalate, but whenever his lips were on mine, it was like my brain was no longer in control of what my body did.

I turned my body to his, quickly straddling his lap as his tongue firmly traced my lower lip. I opened my mouth to release a sigh, and soon our tongues slid languidly against each other. Jensen's left hand ensnared my right hip, his fingers digging in and sending a delightful surge of excitement straight through me. My hands moved down his body until I found the bottom of his shirt and started to raise it between us.

"Mmm, Madison," he mumbled against my ravenous lips. "We need to stop." While I heard his words, his body was telling me an entirely different story.

I shook my head, refusing to relent my attack on his

mouth. I ran my fingers over his muscular chest beneath the shirt I was trying to push up. His grip on my waist tightened, and he shifted his hips up, grinding against me, which caused me to moan shamelessly. He was right; we should stop before we went too far. I still wasn't a hundred percent.

So good ...

Jensen groaned into my mouth, his fingers tightening in my hair, sending tingles shooting down my neck and spine. "I know, but we have to stop."

"Can't," I murmured. "Don't want ..."

With the sexiest growl I had ever heard, Jensen twisted us until he had me pinned to the couch below him, his lips working even more fervently against my own as his left hand snaked up my shirt and gripped my breast over my thin bra. "Do you have any idea what you do to me?" he said before trailing his lips over my jaw, gently nipping along the way.

"I think I have a pretty good idea," I said breathlessly, his lips kissing a trail along the column of my throat.

He pushed his hips forward, and pleasure prickled through me, quickly followed by pain that spider webbed out from my broken ribs. I grunted, but I tried to pass it off as a moan so Jensen wouldn't stop. As much as it hurt, I wanted him so badly.

But he knew. He always knew.

Jensen's body tensed as he raised his lips from mine. "We have to stop. We can't ... not yet. You need to get better. We need time ... take things slow."

I knew he was right. Somewhere deep down inside— past the throbbing between my thighs and the pain that was starting to wane—I *knew* he was right. But my brain was no longer thinking like that. It was in complete cahoots with my body. "Fuck slow," I told him, thrusting my hips up into his.

Jensen leaned down until his lips ghosted mine and his eyes held me captive. "I intend to. But not today. Not like this," he whispered before brushing the tip of his nose over mine and sitting us both up.

My heart stuttered—did hearts do that? Who knew. All I did know was that hearing his words caused my entire body to react in that good-yet-I-wanna-be-so-very-bad kind of way. "I'm sorry," I told him, fixing my hair.

"No need to be. I'm just as much to blame." Jensen fixed his shirt to cover the lower part of his abdomen that was still showing. "It's just, every time I'm around you—"

I quickly snapped my hand up to cover his mouth with the tips of my fingers. "While I understand you're trying to be sweet and noble while maintaining your virtue, I need you to stop talking before I force myself on you."

Jensen smiled beneath my fingertips before kissing them and pulling my hand from his mouth. "It amuses me that you think this has anything to do with my virtue."

"Well, it can't possibly be mine. In case you've forgotten, I was the one who jumped you a few minutes ago," I reminded him, only to have his eyes flash with the same excitement they held when we were mid-bump 'n' grind.

"And I could have stopped you."

I pretended to ponder this before narrowing my eyes jokingly. "Excellent point, you cad."

"Watch it, Landry. You're not too old for a good spanking." He was trying to gain the upperhand, and I wasn't going to allow for it. Not anymore.

I bit my lip and leaned forward until my mouth traced his ear lobe. "You promise?"

Jensen laughed, albeit a little nervously. "You're right. Your virtue is a lost cause. Best do everything I can to protect myself from your corruption." Jensen turned to kiss me quickly, knowing that the last time his lips lingered on mine things had gotten out of hand. "Now, we've missed almost half of this movie already, what do you say we try and enjoy the rest of it?"

For the remainder of the movie, Jensen teased me about my self-admitted crush on Kirk. It would have annoyed me more if his arms weren't wrapped around me securely as I leaned against him, listening to the steady *thump-thump* of his heartbeat. The feeling of his fingers as they traced delicate lines up and down my arms or combed through my hair was delightful, and by the end of the movie, I found myself yawning.

Willow had just appeared as the movie credits started rolling, complaining that she had missed the whole thing. "You guys could have paused it," she stated with her hands placed squarely on her hips.

"Willow, you were gone for over an hour. What would we have done while we waited?"

When she smirked, I wanted to go back in time and *not* ask that question. "Same thing I was doing, but maybe in person?"

"Oooh," I groaned, pushing myself to my feet. "No, I did not need to hear that. No one did."

Jensen chuckled, obviously enjoying our playful teasing of each other, and stood up. "All right, ladies. I'm headed to bed. Early day and all. You two better get some sleep; you've got a big day of shopping ahead of you."

"You bet! Come on, Madi. Sleepover," Willow announced before turning and walking toward my room.

After turning off the TV and all the lights, I walked with Jensen until we stood outside his room. "So, will there be pillow fights?"

"Contrary to what is shown in movies about sorority house slumber parties, we will not be in skimpy lingerie, nor will there be a downpour of feathers from the sky." I paused, taking in his disheartened look before offering him a sly smile. "In fact, I plan to wear *my* new shirt ... and possibly nothing else. So, think about that as you try to fall asleep."

"As much as I'd like to see that," he said. "I'd like to assure you that I already think about that quite often. And as for what the other should be thinking about before falling asleep completely frustrated ..." He leaned in until his lips brushed my ear and his breath tickled my neck. "Know that I will be sleeping without a stitch of clothing on. By the way," he lowered his voice to a whisper, "I've been meaning to tell you all day that I *really* like those jeans on you."

I laughed. "Willow thought you might."

"Hmmm. Well, she was right," he said before walking backward into his room, his eyes moving up and down my body. The smile on his face was quite devilish as he raised his shirt over his head, giving me a brief glimpse of his naked torso before closing his door.

The man did not play fair.

But I *liked* it.

GIRL'S DAY OUT

"Wake up! I'm going to go hop in the shower before breakfast." My eyes opened slowly when I felt the bed shift beneath the slight frame of my best friend. Then she was gone, her bare feet shuffling quickly across the floor toward the bathroom.

Willow wound up passing out in my bed (as I knew she would) around one a.m. We had stayed up a little later than intended when she started asking all sorts of questions about what happened between Jensen and me that afternoon. That, of course, led to me telling her about us making out like a couple of horn-dogs on the living room couch.

I pulled myself out of bed and stretched. My side still hurt, but seemed to be getting better with each day that passed. When I heard the shower start, I stood from the bed and was just about to head out into the hall before I had a simply devilish idea. I removed the shorts I had worn to bed, leaving me in just Jensen's shirt and my panties.

He was gonna flip.

Across the hall, I could see that Jensen's bed was already made, and I was pretty sure I could hear him in the kitchen. I let myself into the bathroom—or, more accurately, I opened the door slightly and poked my head in before calling out for the person I *thought* was inside. Just to be safe.

"Willow?"

"Yup!"

"I'm just going to brush my teeth, okay?" I inquired, hoping I wasn't being too intrusive.

After giving me the go-ahead, I stepped in and did my morning routine. Before leaving, I made sure my hair wasn't too messy, but still looked like sex hair. You know, to give Jensen a taste of his own medicine.

I locked the bathroom door for Willow and made my way to the kitchen. Taking a deep breath, I pressed forward and found Jensen at the stove, flipping pancakes on the griddle. "Good morning," I chirped as I moved behind him and headed for the fridge.

He didn't turn around at first, keeping his eyes on breakfast. "Hey, how'd you sl"—I had just opened the fridge and leaned forward to look for something—I don't know what, really. I just wanted my ass to show from the bottom of the shirt. I could tell by the way his pitch raised that he had looked—"eep?"

I stood up, grabbing the orange juice from the top shelf before turning to face him. "Mmmm," I hummed seductively. "Sooo good." The way his eyes devoured my bare legs thrilled me, and I smiled. "See something you like, Davis?"

"You could say that," he managed to choke out, his voice raspy. I decided he needed to see a little more, so I moved toward the cupboard to grab a glass and reached up for one, the shirt riding up and showing a tiny peek of the side of my panties.

"Hey!" he exclaimed, moving to my side in an instant. When I felt his hand on the hem of my shirt, I moved back and slapped his hand playfully.

"Excuse you!" I cried, backing up until I hit the island.

Jensen continued to advance on me, a dangerously possessive look in his eyes that excited me. "You," he growled, "are a liar, Madison."

My pulse started racing through my veins and my legs trembled when he stopped within inches of my heaving chest. "W — what?" I asked, my voice trembling, and I reached behind me to hold the counter before I melted.

"You said you would be wearing my shirt and nothing else," he reminded me, his finger looping into the side of my underwear and gently snapping them.

I swallowed thickly. "Well," I said. "Willow was sleeping with me. Don't you think that would have been a little inappropriate?"

His lips twisted up into a playful smirk as he gripped my hips lightly. "I suppose I could let it slide this time." His fingers danced on my hips, and it wasn't until I felt a breeze on the exposed skin of my ass that I realized what was happening; he was inching the shirt up slowly.

"What are you doing?" I asked, my voice barely above a whisper.

"I'm going to check your bruises. Is that all right?" I nodded once and he proceeded.

I laughed. "You'd better hope my dad doesn't walk through that door as you're stripping me in our kitchen."

Jensen glared at me. "You really know how to kill the mood, don't you?"

"Just keeping you in line so you don't get carried away as you so often do," I teased.

"Me?" He moved to my left side and pushed the shirt up, grazing the side of my breast as he held it in place. "*You* attacked *me*, remember?" His thumb brushed my nipple, and I sighed, my eyes rolling back.

Jensen's hands moved softly over my skin as he inspected my bruises. There was a part of me that was starting to wonder if this was just his way of getting me slightly naked and just claiming he was "inspecting" my injuries. The other part, though, was all *"Shut up! He's getting you slightly naked!"* She won time and time again; she was a horny little bitch.

Jensen didn't look for long—probably afraid that my father *would* make one of his unannounced morning visits—and replaced my shirt. "Well, it looks good. How does it feel?"

I moved my left shoulder around a little. "A little tight and it hurts when I move certain ways. But all-in-all, it's not too bad."

"Good. We should take you to see my mom next week. She can order another scan and we can see where you're at," Jensen suggested, turning back to his pancakes.

Taking a sip of my juice and grimacing as the taste soured from brushing my teeth, I moved to his side. "Chocolate chips don't seem like a good breakfast staple, Jensen," I scolded lightly as I reached out to pick at the pancake he placed on the empty plate.

"Hey now," he reached out and grabbed my hand before I was successful in scoring a bite. "No picking."

I pulled my bottom lip between my teeth and batted my eyes at him. "Not even if I was going to give you the first taste?" In truth, I wasn't; but now that I had said it, it seemed like a really good idea. Or a bad one, depending on how you looked at it.

He didn't release his grip on me, so I crossed my left hand over and tore a piece of the pancake off and held it up to his mouth. His eyes moved between mine and the warm, fluffy pancake I held out to him. It took less than a second before his lips wrapped around my fingers, causing me to inhale a small gasp.

I eyed my fingers, wet from Jensen's tongue as it slid up them softly before he retrieved the pancake. As he chewed, I tried to tell myself that it was insane to think about never washing that hand again. He finally released my right hand, and I had just reached out to tear another small piece off for myself when he stopped me again.

"That's not fair," I told him, pouting like a three-year-old. "I shared."

The way the right side of his mouth twisted up and his eyes sparkled alerted me that he wasn't actually going to refuse me a bite. Holding my gaze, he reached over and tore a small piece off the pancake and held it out to me. It smelled delicious; sweet and fresh. Without looking away, I stepped into him, wrapped my hands around his wrist to hold his hand steady, and leaned forward to accept his offer.

I watched as his eyes darkened, and I licked my lips before wrapping them softly around the tips of his fingers, taking the warm pancake from him. He released a groan as I moved my mouth up his long, thick fingers suggestively, being sure to run my tongue along them.

Without warning, Jensen dropped the metal spatula to the floor and pulled me to him. His lips were on mine, kissing me deeply, devouring me. I stepped up onto my toes with a whimper, wrapping my arms around Jensen's neck. He lifted me, my legs dangling between his as he walked me back to the island and set me on it.

Stepping forward, he nudged my legs, and I parted them, inviting him closer. I hooked my legs around his, and he held me close, his hands on my ass, groping, kneading. My hip pulsed forward, and I moaned when I felt his cock thicken against me. My hands slid down his neck and shoulders, stopping on his strong, muscular biceps and holding them tightly.

Jensen's right hand came up and cupped my jaw. His fingers tangled in my hair as he held my face in place. The fingernails of his other hand bit into the flesh of my ass, inviting currents of pleasure to ripple through me. His fingers, strong and firm, slipped beneath the edges of my panties. He pulled me forward again until I was balanced on the very edge of the counter. His fingertips grazed the silky wet flesh between my thighs, and we both groaned together before he broke the kiss.

"What?" I asked breathlessly, confused about why he stopped.

Jensen licked his lips. His complexion was flushed, and his chest was heaving.

I could only imagine how I looked.

"That was probably a bad idea," he said, alluding to the pancake sharing. "You have company."

My face blazed with heat. I couldn't believe I'd momentarily forgotten about Willow. "Yeah. Sorry. Breakfast is good, though. If that's any consolation."

"Thanks. You should probably go and get dressed ... just in case your dad stops by."

I hopped off the counter, still extremely turned on and frustrated. Before leaving the kitchen, I kissed Jensen on the cheek. "One of these days, we'll finish what we start," I told him.

He chuckled, turning his head and kissing the tip of my nose. "You can count on it."

Willow and I crossed paths as I made my way back to the bedroom. She was fully dressed in jeans and a lacy black top, her hair and makeup done.

"Hey," she said. "Breakfast smells good. Pancakes?"

"Chocolate chip," I told her with a smirk before closing myself in my room to get ready. I grabbed a fresh pair of jeans and a purple shirt that hugged my figure. As I looked at the way my jeans fit, I decided that maybe investing in a few new pairs might not be so bad. These ones were more than a little worn in around my ass and thighs. Not very flattering.

I stopped by the bathroom and brushed my hair, getting

rid of that messy, bed-head thing I had going on. It was a good thing Jensen shooed me away when he did, because when I arrived in the kitchen, Dad was sitting at the table with Willow, sipping his coffee.

"Hey, Dad," I greeted as Jensen turned from the counter and handed me my own coffee and my pain meds. I smiled appreciatively at him. "Thanks."

"Good morning, Madi. You excited to go into the city today?" Dad asked as I took my seat.

It had been about six months since my last trip to Memphis, and even longer since I had done any major shopping for myself that didn't involve groceries. "Actually, yeah."

"There's this great shop I want to take you to, Madi. They have the most amazing dresses," Willow announced.

Raising an eyebrow, I turned to look at her. "Will, what on earth do I need a dress for? Now, if you wanted to force me into more of those jeans you bought me last time, sure. But a dress?"

Willow smirked, and I really wished I knew what was going through that head of hers. "You never know when you'll need a good party dress, Madi." I was about to protest when she spoke again. "Okay, okay. I saw a dress there I just have to have. And maybe you'll find something, too. You never know. Besides, it's fun to just dress up sometimes."

I conceded, knowing it was a losing battle—especially since Willow would be doing the driving—and we all ate breakfast together. The pancakes were amazing, but every bite I took had me thinking back to Jensen feeding me that one small piece and what it inevitably led to. I smiled. I couldn't help it.

I felt a nudge beneath the table and looked over at Jensen. "Penny for your thoughts?"

My cheeks warmed as both Dad and Willow watched me. "Oh, um. I was just thinking about when I can ride again?" Willow and Dad seemed to buy it, but Jensen looked skeptical. I kicked his shin lightly with my socked foot to thank him for the unwanted attention, but he only chuckled under his breath.

We all helped clean up the kitchen before Dad headed out to start in the barn. Jensen promised he was right behind him.

"Have fun today, girls," Dad said before closing the door behind him.

"Okay! You ready to go, Madi?" Willow asked excitedly.

"As ready as I'll ever be," I joked before turning to Jensen. "You're sure I can't stay home?"

He pondered my request for a moment. "Sorry. I think you'll be okay. Have fun. I'll see you tonight."

"Fine. Maybe I'll get Willow to stop somewhere and I'll bring something home for dinner. Any preferences?" I asked as I slipped on my shoes.

"I'll go wait in the car," Willow announced. "You know, give you two a moment alone. Just a moment, though. Don't make me come back in here." She may have been small, but not even I would mess with her when she used that tone.

"So, any dinner preferences?" I asked again once Willow was outside and climbing behind the wheel of her new Charger.

Shaking his head, Jensen wrapped his arms around my waist. "Surprise me. I'm pretty easy."

I raised my eyebrows. "Oh, really?"

Chuckling, he shrugged and moved his face to mine to kiss me softly. "Your twisted little mind *would* go there, wouldn't it?"

"Don't even try to pretend that's not what you meant," I challenged, and he just feigned shock and continued to claim he had no idea what I was talking about.

Willow was clearly growing annoyed because she began

honking her horn. "Okay, you should go before the half-pint rips us both to shreds. I don't think I would want to go up against her," Jensen joked, before placing one last chaste kiss on my lips. "Have fun. You have your painkillers in case you're gone too long?"

I nodded. "Yup. I'll see you tonight."

Jensen and I left the house together, and he opened my door for me, closing it once I was inside. "Hot car, Willow," he praised as he checked out the interior.

She beamed as she always did when someone complimented her baby. "Thanks! Brandon got it for me when he got promoted."

From across the yard, I heard Jensen's name being called, and we both turned to see my dad walking toward us. "Well," he said, looking back at me with a smile before pushing himself back up. "I guess I should get going before I lose my job."

"I'm pretty sure he's not going to fire you. He pretty much owes you for taking care of me," I reminded him, reaching out and placing my hand on his.

Saying one final good-bye, Willow backed out of her spot and we were on our way to the city for a day of trying on clothes and, I hoped, a day at her spa. After moving to Memphis two years ago, Willow opened up her own salon and spa called *Visions of You*. It was very successful and something she really enjoyed doing. Because she owned the place, a trip to the city was never complete without the two of us going in for facials and full body massages.

"So," Willow said as we drove on the highway. "I think we should do a little bit of shopping then stop for lunch before heading over for massages. What do you think?"

I frowned. "With my ribs, I don't think I can have a massage."

"Oh, pish! We'll figure something out! Beth is amazing

and will take excellent care of you," she promised.

The two-hour drive to Memphis flew by as Willow mapped out all the shops she wanted us to hit. The first store we went into upon arriving was a little dress shop called JJ's House. Willow ran through the store grabbing dress after dress off the racks for me to try on before handing them off to an associate to start me a fitting room.

"Will, I thought we were here for *you*?" I inquired.

She lifted the tiered skirt of a royal blue strapless dress and smirked at me. "Oh, we are. But I know what I want. We need to find you a dress, too."

"Why do I need a dress?" I asked, repeating my question from earlier.

With her hands on her hips, she turned to me. "Madison, please. Just stop being so damn difficult. We're here to have fun. Indulge me. Please?" It was hard to tell her no when she batted those big, blue peepers at me, so I huffed in exasperation and stepped behind the curtain to change, leaving her clapping in my wake.

The first dress I put on was a light pink, lace-covered dress with a really short skirt. The sleeves on it were long and puffy at the shoulder, doing absolutely nothing for my collarbones, and the color completely washed me out. I stepped out from behind the curtain, and Willow scrunched her nose.

"Seriously? Why did you pick this? It can't look good on anyone." As the words left my mouth, a girl two rooms down looked over at me, a bright smile on her face until she heard what I had said — and saw what dress I was talking about.

Smiling sheepishly, I retreated back behind my curtain. "Pay no attention to the lunatic behind the curtain," I said, trying my best attempt at humor. Willow thought it was hilarious as she cackled from her seat outside my room.

The next two dresses were okay. The first was a basic black strapless dress with pockets. I thought I looked great in it, but Willow hemmed and hawed saying she didn't think it was quite right.

"Quite right for what? I have nowhere to wear a dress like this. How can it not be right for hanging in my closet?" I demanded, folding my arms across my chest and glaring at her. She was being awfully cryptic and I didn't like it.

"Next!" was all she said, physically turning me and pushed me back into the room.

Next in line was a purple organza dress with a jeweled collar. It looked pretty frightening, but I trusted Willow when she said it would look better on. It did, which was good. There was a peek-a-boo slit down the chest before it was belted around the waist and then flowed out into an A-Line skirt. It was cute. Not little black dress-cute, but still cute.

I stepped out and Willow vetoed it again within seconds. "You know," I said, making sure the irritation was audible. "You're about to choke on this dress." I was only *half* kidding.

"Come on. Just one more. Try the cobalt one. I think it'll look spectacular with your eyes and skin tone!"

Growing more and more frustrated with her insane need for me to find a dress, I changed out of the purple one and into the blue satin one that was left. The neckline was a plunging V that showed just enough cleavage to not be considered trashy and the back had a zipper that ran all the way from the bottom of the skirt to the top of the mid-rise back. It fit like a glove and I loved how it made me feel. Willow was right (which shouldn't have shocked me, but did), and when I stepped out she nodded emphatically.

"Yes! Yes! Yes!" she cheered. "Madison, you have to get that one."

The smile that I wore gave away just how much I wanted to buy the dress, too. However, when I looked at the tag that was positioned just below my arm, I choked a little. "Willow! It's two hundred dollars!"

Willow got up to inspect the tag herself. "Yeah, marked down from five. Madison, just get it. You look sensational." I couldn't argue with her there. What I could argue with was that she wanted me to pay two *hundred* dollars for a dress I would likely never even wear.

"Where would I wear it?" I asked.

There was an impish grin on her face as she shrugged. I started to think she maybe knew something I didn't. "I don't know. But can you really pass up a deal like that? Come on. Hell, if in a month's time, you still haven't worn it, you can come visit and we'll go out on the town. Okay? Please?" She was begging now — as in literally down-on-her-knees, hands-folded-in-front-of-her begging.

"Fine," I told her, pretending to be annoyed, even though the smile I wore said otherwise.

While I paid for my new dress, Willow had the associate run to the back for the one that she had put on hold the other day. Willow had all the dresses in the world, so I wasn't sure why she needed to add yet *another* one to her insane collection.

"Brandon has a work party. I can't wear something I've already worn." Willow's logic did not resemble that of a sane person. The girl was kooky.

After paying for our purchases, we walked out of the boutique with our white garment bags, laying them flat in Willow's immaculately clean trunk before walking down the sidewalk to browse in a few more shops. I bought three more pairs of jeans, paying more for them than I normally would have — especially since I could have bought three pairs of Levi's for the price of one. Willow assured me that they were great quality and would last a long time. She helped me pick out a few dressier tops that were still casual enough that I could wear them whenever and not just to the clubs I never went to.

We shopped for two hours, and I had to admit, I was having a blast. It was nice to hang out with her and talk about life and guys. We were just leaving the lingerie store when my stomach started rumbling and my side started to ache a little, so Willow decided it was time for lunch. She led the way to a near-by diner where she assured me they had the best vegetarian menu in all of Memphis.

Each of us ordered a veggie burger and a side salad, then talked some more. Whenever I talked about Jensen, Willow donned a grin so wide I knew it had to hurt her cheeks.

"What?" I inquired.

"It's really nothing," she tried to tell me. "I just realized that in the year and a half that you and Dane were together, you never talked about him like this. I mean, you talked about him, but it wasn't with this much emotion. Usually you'd complain about how he didn't clean up after himself, or how much of a dick he was being." She paused. "But, with Jensen. I don't know, you just light up."

I shook my head. "He's a good guy, but we're just fooling around." I paused. "Or, we would be if it weren't for my stupid ribs."

"I still can't believe you haven't slept with him."

I scoffed. "Believe me. It isn't for lack of trying or wanting to."

"Still," Willow said. "You like him."

"Sure. What's not to like?" She held eye contact, her eyebrows arched as though to challenge me. "It's just casual. Neither of us is ready for more. I want to let myself fall for him … I do," I said, still trying to convince that one miniscule part of myself that he *could* be the right one for me. "I'm just afraid that we'd be moving too fast and that the attraction he feels will eventually fizzle out completely."

"Madison, I've spent a little time with the guy, and I'd like to think I'm a pretty good judge of character." Reaching across the table, she rested her hand over mine. "The way he talks about you, how his eyes shine every time I tell him something about you — no matter how silly or embarrassing..." I wanted to smack her for that one "I can tell he's falling for you, but something is holding him back. While I know you guys want to keep things casual, I think the two of you coming together when you did was kismet."

Our lunch arrived just then, giving me a few minutes to reflect on everything we'd talked about. Willow had said that something was holding Jensen back. I already knew about what he'd been through these last few years, but would that effect his outlook on relationships?

Or was he holding something else back?

16
MORE TO THE STORY

Sadness hung over me like a big gray cloud. I watched the orange Charger disappear into the distance, the tail lights swallowed up by the dust of the gravel road. Three days was never enough time, even if Willow promised to come and visit again soon. She even swore to bring Brandon, which was great, because it had been even longer since I had seen him.

"You going to be all right?" Jensen asked softly, coming up behind me and resting his head on my shoulder while his arms encircled me.

I basked in the feeling of being in his arms for a brief moment before working my way free and heading back into the house. "Yeah. I'm fine."

Lost in thought, I found myself in the kitchen. "Hey," Jensen said softly, following me. It was inevitable that he would be concerned. "Did I do something wrong?"

"What?" I asked incredulously. "No, of course not."

The look on his face told me he wasn't entirely convinced. "Are you sure? Because ever since you came back from your shopping trip, you've been ... different."

I closed the fridge, dropping my eyes from his shamefully. "You're right." When I looked back up, I saw fear in his eyes. "No!" I rushed to elaborate. "It's nothing you did, though. It's really all me." Hearing this didn't seem to alleviate any of the confusion in his expression, so I walked to him and took his hand in mine, leading him into the living room before sitting on the couch together.

"It's just," I said quietly before taking a steeling breath. "You know my recent history with relationships is ... colorful. There haven't been many and they were all long*ish*."

Offering me a smile, Jensen gave my hand a squeeze. A spark of electricity moved through me, igniting a fire deep within my belly that only Jensen was capable of. "We've only known each other just a little over a week," I whispered, dropping my eyes to his hands encasing mine. "And yet, I feel so attracted to you."

Jensen chuckled. "And that's a bad thing?"

"Not at all," I assured him. "But it's stronger than anything I've ever felt before, and it's a little scary."

"Yeah," he agreed softly. "I know exactly what you mean."

"I know we're just supposed to be having a good time, and I am — more than I thought I would — but I've been hurt." Tears prickled my eyes as I spoke. "And I can't help that I'm still terrified that it might happen again. I don't know if you know this, but Dane used to work here. You filled the position after my dad fired him."

"Oh?"

I nodded. "Yeah. It was all very similar to how you and I met. Dane got the job, moved into the house. We became friends over the course of the first few weeks. He was funny, charming. It was hard not to fall for his act, actually. One night, we both had entirely too much to drink, and we ..." Jensen nodded his understanding, telling me with his eyes that he didn't need me to elaborate further. "And, I guess from there we were just kind of together."

"Kind of?" Jensen inquired, his eyebrows pushing together.

With a shrug, I carried on. "Things were good in the beginning." I looked at Jensen and smiled sadly. "We were 'having fun.' Our relationship lasted about a year and a half before his behavior changed completely. He became incredibly possessive and angry, always apologizing afterward and saying how he didn't mean to be that way. That I shouldn't do things that I know provoke him. I suspected infidelity for a few weeks prior to our breakup, but never had the confirmation that I needed. Just my gut feelings. Not that they mattered much, because his slamming a fist through my wall was the last straw. I swear, if my dad had been within reaching distance of his shotgun ..."

"He loves you," Jensen said, reaching out a hand to cradle my face, using the pad of his thumb to wipe away a tear that had escaped without my realizing it.

"I guess the reason I'm telling you this is because it's all happening so quickly. It's familiar, and it scares me. I have these fears that are probably irrational, but they don't feel that way to me. They're very real, and the last thing I want to do is project them onto you. I just wanted to be honest." I paused for a moment, biting my lower lip nervously. "And I want you to know that you can do the same."

"What do you want to know?"

That seemed easier than I figured it would be. "When was your last relationship? Were you in love with her?"

He seemed reluctant as he raised an eyebrow and stared at me. "You really want to know this shit?"

"I really do. Unless you don't want to talk about it."

Jensen sighed. "The reason I left Houston, other than to get away from my past and be closer to the rest of my family, was because I broke off my engagement shortly after I'd been incarcerated."

My eyes widened, and I think I even gasped. "Y-you

were *engaged?*"

"*Was,*" he repeated with heavy emphasis. "Her name's Kaylie. We were engaged for a little less than a year, together for just over two."

Trying to push myself past the news that Jensen was engaged, I swallowed thickly. "Why did you break it off?" I managed to croak out with my increasingly dry throat.

"Is that really important?" Hard eyes penetrated mine, and I pulled my body away from his. His eyes softened with remorse immediately. "I'm sorry, it's just kind of a sore spot." With a nod, I moved my eyes to my hands as I pulled them from his and picked at my fingernails. Jensen exhaled heavily and slid closer to me again, using his forefinger on my chin to force my eyes to his. "About two weeks after I'd been sentenced, she found out she was pregnant. She came to visit me one Saturday and told me. I wasn't sure how to feel. I mean, I've always wanted a family, and we were engaged to be married. Sure, the timing wasn't really the greatest, given I was wearing an orange jumpsuit and trying to avoid becoming somebody's bitch, but I figured we might be able to make it work. Three years wasn't that long."

"So what happened?"

Jensen sighed, running his fingers through his hair before nervously rubbing the back of his neck. "I told her we could make it work, but she told me it was too late. She'd taken care of it."

"She ... took care of it?" His meaning hit me like a sack of bricks. "She terminated without you knowing?"

He nodded, his expression turning grim. "She'd always been on the fence about kids, but she said that having a violent offender for a father wasn't something she'd wish upon a child. It didn't seem to matter what triggered my violent outburst toward Robert."

With Jensen's tale of heartbreak fresh in my mind, we sat

in silence. Willow had been right when she told me he had been through something; I just figured it was due to his sister's attack a couple of years ago and his recent release. Never had I imagined he had been betrayed by the one person he planned to be with forever while serving a sentence for something he felt was justified.

Suddenly his reluctance to be in a relationship made sense.

REVENGE: BEST SERVED WET

"You're sure you're feeling okay enough to help out?" Jensen asked as we unlocked the barn door and stepped inside.

It had been a week since we talked everything out. I could tell by the way he stared at me that nothing between us had changed other than our agreement to begin anew.

Dad and Tom had left early for their fishing trip, stopping by to say goodbye and to make sure that Jensen and I were going to be all right without them around to babysit us. Dad still hadn't said anything to confirm my suspicion of whether or not he knew anything. The way he watched us, though—even if we were on our best behavior all week— made me even more certain. Much to my surprise, he didn't seem upset about it; he almost seemed *pleased* by it all.

I pushed the door open and stepped inside the dark barn before hitting the switch to raise the large door. "Your mom said my ribs look great, remember? If she's not worried, then you shouldn't be either."

"It's only been two and a half weeks," Jensen countered.

"Are you a doctor?" Jensen shook his head in response, still uneasy about my being out here. "Well, your mom is. Look, if it makes you feel better, you can do all the hard labor, and I'll fill the water buckets. Deal? I'll ease my way back into things."

"All right. But you don't leave my sight."

Shaking my head, I grabbed Glory's lead and halter before opening her stall. "Always so damn overbearing," I muttered teasingly.

Because it was only Jensen and me, it took a little longer
to empty all the stalls, which made me happy we had yet to
fill up the new barn. I couldn't imagine having to clean out
both of them with no one else around to help. Jensen worked
to clean out the stalls while I hung out in the aisles, watching
him and being sure to tell him when he missed a scrap of
soiled straw. I knew he would get it; it was just so much more
fun to point it out.

"If you don't stop it, Landry, I will throw you in the water trough outside," he threatened. His tone indicated that he
was likely teasing, especially given that he was still highly
protective of me in my condition.

"You would not," I said, calling his bluff. "But, if it really
bothers you, I'll go and start filling the water buckets."

"That would be wise."

Rolling my eyes, I pushed myself off the stall door and
grabbed a few empty buckets to take to the wash stall. Placing them all side-by-side, I put the hose in the first one and
turned on the water to let it fill. As I waited, I thought back
on the week, remembering all the sweet moments Jensen and
I shared — not to mention all the lost naughty-time. Because of
us starting over again, I couldn't deny that it made me want
him more. Absence making the heart grow fonder and all that
other stuff I never believed until now.

Suddenly, there was a loud splash as the water over-
flowed onto the concrete floor. "Shit," I muttered as it
splashed my paddock boots and soaked my feet right
through.

"Tsk, tsk, Landry," Jensen scolded. With narrow eyes, I

looked up to see him leaning against the outer corner of the wash stall. The smirk on his face was both cocky and teasing. "You shouldn't be so wasteful of our natural resources. Do I need to supervise to make sure you do your job properly? Maybe you're out of practice."

Every mocking word out of his mouth pushed me closer to vengeance. I picked up the hose, moving it toward the next bucket, when a thought appeared out of the blue. "You know what, Davis? I've had just about enough of your cocky attitude. I think someone needs to remind you exactly who's running the show around here."

"Oh really?" he responded, crossing his arms and raising his eyebrows confidently. "And just how exactly do you plan to put me in my place, little girl?"

Slowly, I moved my hand down to the nozzle and placed my thumb over it, causing the steady stream to spray quietly beneath the surface of the water.

"I'm waiting, Madison."

I was certain he regretted those words as soon as he said them, because I lifted my hand from the bucket of cold water and sprayed him. It didn't take him long to recover from the shock of my attack and lunge forward. I shrieked and laughed as I tried to keep the water focused on him.

"You are so dead!" he shouted, reaching for me as I evaded him around the three buckets that sat in the middle of the stall. The floor was soaked, and we splashed around in the puddles my genius plan had caused. Jensen must have had trouble seeing through the continual spray of water in his face, because I was able to keep him from retaliating for a few more laps around the small room.

I should have known that my dumb luck would end my reign of power over him, though. The hose wrapped around the three buckets, knocking them all over and causing more water to puddle on the concrete floor. Thankfully, most of it flowed to the drain beneath the wash sink, because I wasn't sure how we would explain flooding the barn to my father. I tried jumping over one of the buckets, but Jensen saw my move and shifted to head the other way, catching me quickly and grabbing at the hose. I laughed hysterically and tried to hold on to it.

"Give it here!" he demanded through his own laughter.

"Neverrrrr!" I cried out, pointing the nozzle at his face briefly before he gained control and pointed it at my chest, effectively soaking my white tank top. It would be safe to assume I didn't expect a full-out water fight when I got dressed that morning.

Because of Jensen's size and his being stronger than me (which I would deny admitting to my death if he ever heard that), he managed to snake the green hose from my grasp and turned it on me again.

"I surrender!" I continued to laugh, the cold water assaulting me from all angles as he held me in place. His left arm was still wrapped around me so I couldn't get away.

"Oh, I don't think so. You fight dirty," he snarled menacingly.

Snickering, I wiped the beads of water from my face, only to have them replaced by new ones when he refused to relent. "Actually, being water, I'd say it's quite the opposite!" I sputtered through the continual spray and my giggles.

"Always a smartass, aren't you? Say you're sorry!" he commanded, stuffing the hose up the back of my shirt so the cold water would shoot up my spine. I screamed and arched my back until my breasts were pressed firmly against his chest.

He'd already accused me of fighting dirty, so what I was about to do—while completely evil—was the only way I was going to get out of his hold. "Ow!" I cried, only once, and he recoiled in an instant, completely horrified by what he thought he'd done.

After removing the hose from the back of my shirt and releasing his hold on me, I bent over, playing it up a little before I struck again. "Oh my God! I'm so sorry! Are you—?"

I moved quickly, snatching the hose from him and spraying him all over again. "I can't believe you fell for that!"

Jensen didn't move. He didn't laugh. He didn't react at all. What he did do was stand as still as a statue as the smile fell from my face. I let my arm fall to my side, the water spilling out onto the floor.

"That wasn't funny," he said, the tone in his voice clearly indicating his hurt over what I had done.

Guilt settled in my gut like a lead weight. I took a step forward, loosening my grip on the hose to let it drop to the floor as I apologized. "You're right. I'm so sorr—"

Jensen didn't let me finish before he sped forward unexpectedly and grabbed me and the hose. He pressed our soaking wet bodies into the corner. The smile returned to my face, and I shrieked as he lightly twisted my arms and held them behind my back while the water sprayed up like a geyser raining down on us both. "And I can't believe you fell for that!"

"You rotten jerk! Okay! All right! Stop! I'm sorry!" I shouted.

Through his laughter, he asked, "What did you say? I didn't quite catch that."

As he held me firmly between his body and the wall, I looked up into his eyes, blinking the water droplets away so I could see better. My breathing was labored, every deep breath I took matching his. I licked the water from my lips, drawing Jensen's focus to them, and a week's buildup of lust suddenly exploded between us.

In a flash, his mouth was on mine. He kissed me with a ferocity that caused a blast of warmth to spread throughout my chilled body. I heard the soft *clank* of the hose's nozzle drop to the concrete floor as I closed my eyes and gave in to Jensen. Releasing my wrists from behind me, he laid his hands flat against my back while my arms moved up to wrap around his neck, my fingers fisting his wet hair tightly.

Warm hands moved down and lifted my shirt. His fingers clawed at the flesh of my back before slowly moving around until his thumbs grazed the swell of my breasts over the thin cotton fabric of my bra. I moaned, opening my mouth just enough for Jensen's tongue to slip inside and move against my own.

It had been too long since I had felt his body pressed to mine in this way. His right hand left my breast for a moment, moving around to the back before unclasping my bra with a single flick of his fingers. Pulling my mouth away, I gasped for air as his hands moved beneath my bra, palming my breasts with his strong hands and nipping at my throat, setting my skin ablaze.

"Oh God," I sighed softly, pushing my hips forward into his.

"Please tell me this is okay?" he pleaded between the feather-like kisses he was trailing down my shoulder.

"'S okay," I murmured breathlessly. "Want this. Want *you*."

In a flash, Jensen groaned, swiftly moving his hands to my ass to lift me. I wrapped my legs around his waist. Our clothes and bodies were completely soaked, making it difficult to move against one another and accomplish anything that would bring us close to what we both wanted.

Deciding to remedy this, I moved one hand between us and tried to undo Jensen's jeans, letting him know it was okay. That I was ready.

Jensen moved back a fraction of a step, letting me slide to the floor, and his hands flew to my button as we both worked frantically to undo each other's jeans. I had barely gotten the zipper on Jensen's pants down when his warm hand slipped inside my pants. Or, almost did. Turned out our water-soaked skin and clothes worked against us.

It was supposed to be our pleasure mounting, but every second spent trying to peel soaked denim from wet skin only made us frustrated. And we were already plenty frustrated from waiting for my body to heal.

He groaned painfully as he pulled his lips from mine. "Shit. This isn't how I saw this happening. It was going to be so hot."

I laughed, letting my head fall back against the wall. Jensen was still holding my jeans open when a chill ripped through me. "Maybe we're just not meant to be spontaneous," I said, finally catching my breath and finding my bearings.

Jensen's deep blue eyes found mine again, his finger hooking into my belt loops and pulling my hips toward him. It awakened my desire for him.

Okay. Truth be told, it hadn't even been extinguished. The embers were always there, just waiting to be stoked.

"We should get some more work done."

I pushed my bottom lip out into a pout. "Really?"

Jensen laughed softly, the corners of his eyes creasing. "Sadly."

His nobility or responsibility—or whatever the hell it was—was really putting a wrench in the works. Feeling bold, I slid the metal button of his pants through its eyelet and brushed my lips over his. "But I want you *now*."

"Soon, I promise." Jensen moved back slowly.

Once we were about a foot apart, he refastened his jeans as I watched hungrily. He caught me eyeing his crotch and chuckled. "Stop it. My self-control is wavering."

Inhaling a deep breath through my nose, I smiled.

"Okay. You're right. But as soon as work is done? All bets are off," I boldly promised. I was able to put on a brave face, but I was still a little bummed that we'd had another almost-earth-shattering round of foreplay, only to be left sexually frustrated again.

Jensen smiled, and I found myself even more drawn to him. I had seen him smile on a number of occasions, but this smile was something else entirely. It was obvious he was happy, but there also seemed to be excitement dancing in his eyes. Maybe he was imagining me jumping him back at the house as much as I was. "Oh yeah? What are we going to do?" he asked in a low, seductive tone.

"That is for me to know and you to find out," I told him mysteriously. Truthfully, I had no idea myself, but I was certain it wouldn't disappoint.

Jensen took several steps backward. "Okay, well I have more work to do around here if we're going to make the most of tonight. But first, I'm soaked to the bone. What do you say we go back to the house and change before finishing up out here?"

Jensen held out his hand to me, and with a smile, I took it, lacing our fingers together. "Sounds like a plan." I smirked, looking up at him.

After changing out of our sopping wet clothes, Jensen made me promise to refrain from starting any more water fights. I agreed, of course, and we headed back out to the barn to finish the stalls. Jensen put fresh straw down while I finished filling the buckets and then squeegeed all the excess water toward the drain in the wash stall. By the time we finished, it was lunch, so we headed back to the house.

With no lessons on the schedule for the weekend, there really wasn't too much to do around the barn. Jensen's mom still thought it would be best if I waited another week or two before I rode, which wasn't what I wanted to hear. I missed it so much. I'd never gone this long without being on a horse before.

"So, what do you want for dinner tonight?" Jensen asked as he flopped down on the couch with his sandwich.

I scooted over next to him. I didn't want that much space between us. In fact, I was trying to figure out just how much time we had before we had to do more work. "Hmm, I'm not entirely sure. All I know is I can't wait to have you in a vulnerable situation."

"Why, Madi," Jensen said, feigning surprise, "are you planning to seduce me?"

I shrugged. "Play your cards right."

Jensen set his plate on the coffee table and turned to me, slipping his right hand between my legs and sliding it up my inner thigh. His thumb pressed against the seam right below my zipper, and I almost dropped my plate on the floor before Jensen took it from me and set it next to his. I gasped as Jensen leaned in and brushed his lips to my neck.

"I assure you I plan to play more than 'my cards' right tonight, Madison."

I shivered, raising my hands to grab onto Jensen's hair when he pulled back suddenly. Leaving me hot and bothered again.

"I'd like to plan something fun for this evening," he told me, piquing my interest.

"Oh?"

"Yeah. Do you trust me?"

"Um, I guess. Considering the source," I teased.

"Look who's being cocky now."

"One of us has to be," I quipped.

His attack on me was sudden and had me doubled over with laughter. His fingers found my sides and started tickling me with no sign of stopping. I tried my hardest to move away from him. Eventually, he had me on my back, wedging him-

self between my thighs as he continued to tickle me merci-
lessly. Our position was the last thing on my mind as I started
to fear wetting my pants.

"You started it!" I screamed, pinching the back of his
bicep in an effort to make him stop. It was no use though, because I couldn't grip enough skin around his muscles.

"What are you? Six?"

I cackled like a hyena as he refused to stop. "Okay! I'm
sorry, okay? Stop! I have to pee!"

I'd have to remember that as an excuse for next time, because as soon as I said it, Jensen sat up, his groin pushed
against me—*that* was when I paid attention to our position.
Swallowing thickly, I lay there fighting the urge to shamelessly rub myself against him. His eyes were dark and clouded
with desire as we gazed longingly at each other.

We had time, right? It wasn't like we had pressing issues
to deal with on the ranch.

"Um," he rasped. "I thought you had to use the bathroom?"

"Right." Jensen didn't move, not that I wanted him to, so
I had to wriggle back on the couch until I was able to swing
my leg around him and stand.

When I finished up, I found Jensen in the kitchen doing
our dishes. I grabbed a towel and started to dry. "So, what
are we doing tonight?"

"So, you *don't* really trust me, then?"

Rolling my eyes, I responded. "I just want to know what
I should wear. Dressy? Casual?" I stepped up onto my toes
and kissed his cheek lightly before ghosting my lips toward
his ear and whispering, "Nothing at all?"

Feeling pretty victorious when I saw his eyes flutter
close, I smiled. "You know, you're making it awfully hard to
behave myself."

"I don't see why we're trying so hard to be good," I said

softly. "I thought the whole point of … *this* was to have fun and let loose."

"Dress casually," he said. I could tell he was fighting the urge to give in to our desire. "That's all I'll tell you."

I glowered playfully at him, but nodded my consent.

"I figure we'll start bringing in the horses around five. That way we'll have plenty of time to get cleaned up."

"So, what do we do for the next three hours?" I inquired, putting the towel down on the counter and turning to him. I slid my hand across his lower back and toyed with the waist of his jeans. "I mean, how can we possibly pass the time?"

Jensen turned to me quickly, throwing me a little off balance. "You know what? I just realized I have to run into town to grab a few bags of feed. Mind if I take the truck?"

"You want me to tag along?"

"No. Why don't you stay here? I shouldn't be gone long. I'll be back soon."

"Okay, yeah. I'll tidy up a bit around here."

Jensen gently gripped my chin between his thumb and forefinger and tilted my face to his. He kissed me sweetly, then left for town.

I flipped the radio on and got out my cleaning supplies, dancing to the tunes of the eighties and nineties as they blared through my house. Within the hour, my kitchen was spotless. Counters were clean, dishes were put away, floors swept, and I was just moving on to dusting the living room when "I Wanna Dance With Somebody" came on. I couldn't help but dance and sing along every time it was on. It was just one of those songs.

Running my duster over my living room shelves, I sang and swayed my hips as the song started out slow. By the time the beat picked up, I had really found my groove, using my duster as a microphone while I literally hopped around the living room. When the chorus finally hit, I was no longer focused on cleaning, completely losing myself to my own performance, dancing around the living room like a total pro.

Okay, so it was probably more spastic. I was actually glad that I was alone, because if anyone saw my little show, I was sure to be humiliated — or committed.

I took a deep breath, knowing that there was a high note coming, and while it was likely I was about to butcher it completely, I didn't really have any shits to give. I was having a blast belting out this song and dancing around the house. It was the happiest I'd been in a very long time.

"Well, judging by how you're moving, I'd say you're definitely feeling better."

I jumped, slapping my hand over my chest. My breath caught in my throat in preparation to scream when my eyes locked on Jensen's, and I let out a breath of relief. "Shit! You scared me."

My heart pounded loudly in my ears, drowning out the music that continued to play in the background. I looked at Jensen leaning up against the wall. A wide smile stretched across his face as he stood there with his arms crossed.

"I don't know that I've ever heard you sing before," he noted, pushing off the wall and walking to me.

I stayed put as he made his way across the room, my heart racing with his every step. "I'm pretty sure that wasn't singing. A dying cat probably sounds better."

Grimacing at the thought, he pulled me to him. "Somehow, I doubt that." He started to move his hips to the beat of the slow song that came on the radio next, and I just stared at him dumbly. "What?" he asked.

"Um, I don't dance."

Laughing, he kissed me softly. "That's a load of horse shit. I just walked *in* on you dancing."

"Okaaay," I said, dragging the word out. "I only dance when I'm alone. Or drunk. Yeah, I also dance when I'm drunk."

He pulled away from me with a sly grin. "Good to know." I regretted divulging that little nugget immediately, being sure to mentally note that I should probably never partake in excessive drinking when Jensen was around. Taking my hand he began to pull me toward the door, taking my makeshift microphone from me and setting it on the bench on the way out.

"Where are we going?" I asked.

"Well, it's five. I figured we should get our work done so we can ... *play*." The way he said that word made me tremble with excitement.

Jensen and I grabbed a couple of halters each and headed out to the farthest paddock first, deciding it made more sense to work inward. I must have been anxious to see what Jensen had planned for tonight, because it didn't seem like it took all that long to get the work done. We brought Halley and Ransom in last, and I spent a little time with her, promising to ride her as soon as I was able, before exiting and locking her stall.

"Okay," Jensen said on the way to the house. "You shower first. I'm going to run out to the office to check on a few things. I'll be back shortly, and then I'll have my shower."

"Should I start dinner?" I asked, still unsure what exactly he had planned.

Shaking his head, he opened the front door. "Absolutely not. I've got everything under control." He moved behind me, gripping my hips right above my ass and pushing me along to the bathroom. "Now, go."

I closed the bathroom door, deciding to leave it unlocked and see if his self-restraint was intact (I secretly hoped it wasn't) and undressed before hopping in the shower. I made sure to take care of any and all personal grooming. I usually did anyway, but I was extra careful to get *everything* this time.

I wrapped my towel around my wet body, and had just entered my bedroom when I heard the front door open. "I'm all done with the shower!" I called out as I grabbed the matching black lace bra and panty set that I bought in Memphis with Willow.

Turning toward my bed, I laid the scanty undergarments on the bedspread, and was just about to drop the towel when arms wrapped around me. I smiled, relaxing into the embrace.

"Did you get everything in order?" I asked, running my hands along his forearms.

A chill ran up my spine as his embrace tightened around me, but my blood turned to ice in my veins when a dangerously familiar voice said, "Those are new."

FIGHT OR FLIGHT

I moved to pull free of Dane's restrictive hold on me, but he didn't relent so easily. His grip around me tightened, resulting in the towel shifting. The terrycloth was the only thing keeping my body covered.

"I missed you," he murmured into my ear.

Panic knotted in my belly. I gripped the top of my towel with my left hand and tried to wrestle free with the other.

"Get off me!" I shouted, twisting my body and wrenching free. My legs were against the bed, and I held the towel tight to my chest. "Get the hell out of my house," I demanded through clenched teeth, chest heaving and hands shaking.

Dane made no indication he was going to leave. "Relax," he demanded. The tone he used sounded menacing.

"Wh—what are you doing here?" I asked, secretly wishing that my voice hadn't cracked.

"What do you think?" he shouted, making me jump slightly. "I'm pissed that you kicked me out and made your dad fire me!"

The man wasn't capable of letting go of anything; what happened between us was *months* ago, and he was still pining away over losing me and his job? Even though he had constantly blamed me for how angry he was all the time?

"I didn't *make* my dad do anything. He's a big boy, Dane. He's fully capable of making decisions all by himself—just like when you made the conscious decision to raise your hand to me." Apparently my balls of steel had dropped, which was nice, because I was finally able to stand up to him.

The courage I felt was short-lived though as he took a heavy step toward me, forcing me back into my room. "I'm taking what I *deserve*."

Feeling cornered, I stepped to the left and tried to dash around him, but he expected it. His hands gripped my shoulders roughly, and he used more strength than he'd ever used with me before to toss me onto the bed. The towel shifted when I landed, and I scrambled to right it as I moved to stand.

Dane rushed forward and climbed onto the bed. His legs straddled my bare thighs and his left hand wrapped around my right forearm, forcing it above my head where he pinned it to the mattress. Then he yanked the other from my towel and raised it also. His hands were so big, he was able to use only one to hold both of my arms above my head.

"Stop fighting," he ordered.

I stopped struggling, not because he told me to, but because I was hoping to keep the towel from slipping even more. That didn't matter, because he used the fingers of his free hand to fiddle with the edge of the towel, inching it away from my breasts.

"Dane, stop, *please*," I pleaded. Tears burned my eyes, and I couldn't keep the tremble from my voice as a sob steadily built in my chest.

His bloodshot eyes burned with anger and rejection, and his breath smelled of cheap whisky. "You think I'd just let you do that to me? Kick me out like that? Humiliate me by fucking around on me with that guy?" He tightened his grip around my wrists until my bones ached and my skin burned.

"You belong to *me*, Madison."

"Dane, please! You're hurting me!" The tears fell freely over my temples and pooled in my ears before spilling onto my bed.

His eyes were on me, but I could tell he wasn't really seeing me. He was too lost to his rage. I'd seen this look before. "You know you shouldn't upset me, Madison."

"I didn't do anything!" I screamed, raising my head off the bed and getting as in his face as I could.

His free hand came up from where it hovered above my almost naked chest, and I flinched. I tried not to, but I was terrified. He didn't hit me, though. Instead, he gripped my face between his thumb and fingers and squeezed my cheeks hard. I tasted blood when my teeth cut through the inside of my mouth.

His eyes held mine, and I couldn't even recognize him. This wasn't the man I'd lived with, or the one who used to share my bed. This was a much darker version of the man Dane had become toward the end of our relationship when his drinking became more important to him.

"Dane, please," I pleaded once more, my cheeks hurting in his harsh grip.

A smile slowly spread across his face. "That's my girl," he whispered, lowering his face next to mine. His lips brushed my ear, and I tried to pull away. "Always begging to come back to me."

He released my face and pushed my head back toward the mattress. His hand quickly moved to his belt and he started to undo it.

"No, Dane. Don't."

The anger returned to his eyes when he pulled his belt free and folded it in half, using the bed to assist. "Did you just tell me no?"

I suspected there was no right answer, and while I was

extremely fucking scared, I felt my instinct of self-preservation kick in. I started struggling again, screaming and yelling at him to get off me and get the fuck out of my house.

He hated that I was trying to fight back, and he raised his hand, the buckle of his belt gleaming in the last remaining rays of sunlight from the window. I closed my eyes and braced myself for the strike when suddenly Dane's body flew backward as though he'd been pulled on some kind of pulley system.

I scrambled to cover myself with the towel and rolled off my bed. My body shook as I backed into the night stand, sending the lamp crashing to the floor. All I could hear was the roar of blood in my ears. Then I heard shouting. And fists hitting skin.

I looked around my room. It was empty. I raced out into the hall and found Jensen standing over Dane. Specks of blood were spattered on the walls, and Jensen was holding Dane by the front of his shirt as he hit him over and over and over.

Tears continued to fall down my cheeks as I registered exactly what was happening.

"You hard of hearing, asshole?" Jensen demanded, punctuating his question with a fist to Dane's face. "Because I distinctly remember her telling you it was over." Another punch. A sickening crack.

There was a garbled response from Dane. I couldn't make it out, but it upset Jensen nonetheless. He raised his arm again.

"Jensen," I called out, my voice trembling. His anger forced conflicting emotions in me. There was a part of me that was a little scared at his loss of control, but another appreciated his protective nature. Judging by the way he refused to let up on Dane, I knew he hadn't heard me, so I stepped forward and placed my hand on his upper arm hesitantly, still a little afraid. I'd never seen him like this, but based on what he told me about his past, I always knew it was a possibility.

Thankfully, his firm hold on Dane slackened, and he took a step back, his eyes still full of rage and never leaving our intruder. His upper body heaved with each angry breath he took, and his hands remained clenched at his sides. Dane stayed down, moaning and unable to move.

When Jensen moved, I flinched. I was glad his back was to me, because I hated that he elicited this response. He pulled out his cellphone and called the cops to report a break-in and attack. By the time he hung up, Dane was unconscious.

I wasn't sure what to expect when Jensen turned and took his first couple of steps toward me. I waited, holding my breath and clutching my towel to me tightly.

His hard, angry stare softened. "Madison," he said in a soft, soothing tenor. "It's okay, I'm not going to hurt you."

What? My eyebrows pulled together in confusion. "What?" I asked, mirroring my thoughts. "I never thought that." Suddenly, I shook my head.

"Are you okay?" His right hand cradled my face, his eyes taking inventory of my appearance, and his left rested on my hip.

I lifted a hand and pressed it to his chest, confirming his presence was real. "I'm fine. Just ... a little rattled."

Jensen pulled me to him, his right hand moving over my damp hair. "I'm so glad he didn't get a chance to ..." He struggled to finish the sentence, kissing the top of my wet head instead and inhaling deeply. I swear, I even felt his intake of breath shudder. "You should get dressed before the cops show up."

Dane was just coming to when the cops arrived, and after they hauled him away, they took statements from both Jensen and me. When they had everything they needed, they left, telling us they may need to contact us again.

"So much for tonight," Jensen said with a heavy sigh, running his hand through his hair.

I nodded solemnly, still reeling from everything that had happened, when his statement registered. My gaze snapped to him, eyebrows pulled together. "Wait, what?"

Jensen shrugged. "I was hoping we could get off the ranch tonight, but I guess that's been shot to hell."

He turned to walk away when my arm shot out and I grabbed him by the wrist. "Wait," I tell him, my hoarse from all the screaming at Dane. "I'd still very much like to go out."

"Madi, I don't think it's a good idea. After everything that just happened ..."

"Now is the perfect time," I argued. "Please don't make me sit in this house. I'd rather end the day on a high note than where I am right now, emotionally."

Jensen's blue eyes regarded me carefully before he acquiesced with a nod. A smile slowly spread across his lips. "Okay. Mind if I go have a quick shower first?"

Even though I was still pretty shaken up, I nodded. He must have sensed my nerves, because he pressed a kiss to the top of my head and told me he wouldn't be long.

When I heard the bathroom door shut, I went back to my room and checked my appearance. Before the cops arrived, I'd pulled on a pair of my new jeans and a fitted, light blue, plaid button-up. My hair was a little tousled, so I ran my fingers through it to make it look a little nicer, then I applied a little makeup to hide the red blotches around my eyes.

I finally felt a little more human, and I was just putting my mascara away when I heard the phone ring and rushed out to the kitchen where it was resting on the charger.

"Hello?"

"Hi, Madison. Is Jensen in, please?"

I immediately recognized the voice on the other end of

the telephone as Jensen's mom. "Um, he's just in the shower. He should be done soon though," I told her, walking to the living room and relaxing onto the couch.

"How are you feeling?"

I knew she was talking about my injuries and not what had happened earlier tonight, but it was a loaded question that made my body tense and my eyes warm with tears. She sounded genuinely concerned, and I didn't want to alarm her, so I tamped it down and responded.

"I'm still doing great. Better every day. Thanks for asking," I told her with a shrug. "Jensen's been great."

"Good. I'm glad. You'll let him know I called?" she inquired.

"You bet. It was nice talking to you, Dr. Davis."

About five minutes after hanging up, Jensen emerged from the shower, stopping in the doorway to my bedroom in just his towel.

"I should be ready in about ten more minutes."

"Sure," I said. While I had seen Jensen in a towel—and less—before, I couldn't help but take in the sight before me. Water beaded off the ends of his disheveled hair and trickled down his brawny body, disappearing once they met the terrycloth towel, and his colorful sleeve seemed even brighter beneath the slick water on his skin.

When I looked back up, his eyes dropped to the phone still in my hands. "Did somebody call?"

"Oh, your mom. She wants you to call her back."

"Okay. Thanks." I handed him the phone and watched him saunter his towel-covered ass out of the room.

Alone again, I stood in my room for a few minutes, staring at my bed and reliving Dane's attack. I couldn't stand it anymore, and I quickly left, seeking refuge in the kitchen until Jensen was ready.

"Madi?" he called out.

"Kitchen!" I turned around from where I was leaning on the island, and all the breath left my body when I took in the man who stood before me. Dark denim jeans and a lightweight, black cable-knit sweater never looked so good on a man. The brown hair atop his head was still slightly damp from his shower and his blue eyes sparkled. I allowed my gaze to roam over his body appreciatively.

"Are you ready to go?"

I nodded, my nerves slowly being replaced by excitement.

"Come on, put your boots on and come with me." He was being very cryptic. What could he possibly have planned? Was he going to take me into Savannah for dinner and a movie? I would admit it would be kind of fun, just not what either of us initially wanted.

Once my boots were on, Jensen took me by the hand and led me out of the house, past our vehicles, and toward the barn. "Jensen, where are we going?"

He winked at me once as he led me in through the large barn door. "You'll see."

Boy, did I ever.

TRYING TO FORGET

As soon as we stepped into the barn, I saw both Halley and Ransom tethered and tacked up in the aisle. "Jensen, I can't. Your mom said ..."

"I talked to her when I called. She said a little trail ride probably wouldn't be bad" — he looked down at me, that same teasing glint in his eyes — "as long as you think you can stay in the saddle."

"Funny," I said, shoving him lightly as we got closer to the two horses. "So, we're really going for a ride? Together?"

Jensen quickly took Halley's halter off and bridled her before handing her reins to me and doing the same to Ransom. "As long as you think you can keep up."

"I could ride circles around you," I boasted confidently as we led our horses outside where I mounted with ease. The pain in my ribs was almost completely gone. It was a relief, and as soon as both feet were in the stirrups, I closed my eyes and sighed.

"You ready? There's somewhere I want to show you. You've probably already found this little slice of heaven, but I thought it would be perfect for tonight." When I opened my eyes, I saw Jensen on Ransom to my right. In the last week I had seen them together a few times now, but under no uncertain terms was it any less sexy. The man looked good on a horse, and he knew what he was doing. My legs trembled, but not in an I'm-going-to-fall-off kind of way. No, it was a very good, excited tremble. It helped me put Dane out of my mind for the time being.

"Yeah. Let's go."

Jensen led the way, taking the trail I was familiar with, but then veering off completely until we were going down paths I didn't recognize. Trusting that he knew what he was doing, I stayed close and let him make all the decisions. I was just enjoying being allowed to ride again; and to be riding alongside Jensen? It was exhilarating.

"Do you think you could handle a trot?" Jensen asked, turning to me. "I want to get there with enough time."

"Time for what?" I inquired, really wishing he'd tell me what he had planned.

"Just, yes or no?" he prodded, somewhat impatiently.

With a nod, I nudged Hails into a trot. "All right, Mr. Impatient. Lead the way."

Chuckling, Jensen instructed Ransom forward, his extended gait easily allowing him to take the lead again. "It's not much farther." It was kind of disheartening to know we were almost where Jensen had planned to take us because I wasn't quite ready for our ride to end.

When Jensen slowed Ransom to a walk, I followed suit, noticing that the trail we were on had become narrower and the massive branches of the trees native to these parts curved overhead like a natural canopy. Jensen led me through some low-hanging branches, instructing me to duck down and lift the smaller ones out of the way.

When we made it through, I gasped as we entered the most breathtaking clearing I had ever seen. There were beautiful wild flowers everywhere and some of the leaves of the trees around the perimeter of the area were beginning to change as fall approached. Fireflies completed the ambiance as they bobbed and weaved above the tall grass.

"Wow," I said breathlessly. "Jensen, this is ... How did you ...? Wow ..."

I couldn't take my eyes off of the breathtaking beauty of the hidden thicket, but I heard Jensen dismount to my left. "So, you like it, then?"

I felt his hand gently touch my left thigh, and I looked down at him. "It's beautiful. When did you find this place?"

"Last week after one of my training sessions with Ransom. I knew I wanted to bring you here when you were able to ride again." His smile widened as he took a step back. "Why don't you come down so we can get settled?"

"What are you talking about?" I asked as I swung my right leg over and dismounted to Halley's left. Once I was on the ground, I noticed a large insulated cooler a few feet away. "What is this?"

"A picnic, Madison." The man was too much for words.

"When did you do all this?" I asked, leading Halley behind him and Ransom as they made their way toward the cooler.

"I may have stopped on my way back from town and set everything up," he said, replacing Ransom's reins over his neck and pulled a halter off the blanket before putting it over his face, then moved away from him without fear.

"Aren't you afraid he'll take off?" I asked, watching warily as Ransom dropped his head and started eating some of the grass near the blanket.

"Nah. He'll be okay. So will Halley. Trust me." He grabbed a second halter and repeated what he did with Ransom before taking me by the hand and pulling me down onto the blanket. There was a small iDock on the blanket with a slim black iPod nestled in it, and Jensen turned it on. Soothing and familiar instrumental music filled the silence as I continued to bask in the majestic beauty of this place. I was in complete awe.

"If I didn't know any better, I'd think this was a date."

"Wine?" Jensen asked, opening the tightly sealed cooler and grabbing the wine and two glasses.

I laughed. "You've really thought of everything, haven't you?" I asked, completely amazed by his effort to execute the perfect evening. Jensen handed me the glass he had just filled before filling his own, and that's when I noticed the pillows on the blanket behind him. "Pillows? Why, Jensen Davis, do you plan on seducing me out here?"

He hummed as he took a sip of his wine. "I figured we'd see where the night took us." He moved to his left a few inches and patted the empty space to his right. "Why don't you come over here?"

There was no need to ask me more than once. Even though I wasn't terribly far from him, I definitely wasn't close enough, either. Biting my lip, I got up onto my knees and maneuvered until I sat next to him. "This is amazing," I whispered, turning my head to look into his eyes in hopes of being able to express just how much this entire night meant to me.

He stared at me a moment, but I could see what looked like regret in his eyes. "I'm so sorry about earlier," he said. "I shouldn't have lost control like that. I never wanted you to see that side of me."

"Jensen," I started to interject.

"I thought I'd left that part of me behind when I was released." He lowered his eyes. "But when I heard you screaming, and then saw him on top of you, ready to—"

"You stopped him," I interrupted, drawing his attention back to me. "Jensen, if you hadn't gotten there when you did …" My voice broke, and nausea rolled in my belly. I couldn't bring myself to finish my sentence, and a tear slipped down my cheek.

Jensen's warm hand slid over my cheek, his fingers slipping into my hair, and he rested his forehead to mine. With his face mere inches from mine, and his lips irresistible in the faint glow of the setting sun, I leaned in to kiss him softly. While I felt the need to deepen the kiss, I was quite content to just allow our lips to move tenderly together, his delectable bottom lip between mine, and my top lip between his.

His right hand moved to my neck, his fingers threading into my hair, sending a wave of desire straight through me. The kiss was soft and sweet and exactly the kind of kiss that could make a person melt. It wasn't pushy or insistent. There was no pressure for more behind it. After my evening, it was exactly what I needed.

With a sigh, I broke the tender kiss and rested my forehead to his. When I opened my heavy-lidded eyes, I was met with his own passion-filled stare. "That was nice."

"Just nice?"

A smile broke across my face. "It was what I needed."

"There's more where that came from," he whispered, his warm, sweet-smelling breath wafting over me and filling my head with a delightful fog of desire. I nodded, my forehead still against his, before he moved his mouth to capture mine in one more innocent kiss and laid us back on the pillows.

As soon as we were horizontal, conflict set in. I had been waiting not-so-patiently for my injuries to heal so Jensen and I could finally give in to our urges. It had been a long few weeks of repressed sexual tension, with very few opportunities for release. We were both ready to burst.

Then Dane showed up, drunk and trying to force himself on me. The memory of that wouldn't leave me any time soon, but I told myself I could try to forget with Jensen. It was what we agreed on, right? To use each other in order to move on from our pasts.

Jensen's fingers wound into my hair while moving his right arm until his hand was flat on my back and urging me toward him. Our lips moved eagerly, and I shifted my body to straddle him, cupping his jaw as our mouths opened and our tongues slid smoothly against each other.

Our zeal for one another climbed with each second that passed. Without a second thought, I moved my hands between us and tugged on his shirt, lifting it so I could see and feel him without the barrier of cotton between us.

"Mmmf, Madison," he mumbled, his tongue still sliding against mine making it difficult to enunciate correctly. The minute my hands touched the bare flesh of his stomach, he stopped trying to speak, instead choosing to groan and pull me closer as he flipped us until he had me flat on my back, pressing himself firmly between my legs.

Everything was forgotten. Nothing else in the world mattered when Jensen kissed me.

I continued to work the shirt up his body, getting it to his chest before he removed his lips from mine and discarded it to the corner of the blanket. He looked around the meadow once. My eyes followed his, stopping when we found our horses several feet away, still grazing happily.

His hands rested on my jean-covered legs, moving up my calves. He hooked his fingers behind my knees and pulled my body roughly toward him, causing me to whimper when I made contact with him again.

When he was satisfied with my position against him, his hands traveled up the outside of my thighs, sliding to the top and continuing up toward my hips. The wide span of his hand had his pinkies still running along the outer seam of my jeans while his thumbs came dangerously and deliciously close to the juncture between my legs. I squirmed beneath him, thrusting my hips up in an effort to force his touch. When his right thumb made contact, my legs tightened around him, holding him even closer still.

While I wanted his hands to remain where they were, I also needed his hands on my heated flesh. Lowering his body again and reclaiming my lips with his own, his fingers teased the skin of my belly before swooping beneath my blue shirt and toward my breasts.

Everything was going well. Jensen and I were finally going to get what we'd both been wanting for so long. Then the flashes started. It was nothing Jensen did that set it off, but all I could see was the look in Dane's eyes, feel the weight of his body on mine, and the way my skin crawled.

My body tensed below Jensen, and he immediately pulled back, slipping his hands under me to help me sit up as I struggled to catch my breath.

"I'm sorry," I mumbled, covering my face.

"Why are you apologizing? You have nothing to be sorry for." He wrapped an arm around me and let me lean on him.

"I know. But this can't be what you had planned for tonight."

Jensen laughed. "Madi, there was no concrete plan for how tonight would go. Truthfully, I only brought you out here to get you out of the house."

"Yeah, but—"

"Do I want to sleep with you? I'd be stupid not to, but I'm not going to risk your emotional well-being. I'm not a complete fuckwad."

I glanced up at him and smiled. "You know, when you say stuff like that, it makes me want you even more."

"Yeah? The term 'fuckwad' gets you hot?"

I laughed loudly, grateful for his ability to lighten the heavy mood. "Sure. Let's go with that."

"So, uh," he stammered somewhat awkwardly in the wake of our almost-sex as he pulled his shirt back on. "You hungry?"

I nodded, pulling my knees up to my chest and clenching my legs together to quell the undeniable ache that still
lingered there. Jensen leaned forward and reached into the
cooler again, pulling out two covered containers.

"I stopped at a little Italian restaurant and picked this
up." He opened the container and the smell was amazing.
"It's not as warm as it should be, but it's not cold, either. It's
vegetarian lasagna."

The first bite was incredible. "I didn't know that there
was an Italian restaurant in town."

"Well, it's relatively new. Do you like it?" Jensen
watched me carefully as I slid my fork into my mouth again,
closing my eyes as I savored the taste.

"Mmm hmm." He seemed pleased with my reaction and
set his dish down to refill our wine glasses.

As the sky darkened above us, Jensen reached into his
cooler of magic and grabbed several thick-pillared candles
and a lighter, placing them between us so we could see. Even
though we were supposed to be keeping things between us
casual, I couldn't help but notice just how much thought
went into tonight. It was equal parts scary and exciting.

After clearing away our empty dishes, he moved the
candles to the edge of our blanket and pulled me down into
his arms so we could stare up at the stars for a bit while we
let our food digest. Halley and Ransom continued to roam the
field, never going too far—and even when they tried to, Jensen would pull an apple or carrots out of that bottomless
cooler and coax them back over to us.

We stayed wrapped up in each other's arms for another
half hour before Jensen suggested we head home. "We
should get the horses back, and then I'll come back with the
truck to pick this stuff up before I turn in for the night."

"I'm not going to make you come all the way back out
here by yourself. I'll come with you."

Shaking his head, he helped me to my feet. "No, it's fine. I don't mind."

"Maybe not," I argued. "But I want to help. Don't be such a guy." The truth of the matter was I didn't want to be home alone, but I couldn't admit it aloud.

After folding the blanket and fitting everything securely in the cooler, we removed the halters from Ransom and Halley and put them inside before Jensen made sure it was shut tightly. Once satisfied with our cleanup, he moved to Ransom's side, and we mounted before he led us back toward the ranch. While it was sad to leave this secret place of ours, I looked forward to revisiting it together one day soon.

The ride back was good, the sexual tension between the two of us gone for the time being, and we joked around with one another, laughing genuinely as we reentered the ranch grounds. After brushing Halley and Ransom down, we walked hand-in-hand to the truck so we could drive back out and pick up the cooler.

"You can stay here. I'll be back before you know it," he told me, unbuckling and opening his door.

Matching his actions move-for-move, I stepped out of the car with him. "No way. I'm coming."

Jensen smirked and shook his head, chuckling as he closed his car door and circled around to me. "Fine. If you insist. *Come.*" He was such a guy.

I narrowed my eyes but took his hand in mine and walked with my body right against him. He was right; it didn't take long thanks to how he was able to drive down a gravel road that got us pretty close to another entry point. Once we had the cooler tucked away in the back of the truck, we headed home and got ready for bed.

I had just pulled Jensen's shirt on, and was preparing to climb into bed when I froze. I stared at the bed, at the black underwear set that was still there from earlier, and fought the flashes. Forcing my eyes closed, I found the strength to walk away.

Jensen was in his room, turning down his blankets for bed. "Hey," he said, abandoning his comforter and meeting me in his doorway, his eyes taking in my attire appreciatively as they roamed over my bare legs. "What's up?"

Like earlier, just being with him calmed me. I felt safe with him. I took his hands in mine and allowed myself to get lost in his eyes again. "I just wanted to thank you again for tonight. I had a really great time." Jensen beamed, folding his arms and mine around me while I still held his hands.

Tilting his head down, he kissed me softly. "I'm glad. I did, too."

"I don't …" I knew I should tell him what was really going on with me, but I just couldn't. Not yet. "I don't want the night to end. Can I …" I paused, digging deep down for the strength to voice the rest of my question. "… stay with you?"

I could tell he sensed something was off. "Madison—" he started to dispute before I worked one of my hands free and silenced him with my fingers on his lips.

Shaking my head, I spoke again. "No sex. I just …" I sighed. I needed to be honest. "I can't sleep in there." I looked up in his eyes, silently pleading with him. "I need to be with you. Please."

Nodding against my touch, he led me to his bed, ushering me beneath the covers on the side farthest from the door. I laid back on one of his fluffy pillows and brought the blanket up to my chin. I watched as he removed his shirt again and tossed it in his hamper before he unbuttoned his jeans. His eyes caught mine as I ogled him stripping.

"You know, it's not fair that you get to watch me get undressed, but I don't get the same pleasure," he teased as he tossed his jeans and socks to the hamper and walked over in his boxer briefs before lying next to me and pulling me against him.

"Well, then I guess I'll have to remedy that soon, huh?" I ribbed, angling my face to kiss his jaw softly before letting my heavy eyes close.

With a chuckle, he kissed my forehead. "Agreed."

Silence surrounded us, and I was just dozing off when Jensen kissed the back of my neck.

"What are you doing next weekend?" he whispered.

"Hmmm?" I hummed, not sure I heard him right.

"Madison, I'd love it if you'd come with me to my sister's wedding."

My eyes snapped open and I sat up, startling him. "What?"

"I just thought we could have fun together. It wouldn't be a date." He cleared his throat, and I could see how nervous he was about how I might misunderstand the invitation.

I couldn't explain it, but hearing this felt like a kick to the gut. It shouldn't have. I knew that. I needed to rein that shit in, because that was all our "relationship" was supposed to be based on. Casual. Fun. No strings. No feelings.

When the feeling dissolved, I smiled. "That sounds like a lot of fun."

The smile that appeared on Jensen's face was adorable. "Cool. I'll tell my sister."

Even though we wouldn't be attending as a couple, I found myself really excited for a weekend away with Jensen. I could just imagine the possibility for all the "fun" we might have away from the ranch.

"Come on," Jensen said softly after I yawned. He placed another soft kiss onto the top of my head. "Let's get some sleep."

Taking a deep breath, I rested my head on Jensen's chest and let myself get lost in his scent. His presence, allowed me to relax and forget about earlier long enough to fall asleep.

20

THE TRUTH COMES OUT

Dark, starry skies filled my dreams that night. Jensen and I lay on the ground in the field, arms around each other as we stared up into the night sky, occasionally stealing a kiss here and there. There was no better feeling than being in his arms, and that feeling only amplified as my eyes fluttered open and I felt the reality of actually being in his arms.

His warm, mostly naked body was pressed firmly to my back; I could feel the hair on his legs against the backs of my calves as we spooned beneath the thick comforter on his bed. I moved slightly, enjoying the feeling of him positioned against my body, and he tightened his grip on me to keep me from pulling away—not that I intended to. I remained still, waiting for his breathing to even out again and his hold on me to relax before I attempted to roll over to face him.

Not anxious to break our connection, I made sure I moved beneath the arm he had draped over my waist so it stayed in place. Resting my hands under my cheek, I observed him, taking in absolutely everything. There was a peaceful look on his face as he continued to sleep, and his dark hair was in complete disarray, causing my fingers to twitch with the urge to reach out and touch it. I didn't want to tame it, per se; I just wanted to *feel* it. As my eyes continued on their journey over his features, I took note of the subtle scruff that had appeared overnight and I wondered what it would feel like against my skin. Not on my hand, but everywhere else as he covered my entire body with tender kisses, occasionally nibbling the more sensitive areas.

Unable to control myself anymore, I moved my left hand from under my cheek and reached out, moving a stray piece of his unruly hair off of his forehead before allowing my fingers to ghost over his scruff. He shivered beneath my light touch, and I pulled back immediately, not wanting to wake him or have this moment end. I enjoyed looking at him every day, but I had never seen him like this. So peaceful. So innocent. So delightfully happy.

I remained in his bed for a few more minutes, just enjoying the moment when I finally felt that annoying morning urge to use the bathroom. Very slowly, I shimmied back toward the edge, being sure to not let his arm fall hard to the mattress so he could remain asleep. After taking care of business and brushing my teeth, I ventured barefoot out to the kitchen to put a pot of coffee on and find something for breakfast. Remembering that Jensen quite enjoyed my French toast casserole, I decided on that.

After turning the radio on and keeping the volume at a reasonable level so I didn't wake him, I began cutting and mixing everything up before putting the casserole in the preheated oven. While it baked, I grabbed a pad of paper and a pen so I could make a grocery list. It hadn't occurred to me until I was grabbing everything I needed that we were running pretty low on a lot of things; a run to the market was definitely in order.

With my list made and sitting on the island counter for later, I poured a cup of fresh coffee and added my cream and sugar before sipping it slowly. Warmth spread through me as the caffeine kicked in, my heart pumping a little faster, waking me up. Enjoying the early morning buzz, I thought back on the night before. Not the Dane stuff—though it made a brief cameo before I shoved it back down. I focused on the trail ride out to a secluded field with Jensen where we dined and drank wine as we watched the sun set. It was almost too good to be real.

The memory of him asking me to his sister's wedding made me smile. I couldn't wait to see what our weekend away might bring. Even though we weren't together, I wanted to look incredible for him—really drive him wild to make the weekend even more memorable. That was when I remembered I had just bought the perfect dress. How convenient ...

Or was it?

I suddenly realized that Willow and Jensen had been alone for a bit during her visit. Could Jensen have said something to her? I wouldn't be surprised, and she did seem adamant I buy a new dress without an actual reason. That was all the convincing I needed.

"Meddling little fibber," I muttered, setting my coffee cup down and reaching for the phone to dial Willow. Yes, it was only just after six a.m., but she was likely to be up anyway.

"Hey, Madi!" she chirped into the phone. "What's up?"

I shrugged, hopping up onto the island and allowing my legs to swing back and forth. "Not much. Jensen and I went on a trail ride last night," I confessed, my foolish grin returning to my face as I told her everything about our date. Willow ooohed and aaahed, also being sure to reiterate everything to Brandon who had woken up only minutes after I had called.

"Also, I've realized that someone *claiming* to be my best friend kept something fairly huge from me," I said, my tone only half-serious.

Willow squealed excitedly. "Oh! He asked you! What did

you say?"

"I told him it sounded like fun," I said, the smile on my face so wide it hurt my cheeks. Realizing I still hadn't confronted Willow for her involvement, I redirected my attention to her. "Wait a minute! How could you not tell me?"

She only giggled. "Well, he never actually told me he was planning to ask you. I just thought you should have a dress on stand-by, just in case."

Just then Jensen appeared in the kitchen wearing nothing more than a pair of black flannel pajama pants and running his fingers through his hair as his sleepy eyes found mine. "Hey," he said quietly as he approached me with a sly smile, pushing himself between my legs and kissing me softly while Willow started talking about Brandon's office party the night before.

"It's barely seven a.m. Who are you talking to?" he asked quietly, reaching his left hand out for my coffee and taking a sip—a dangerous gesture for most people. His right hand rested on my bare thigh, sending fire through my veins that started where his fingers rested.

"Will," I whispered before leaning forward and kissing him softly. His breath tasted of mint and coffee, and the scruff that remained on his face delightfully scratched at my skin as he let his lips linger on mine for a moment.

"Mmm," he moaned quietly before turning toward the phone. "Willow, Madi has to go now."

Willow's laugh trilled in my ear as Jensen's mouth returned to mine. "Okay, Madi. I'll talk to you later. Have fun," she sang before hanging up.

After hitting the off button, I let the hand holding the phone fall from my ear, not really hearing the handheld clatter to the floor when I dropped it to fist Jensen's soft hair. Simultaneously, our mouths opened and our tongues met enthusiastically as my legs tightened and pulled Jensen closer to me. His hands gripped my bare thighs before moving up and under the bottom of our shirt (so maybe I was willing to share it … as long as it smelled like him) until he was tugging at the sides of my panties.

Scooting toward the edge of the island's countertop, I moaned when I felt Jensen's thumbs move under the thin cotton fabric and toward the pulsing between my legs. "Fuck," I mumbled into his mouth as I thrust my hips forward, forcing his right thumb to make first contact. It was like the motherfucking moon landing, and I wanted him to plant his flag in me.

He started to pull back, almost as though he realized this was quickly escalating to something we both knew we shouldn't be doing. "Madison, I hate to admit this, but I don't have any condoms." He seemed so upset with himself, which could only mean he wanted to have his way with me just as much as I did.

In a flash, my left hand moved up to the back of his bicep, holding his right hand in place inside my panties. I grunted, resisting the urge to unabashedly hump his hand again. "We can do other things—non-sex things—to each other. *Please*," I whined pathetically. "I can't take this anymore."

Without any further hesitation, Jensen stopped trying to pull away, instead pressing his lips to mine with need as his fingers travelled to where I had been craving his touch for weeks.

"Oh, god," he sighed into my open mouth before his fingers slid slowly—deliciously and painfully slow—between my legs, pushing me further and further toward the release that would swallow me whole soon enough.

As his fingers played me like a piano, his hips moved of their own accord, seeking anything they could to feel half as good as he was making me feel in that moment. Releasing his hair from my grasp, I moved my hand down his neck, his arm, and over his abs before I teased the waist of his pants, tugging on them lightly.

"Do it," he demanded gruffly, biting my lower lip hard and making me whimper as I plunged my hand into his pants, wrapping it around his thick length for the first time ever.

It twitched in my grasp as I thrust toward the base, and Jensen grunted as he released my lip from his teeth. Upon opening my eyes, I saw that his were more intense than I'd ever seen them. Holding his stare, I continued to move my hand up and down his length, watching him fight the natural urge to let his eyes roll back in his head with every pass my palm made over the head.

There was only one thing that could make this even more enjoyable for him without *actually* having sex with him.

Removing my hand from his pants, Jensen's eyes widened with confusion and what looked like panic. "What are you —?" His eyes quickly drifted down to my hand, widening more than should have been possible, as I slipped it between my legs. Strangled sounds escaped his strained vocal chords as I slipped my fingers beneath his palm to gather some of the slick moisture there before thrusting my hand back into his pants.

"Ooooh shiiiiit," he groaned, his left hand squeezing my thigh almost painfully as my hand slid over his erection with ease. He was so lost to the sensation of my wet hand pumping him that he seemed to have forgotten about my own pleasure. Moving my left leg slightly, I nudged his hand back over so he could resume his previous actions.

He matched my every move with one of his own, sweeping his fingers over that most-sensitive bundle of nerves before gliding it through the silken flesh and pressing firmly when he arrived at his final destination. "Shit, baby. You feel so good," he whispered as he teased me a little bit more than was entirely necessary.

"Yeah," I moaned, sounding more like a porn star than anything. I tightened my hand around him and pumped him once more. "You, too. So *fucking* good." Apparently my swearing pushed him that much closer toward the edge, because he groaned and let his forehead fall to my shoulder.

Resting my head against his until my mouth was right by his ear, I let the sensation of his long, talented fingers pleasuring me take over. "More, Jensen," I panted. "I need more."

I felt the sting of his teeth nipping at my neck at the exact moment he pushed his fingers into me. Biting was never something I would have thought to be erotic in real life, but there was something about it in that exact moment that did wonderful, tingly things to my entire body. Of course, those feelings could have been because his fingers were buried deep, stroking the shit out of that elusive little hot-spot inside me.

"Yes ... Yes ..." I moaned over and over again as he moved in and out of me. "Shit ... Fuck ... Don't ... *Ohhhh* ... Don't stop ..." My voice grew louder and louder as his hand moved faster and fucking faster between my thighs.

Even though I was so focused on the things Jensen was doing to my body, I remained aware of what *I* was doing to *his*. As his speed increased, so did mine. I could tell he was nearing his orgasm as his hips thrust, short and fast, into my hand. "Look at me?" I murmured.

Lifting his head from my shoulder, he placed kisses along the side of my neck and jaw before planting a deep, passionate kiss on my lips. Our mouths parted, eyes meeting and our labored breathing synching up. With his hair falling over his sweat-dampened forehead, I watched as his eyebrows furrowed and felt his body tense between my legs.

"Shit, Madison ... I'm going to ..."

I nodded, scooting my ass forward on the counter and forcing his fingers just a little deeper, encouraging him to take me with him as he fell into pure ecstasy. His fingers worked their magic inside of me, and his thumb resumed its work externally, bringing me that much closer. The orgasm swelled, my body tensing in preparation, and I tightened my legs around him, digging my heels into his ass as we continued on toward our final destination.

Jensen brought his face forward, our eyes still only on each other, and rested his forehead to mine. His warm breath wafted over my face as I moved minutely to brush my lips against his. Our soft kiss was broken by our moans as I felt the first wave of rhapsody wash over me, my stomach muscles tightening in its wake, preparing for the next set that I could already feel swelling on the horizon. I could feel his forehead wrinkle against mine, and his eyes hooded further as I continued moving my hand.

"Yes ..." I moaned, nodding my head to let him know what I wanted. The next onslaught of pleasure that crashed down around me was my undoing; I cried out, my voice echoing in the tiny kitchen as I felt Jensen pulse and release in my palm.

With our bodies physically spent, we sat, unmoving, for what seemed like an eternity, remaining locked in each other's stare. Jensen's eyes reflected a kind of peace there that could only come after an orgasm; the calm after the storm. His lips were plump and reddened from the frenzied kisses, and his hair was ... well, it was as unruly as ever, but this time it was because I had been running my fingers through it.

Tilting his head, he kissed the tip of my nose. "That was ..." His eyes closed and the corners of his mouth twisted up into a smirk as he remembered. "Fuck, it was amazing." Removing his hand from my panties, Jensen shifted to the right and grabbed a tea towel from the last drawer in the island counter and handed it to me as I removed my hand from his pants so I could clean it off.

Smiling lazily as I finished wiping my hand, I sighed. "Yeah. It really was. It's like weeks of sexual frustration is just ... *gone.*" I glanced up at him again. "Thank you."

Shaking his head, he moved and kissed me softly. "No. Thank *you.* I probably would have tried to stop us again."

I laughed and hopped down from the counter, my legs still a little weak from the pleasure that was still coursing through my veins. "Probably. But I wouldn't have done anything different. I always get my way." I grabbed the waist of his pants again and tugged him toward me before standing on the tips of my toes and planting a hard kiss on his lips. "Are you hungry?"

Jensen nodded. "Famished."

"Good. Breakfast should be ready in a few minutes. I'm going to go wash up really quick. I'll be back." Jensen tapped my ass lightly as I turned to walk from the room, causing me to giggle like a schoolgirl.

After locking myself in the bathroom, I washed my hands and brushed my hair again. With a smile permanently plastered on my face, I pulled my hair over my left shoulder and noticed a red welt starting to form on the right side of my neck.

"Oh shit," I whispered, leaning in to get a good look at the hickey. The mark, while it excited me in the moment—and a little currently, if I'm being completely honest—was going to be a bitch to hide from my dad. How the hell was I going to explain it if he were to see it? Was I going to be confined to turtleneck sweaters and scarves until it faded? It was too damn hot for that nonsense.

Still not sure how I would explain it, I headed to my

room and changed my underwear before pulling on a pair of jeans and changing out of my shirt, trading it for a light blue tank top. While I really enjoyed the way Jensen eyed me hungrily when I wasn't wearing much of anything, I knew that we had a morning full of chores to get done in the barn before Dad returned later.

When I reached the kitchen again, I saw Jensen had gotten dressed, too. I stood in the doorway, eyeing the island countertop, and I could feel the blush filling my cheeks.

Jensen looked up from setting the table and smirked when he realized what I was staring at. "Yeah, I don't know if I'll ever be able to look at the kitchen the same way again, either."

"That really just happened, huh? It wasn't some incredibly vivid dream that my sexually-frustrated brain cooked up?" I asked as the timer on the stove sounded.

After he finished setting the table, Jensen came and stood behind me as I put my oven mitts on, wrapping his arms around my waist and pressing his groin right against my ass. "I'm sorry for leaving you frustrated, baby," he crooned, kissing the sweet spot just behind my right ear before gasping. "Shit! Did I do that?"

I laughed. "Well, it wasn't the mailman."

"What the hell? Who does shit like that?" He was getting so worked up over something that would likely be gone in two days' time.

Working against his hold on me, I turned and placed my oven mitt-covered hands on his cheeks. "I'm fine. And, if I'm being completely honest, I kind of liked it." I pulled his face down to mine for a kiss.

"You kinky little freak," he teased, gripping my hips and meeting me halfway, letting our lips touch briefly before I had to grab breakfast.

As we ate, I couldn't stop the memory of what we'd

done from playing in my head on a loop. Unfortunately, it was affecting my lower body, forcing me to cross my legs tightly to quell the sudden need that had sprung to life again. The sounds Jensen made with every bite he took wasn't helping my problem, either. In fact, they were very reminiscent to the ones he made when I made him come.

Jensen's head snapped up, his eyes wide with surprise. "What?" I asked, suddenly feeling a little nervous.

Swallowing thickly and blinking rapidly a few times, he set his fork down. "You ... um ..." He nervously swallowed again. "That noise ..."

I was instantly mortified as I realized what it was he was trying to say. At some point in my silent reverie I had moaned or whimpered or *something*. I dropped my fork and covered my mouth. "Sorry."

He half-laughed and shook his head before shifting his chair and taking my hand in his. He tugged, forcing me to stand and then pulling me down onto his lap. "Don't be. Maybe it's completely narcissistic, but to know that it's *me* you're thinking of when you make those sexy sounds? Well, it makes me want to do things to you that make those memories seem dull."

"Fuck me," I whispered, not meaning it literally — or, kind of not.

Jensen chuckled, brushing the tip of my nose with his. "Soon, Madison. Until then ..." After one last, simple kiss, I went back to my chair so Jensen and I could finish breakfast before heading out to the barn.

A little over an hour later, all the horses were taken out, so Jensen and I worked at cleaning out the stalls. I assured him I was feeling well enough to get back to more of the physically demanding parts of my job, and after making me promise to let him know if I was feeling any pain, he conceded. We worked through the morning before heading to the

235

house for lunch.

"So," I started to say as we walked hand-in-hand through the door. "What do you say we go for a ride this afternoon? Nothing strenuous, maybe just out to our spot?"

Nodding, Jensen opened the fridge. "Sounds good. First, though? I think we should head to town for some groceries."

"Yeah, I have a list." I grabbed the list off the counter, looked it over once more before folding it, and then pushed it into my pocket. "You know what? Since we'll already be heading into town, why don't we just eat out?" Jensen's eyebrows rose suggestively, and I saw that damn devious glint in his eyes as he took my suggestion and turned it into something perverted. *Typical.* "Oh, grow up. You really must be fifteen."

Jensen quickly closed the gap between us and gathered me in his arms. "If you want to stay out of jail, you'd better hope not."

All I could do was roll my eyes and kiss him before dragging him through the front door so we wouldn't get caught up in each other again. The passion between us was powerful, and I knew that if we weren't careful we would find ourselves in a very similar situation as earlier. Not that it would have been a bad thing.

SMILE, YOU'RE ON CANDID CAMERA

Ever the gentleman, Jensen opened my truck door for me and closed it once I was safely inside. Apparently his parents had raised him right, because I had never known a man to open doors for me. Not even on first dates when they were trying to impress me.

"What?" Jensen inquired with a smile as he fastened his seat belt.

I shook my head. "It's silly." The look in Jensen's eyes told me we weren't going anywhere until I told him what I was thinking. "The whole opening-doors thing. It's all very sweet. No one's ever done that for me before."

Chuckling, Jensen pushed the key into the ignition and started the ancient truck. It came to life with a roar. "My mother was a stickler for making sure I knew how to treat a lady."

"Well, I'm glad. While I never thought of myself as the type who needed to be doted on, I quite like how it makes me feel. Keep it up and eventually you'll get lucky," I teased, poking his muscular thigh as we turned out of the driveway.

"Eventually, huh?"

I laughed. "Well, you're the one who said your virtue needed to be protected from my corruption. *But*, I'm sure I'll eventually be able to bring you around to the dark side."

Reaching over the console, Jensen held my hand, lacing our fingers together. "First *Star Trek* and now *Star Wars*." He took a deep breath, releasing it with a chuckle. "Landry, if you're not careful, I will have to pull this car over and show you just how susceptible I am to your personal brand of corruption."

Curious to see just how serious he was, I smirked. "You think making mention of *Star Wars* is arousing? Makes me wonder how you'd feel about my gold bikini get up."

Stifling my laughter, I watched him carefully as he swallowed thickly and kept his wide eyes trained on the road so as not to kill us as he sped down the highway toward Savannah. "Please, for the love of everything sci-fi, don't let that be a joke."

"Baby," I cooed, stroking the back of his thumb with mine. "I assure you it most definitely is *not*."

He exhaled another shaky breath. "May I ask how you came to acquire said bikini?"

"Willow. We went to a Halloween party a few years back. She knew all the guys would dig it—fans of the franchise or not." As Jensen shifted in his seat in what I assumed was an attempt to hide his *appreciation* for my little story, I laughed. "Play your cards right and I'll show you sometime."

"That," he rasped, "would be *awesome*." Jensen quickly changed the subject to something a little less stimulating for him so that we could safely get out of the car without being the talk of the town.

"So, where do you want to eat?" he asked as the car entered the town limits.

"Well, there's the diner," I suggested. "It's always pretty great." Having visited the area when he was younger, he didn't need directions and found the diner within minutes.

Jensen parked the car, and I had just unbuckled and reached for the release on my door when he rushed around to open it the rest of the way. "You're killing my efforts to remain chivalrous, here."

"Sorry," I said, genuinely apologetic. "Like I said, I'm just not used to it."

Holding out his hand for me, he winked. "Well, *get* used to it."

With our hands tightly twisted together, we walked into the diner and found a booth by the window. Deciding to sit across from one another, we waited for the server to come and take our drink order.

"Hi there!" a cheerful voice said to my right. "What can I get for yo— Oh. My. God! Madison? Madison Landry?"

Raising my eyes, I met the deep brown stare of Tiff Thorne, one of my old high school classmates. "Tiff, hi. How are you?"

In high school, Tiff and I weren't friends, but we weren't *exactly* enemies, either. While I was focused on my studies and self-deemed too klutzy for anything that required coordination, Tiff was Little Miss Everything. Cheerleader, outstanding athlete, class president. There was nothing she wasn't good at. It was a classic case of keeping your friends close and enemies closer. I often tutored Tiff in Algebra — and by tutored, I mean she paid me to do her assignments. I didn't mind, actually. The reason being because when the time came for tests, she had no clue what she was doing, and that wasn't my problem. I tried to teach her. Multiple times.

Even with all of her successes in high school, here she was … waiting tables. Not that I was judging; maybe she enjoyed her job. Anything was possible.

"I'm good! How about you? No longer single, I see?" Her eyes drifted to Jensen, and I *definitely* saw the look she gave him. She was looking at him like he was something to eat.

The only thing that kept me from not jumping up and shredding her corneas was Jensen. The entire time Tiff was eyeballing him, he was staring at me, holding my hands in his across the table so I would focus on him.

"No," I told her, even though it was a lie. Jensen and I weren't an item, but I felt like I had something to prove to her. Like I could be capable of having something she didn't for once. Besides, I didn't hear Jensen object. "Not single."

"How long have the two of you been together?" she asked, and through my periphery I could see that she was still staring at Jensen. I may have wanted to punch her in the throat.

"Um, not long. A couple weeks?"

"Still time for everything to go south then, huh?" she asked, trying to pass her tone off as a joke, when really I knew she was just being a total bitch.

Jensen's eyes narrowed before he turned to her for the first time. "Here's an idea, how about you take our order before you cut your tip in half ... *again*." My stomach flipped and my heart pounded excitedly in my veins as I watched Jensen put Tiff in her place. "And then, if you can manage to keep focused on your work, I *won't* feel the need to talk to your manager about your shitty job performance and etiquette."

Tiff was still staring at Jensen, but it was no longer in an attempt to seduce him. She. Was. *Pissed*. After jotting down our drink order, she turned on her heel and stormed off.

"I'm sorry," I said, releasing his hand and sitting back in the booth.

Jensen looked at his empty hands before folding them on the tabletop. "For what?"

"Using you like that. Saying we were together when we're not."

"Oh." He smiled. "Don't worry about it. I didn't mind."

"Still wasn't fair to you. I acted like a dog marking its territory."

"Madi, really, it's fine."

I glanced back over to where Tiff stood, glaring at me, then I looked at Jensen and leaned in to keep from being overheard. "You know she's probably going to spit in our food now, right?" I told him, knowing exactly what kind of person Tiff was. In a word: vindictive.

Jensen shook his head. "Nah. She wouldn't dare. She's not too hard to read. In fact, I guarantee she's back there right now trying to find someone to take our table from her." Jensen paused, looking over toward the back counter. When I followed his gaze, I smiled upon seeing her talking heatedly to a male server as they both glanced over in our direction. "Now, if it had been just you who had spoken to her that way, she likely would have reacted the way you expected. But she's not used to being rejected. She won't want to come back to that."

Sure enough, as Jensen finished speaking, a male server came over with our drinks. "Hi there. I'm Alex. First, I'd like to apologize for Tiff. She's not really the easiest person to deal with, and I can only imagine what *really* happened."

"Oh, it was nothing," I assured him.

Alex was great. He took our order and checked on us whenever he noticed our drinks had gotten low, and also in a way that didn't feel intrusive when we were eating or talking. As we stood from the table after eating, Jensen tipped him generously before wrapping his arm around me and leading me from the diner and to the car. I thought it was sweet, and maybe even read a little too much into the gesture until I looked over my shoulder and saw Tiff. He'd done it to keep up the façade I'd established. Nothing more.

So why did it kind of bum me out?

We roamed the aisles of the grocery store slowly, grabbing both things that were on the list and others that weren't. As I pushed the cart, I paid close attention to a lot of Jensen's impulse buys. As it turned out, the man had quite the sweet tooth. With a couple bags of chocolate chip cookies—the good, chunky chocolate chip cookies—and the ingredients to make homemade brownies in our cart, I watched as he stood and debated which ice cream he wanted.

"You are going to wind up in a sugar-induced coma, Jensen Davis," I teased.

He laughed, keeping his eyes ahead on the freezer. "Not if you help me eat it."

"Mmmm ..." I said contemplatively. "I'll be honest, if you want me to eat ice cream, it has to be vanilla."

Jensen grimaced. "Vanilla? Isn't that kind of boring?"

"Hardly!" I countered as I left the cart and moved in front of him to grab a carton of vanilla ice cream. "I mean, on its own? Sure, it can be." I dropped the ice cream in the cart next to all the other junk. "But, with the right toppings it can be anything but dull. Trust me."

Jensen seemed skeptical, but he walked away from the freezer. "What kind of toppings?" There was something in his tone that led me to believe we weren't *just* talking about ice cream.

Deciding to play along, I shrugged. "Well, your chocolate chip cookies would be amazing crumbled up on top of a chocolate sundae. There's also the brownies you'll bake. Add a few bits of that and I guarantee you'd be in heaven." We resumed walking so we could go and pick up a few of these toppings. "Then, we've got the classics: strawberries, caramel, chocolate sauce ... whipped cream ..."

Through the corner of my eye I caught Jensen smirking, and I could only assume he was coming up with some deliciously kinky idea of eating an ice cream sundae off my body. While I imagined it would be quite sticky, the idea of hopping in my over-sized bathtub with him afterward seemed even more appealing and worth the mess.

Feeling the need to know if he was thinking what I was now thinking, I nudged him with my elbow. "You know, we wouldn't even need bowls."

"Are you trying to kill me?"

"Asks the man who bought enough junk food to force an elephant into diabetic shock," I challenged. "You said vanilla was boring. I'm just showing you that just because something seems plain doesn't mean it has to be."

Jensen grabbed my arm gently to stop me and turned me to face him. "Finally able to see that, huh?" Placing his thumb and forefinger under my chin, he tilted my face up to his, kissing me softly.

If he wasn't careful, he was going to make me think he had feelings for me. Or worse, treat me so well that mine developed for him.

With a breathless sigh, I thought about what he said in regards to my statement. "I wasn't talking about me," I confessed, grabbing the front of his shirt to keep him close. "But, I suppose with the right things on top, even *I* could be a little more exciting."

"You're terrible," he told me with a laugh. "Come on, there are only a few more things on the list."

After paying, Jensen and I loaded everything into the box of the truck and headed for home. We had just left Savannah when Jensen's phone rang between us. His eyes lit up as he recognized the number on the navigation screen in his dashboard and he connected the call on the touch screen, activating his Bluetooth system. "Lilah-Bean! How's it going?"

"Ugh! I wish you'd stop calling me that." Her voice as it rang through the car was beautiful. Instantly I pictured someone tall—but not as tall as Jensen or his father—with lighter hair than Jensen's … not quite the same brown, maybe

a little warmer and on the chocolaty side ... and the same blue eyes as him.

I watched Jensen as he reacted to what his sister said with a smile so big it caused the outer corners of his eyes to crinkle. "Come on, I've been calling you that since you were three. It can't bother you that much?"

She let out a loud, exasperated sigh. *"No, what bothers me is that Kyle has taken to calling me that now, too."*

Jensen laughed loudly. "Well, I can't help that. I'm not his keeper."

"You encourage it!" she argued.

Scoffing, Jensen looked at me as I silently giggled at their exchange. "Please! I do not encourage his behavior. Besides, it's not my fault you used to hide your beans up your nose."

Lilah groaned, and I stifled a laugh. As an only child, I was completely fascinated by their banter. Willow and I were close, and had been since we were both in elementary school, but this was something unlike what the two of us shared.

"So, what's up?" Jensen asked. "With the wedding coming up, I know you can't be calling just to chat. You have to have a ton of shit to get done."

"Shit? My wedding plans are not 'shit'!" she screamed into the phone, sounding genuinely offended.

Turning to me with fear in his eyes, I giggled. "I'm sorry, you're right. You must have a ton of *important things* to do. Not shit. Definitely not shit." He shook his head and mouthed "wow."

Silence filled the car on our end for a moment as I assumed Lilah was calming herself down. *"Um, I just wanted to make sure that things weren't going to be weird ... at the wedding, I mean."*

"Weird? Why would things be weird?" he inquired, furrowing his brow with confusion.

"Well," she whispered. *"Because Kaylie will be there ... re-*

member? And Mom says you're bringing a date."

Jensen's face instantly hardened into an angry scowl. "What?" he demanded. "You can't be fucking serious, Lilah. No. Absolutely not—!" I reached over and placed my hand over Jensen's as it remained stationary on the gear shift.

"Please, Jensen. This is my wedding day. I know things didn't work out between you two, and I'm happy that you're finally getting settled into your new life after what happened. But whatever it was that happened between the two of you, I need you to forget about it for one day, okay? She's my friend."

My head snapped to Jensen, and I could see his jaw clenching tightly as he tried to keep himself calm*ish*. Squeezing his hand seemed to relax him a little, and he looked at me appreciatively. "They don't know?" I mouthed, only to have Jensen shrug sadly and move his hand to twine our fingers together. He needed support, and I was only too happy to lend him some.

"Jensen?" Lilah asked, panic in her voice.

"Yeah," he responded. "I'll, uh … *forget* about it. For you. Can I ask one favor, though?" There was no answer, so Jensen took that as his cue to continue. "If you're planning a seating chart for the reception, don't put me anywhere near her. I may be able to play nice, but I can't imagine—"

"Oh! Yeah. Done. However …"

Jensen groaned. "I don't like where this is going, Lilah," he warned.

From the other end of the call, she laughed nervously. *"Yes, well there's usually never any pleasing you, now is there?"*

"Spit it out."

"You do realize you'll probably see her at some point. Talk to her, even."

Jensen groaned. "Not if I can help it," he muttered. Sighing with defeat when he realized she was right, he conceded. "I'll be on my best behavior. Cross my heart. But you might want to tell *your* friend to keep her distance from me as well."

"*Thank you!*" she exclaimed. "*Oh ... What?*" she whispered to someone on her end of the phone. "*Right, right. Jensen? Kyle wants me to ask if you're going to be at the hotel to get ready with him and Gavin?*"

Jensen looked to me for my reaction; I simply nodded. "Um, yeah. Madison and I will get into Memphis the night before the wedding and check in. Just have Kyle text me with the hotel suite number."

After Jensen and Lilah ended their call, Jensen looked over at me briefly. "I know you don't know anyone who's going to be at the wedding, so you are probably welcome to hang out with me and the guys. It's just, as Kyle's best man, I should probably be there."

"No, of course. It's fine. I can even stay in our room and get ready while you guys are doing your thing. It's fine." A thought suddenly occurred to me. "Actually, since it's in the city, I can maybe sneak over to Willow's spa and get my hair done."

Jensen nodded a few times, keeping his focus on the road ahead before something flashed in his eyes. "*Our* room?"

"Oh ... uh ..." I stammered nervously, my face burning bright. "Sorry, I just assumed. Of course we'll be getting separate rooms."

Chuckling, Jensen squeezed my hand. "Relax. I would love it if we shared a room. I just wasn't sure how to bring it up."

"Speaking of being unsure how to broach a subject," I interjected, biting my bottom lip as I thought about keeping my next thoughts to myself.

Jensen sighed, releasing my hand so he could place his back on the wheel with the other. "You're wondering why I never told my family what Kaylie did?" I nodded. "Kaylie is one of the only friends Lilah had left after the attack."

"Do you ..." I took a deep breath, afraid of the answer to the question that burned the tip of my tongue like acid "... still, um, *love* her?"

Jensen shook his head emphatically. "There was a time I loved her. But her betrayal destroyed any feelings I had for her. Even though I hate Kaylie for what she did, I can't take Lilah's friendship away from her. She's already lost so much."

Uncomfortable silence filled the empty spaces where Jensen's pain had left room. Having not been through what he had, I wasn't sure what I could say or do to offer him any solace. I could think of plenty of things to do to take his mind off of it for the moment, but nothing that would help him move forward to get past Kaylie's betrayal.

"I want two," I blurted out without even thinking, causing Jensen's head to turn suddenly. I really hadn't been meaning to say anything, not knowing what it was I *should* say as a follow-up. But, now that the cat was out of the bag, I just decided to go with it.

"You want to what?" he asked, clearly misunderstanding what I was saying.

"Kids. I've always pictured having two." Dropping my eyes to my lap, I fidgeted with my short nails. "I'm an only child, and I always wondered what having a sibling would be like. My mom died when I was young, so they never got around to having another one—obviously. Willow is as close to a sister as I'll get, and I'm grateful for her, but I still always wondered." I sucked in a deep breath and waited for his reaction to my confession. God, we had only known each other a few weeks. He moved in the first day we met. We weren't even dating, yet we'd done unspeakably dirty things to each other in our kitchen, and now I was talking kids with him.

Jensen chuckled, and through the corner of my eye I watched him return his complete attention to the road instead of multi-tasking between me and his driving. "Five."

"Five?" I squeaked. "You do know how children are born, right?" My breaths grew shallow, my chest tightening as an anxiety attack started to rear its ugly head. There was no way I could birth *five* children. "I'd be willing to compromise."

"Why, Madison Landry, are you telling me *you* want to bear my five children?" *Oh fuck.* Were we just sharing numbers? We weren't even together, and here I am acting like we've got this huge elaborate future together. My foot should just relocate to my mouth permanently.

Swallowing thickly, I tried to find a way to backpedal my way out of this situation. "Um, well. You said that you and Kaylie never had this conversation until … well, until it was too late. And I figured that … um … well …"

"You are so adorable when you're freaking out." He laughed. "What's your compromise? It could make-or-break whether or not we could ever have a real relationship beyond this," he joked, winking at me.

While I knew what we had was just a fling, hearing him say that there was a possibility for a relationship made me want to jump out of the car and do back flips and cartwheels … well, if I was coordinated enough *to* do them, I suppose. However, I held my composure and answered his question. "Three. Three and a dog would be my compromise."

Seeming happy with my answer, he nodded. "All right. I think I can agree to three. And a dog, of course."

"Should we shake on it?" I asked with a laugh, relaxing a little as we pulled into our driveway and parked in front of the house.

"That seems so impersonal. Especially when negotiating how many children you're promising to give me," Jensen said slyly as he unbuckled his seat belt and leaned across the console. Our lips were mere inches apart as he clicked the release on my seat belt, eyeing me intensely. "I think a kiss would be much more appropriate."

I nodded lightly as Jensen's left hand cradled my face and pulled it toward his, our lips moving together tenderly. Chuckling, Jensen pulled back, his blue eyes sparkling. "Now remember, an oral contract is binding in the state of Tennessee."

Unable to contain my laughter, I shoved him back and opened my car door to start taking the groceries inside. "You're twisted. I don't know what I ever saw in you."

Jensen closed his own door after getting out. "I'm not going to lie, your love of all things sci-fi seems to be your only positive attribute right now."

"Oh, really?" I demanded, raising my eyebrows and grabbing three bags from the box of the truck.

Shrugging, he grabbed the final four bags and followed me to the house. "Okay, and your ass. You have a great ass."

"Ha!" I cried as I walked into the kitchen and set my bags on the counter next to the fridge. "And *I'm* terrible. You, Jensen Davis are—"

Before I could finish, Jensen dropped his bags to the floor and spun me around until he had me pinned between him and the island. My body started trembling as the memories from this morning came back strong, and I wanted nothing more than for him to give an encore of this morning's performance.

"What? What am I, Madison?" His lips ghosted mine, never touching down fully before brushing over my jaw and down my neck, where he lightly kissed the darkening mark he had left earlier.

"Huh? I … um …" All conscious thought had left my brain as his mouth continued to kiss my throat. "What was the question?"

With a satisfied snicker, Jensen pushed away from me,

causing me to shake my head clear of his spell. "Yeah, that's what I thought," he told me cockily as he bent down to retrieve his bags of groceries and put them away.

Staring at him for a few minutes, I tried to slow my racing heart before I went into cardiac arrest. I thought back to what I was trying to say — amending it to fit with recent events. "A tease. You, Jensen Davis, are a *tease*." He didn't try to deny my accusation at all; instead, he winked and continued to put food in the fridge and pantry.

"Come on," Jensen said, grabbing my hand and pulling me toward the groceries that still needed to be put away. "If you want to go for a ride this afternoon, we need to get all of this put away."

"Sorry, *Dad*."

Jensen cringed. "Please, don't ever call me that. Don't get me wrong, your dad's a great guy, but I've done things to you that takes that to a whole new level of disturbing."

With a disturbed laugh, I concurred. "Okay, I see your point. I'm sorry."

When the groceries were put away, Jensen and I headed outside to check on everything before we grabbed Ransom and Halley and went for our afternoon ride. I was excited to go back out to the field with Jensen.

Of course, I should have known it was too good to be true. As soon as we got Ransom and Halley inside, the skies opened up with a torrential downpour. It was rare to get this much rain this time of year, but not unheard of.

"It's okay," Jensen assured me. "We'll go again before winter. I promise."

Heartbroken, I looked at him. "I know, I was just excited. To ride. To be with you."

"Well, one out of two of those things isn't so bad, is it?" With wide, innocent eyes, he awaited my answer, and I saw this as the perfect opportunity to get him back for when we were in the kitchen. Sure, I wasn't going to tease him sexually, but teasing was teasing. It didn't always have to be about sex. Plus, when I teased *him* about sex, it only teased me too. Why would I do that to myself?

I placed my hand on his cheek, rubbing the scruff he had left there this morning and smiled. "You're right. I think I'll go ride in the indoor arena." I turned and headed for the locker room because I was serious about riding inside.

His heavy footsteps were heard behind me, and I smiled. "Oh, funny," he said as he helped me grab my saddle and brushes from my top locker before grabbing Ransom's tack.

"Thanks," I said cheerfully. "I have my moments."

Jensen and I rode for an hour, and as we did, we talked and worked on training Ransom while I allowed Halley to get used to being ridden again. Cantering was still a little too much on my ribs, but I knew well enough not to push myself if I wanted to stay out of the ER. Thankfully, it wasn't as bad as it used to be.

After we brushed the horses down, it was five and still pouring outside. We would have to bring the horses inside in this weather; it was days like this that made me dislike my job. With Glory and Starla soaked and happily eating in their stalls, I turned to find Jensen bringing in Oscar. His dark hair fell down his forehead and dripped over his eyes, and his light-colored jacket was drenched with water, making him look chilled to the bone.

"Okay, I think Oscar was the last. You ready to go home and dry off? Maybe make a light dinner and curl up on the couch?" he suggested as he sauntered over to me.

I nodded, meeting him halfway. "Um, yeah. Just let me do a quick walk-thru of the barn and make sure all the lights are off." Jensen nodded, and I headed off to shut off all the lights. After checking the viewing gallery and the locker room, I went into the wash stall and turned off the lights. As I turned to walk out, I noticed a red blinking light in the upper corner of the large room. Quickly, I turned the light back on and my heart leaped into my throat when I realized what it was.

"Shit. Fuck. *Shit!*" I cried, turning the light off again and running full tilt out of there. Horses spooked in their stalls as my loud footsteps echoed off the walls, and Jensen turned to me with mild panic that would soon mirror my own.

"Madi?" he asked, catching me by my biceps and holding me in place. "What is it?"

I gasped for air and tried to swallow my heart back down. From the way it felt, I was sure it had leapt right up into my throat. "Cameras," I wheezed painfully. "Dad. Cameras." Jensen searched my eyes, trying to make sense of what I was telling him. "Dad installed security cameras!"

"Yeah, he told me he was going to. Something about a discount on the insurance."

I shook my head violently, clenching my eyes shut. "No! There's one in the wash stall, Jensen."

When my eyes opened and found his again, I watched all of the color drain from his face. He released me from his grip. "Oh, shit."

"Come on. We have to check his office for where they feed to. Jensen, he can't see us like that! N-not before I can tell him." He seemed to be staring right through me, his skin so white he could have passed for dead — which could be a reality if my dad found that footage.

Moving faster than should be humanly possible, I yanked Jensen toward Dad's office in the barn and fumbled in my pocket for the key ring that held the spare. I dropped them on the floor several times as the adrenaline from my fear pumped furiously through my veins in an effort to keep me upright. Every time I looked at Jensen, he tried offering me an "it'll be okay" or an "I'm sure they're not even feeding live yet." However, they all fell flat in light of the terror in his eyes.

After what seemed like entirely too long, I got the door open, the brass knob slamming into the wooden wall behind it with a loud bang. I flipped the switch and looked around. Dad's desk was immaculately cleaned of clutter; he had a tall filing cabinet in the corner where he kept the contracts and waivers of our clients, and his chair was tucked tightly into his desk. Then, up in the far right corner, was another fucking camera.

"Son of a bitch, this isn't where it feeds to." I turned to Jensen, who finally regained a little color. "It has to be at his house." Looking at the clock above the door, I sucked in a deep breath. "It's seven now. Dad should be home around eight. We have to go get rid of the tape."

Jensen finally relaxed enough to laugh. Sure, it wasn't a full-out laugh, but something I had said was funny to him. "All right, Bugsy, settle down." Was he seriously trying to joke with me at a time like this? His junk was about to become well acquainted with my knee in about three ... two ... "Madison, everything's digital now. I don't know that there will be 'tapes' to get rid of," he explained, taking me by the hand and leading me back out of Dad's office.

"This is no time to joke around!" I shouted, my cheeks flaming beneath what I could only assume was an unflattering and unnatural shade of red.

Jensen nodded, knowing I was right. We ran out of the barn, still sharp enough to remember to lock the door before running through the rain that was still coming down in sheets. On several occasions, I slipped only to have Jensen rescue me before I took a fully-clothed mud bath, complete with gravel exfoliation.

When we reached Dad's front door, I grabbed my keys again and was shocked that I didn't fumble them this time.

Especially considering just how much fear flooded my body. With the key in the lock, I disengaged it before throwing it open. Jensen and I rushed in, hastily kicking off our muddy boots before I grabbed the wet arm of his jacket and ran quickly toward the den where Dad's in-home office was.

Water poured off our clothes and onto Dad's clean floors, and I very briefly noted in my frantic brain that I would have to be sure to clean it up as soon as we had what we came here for. Nothing else in the house immediately registered in my mind as I ran through the house until I came to a sudden, would-have-been-screeching-had-I-been-wearing-shoes, halt in the threshold of the den. With Jensen right behind me, I threw my open hand up until it landed flat against the spot where his abs and his chest met, stopping him. My fingers curled, tugging the fabric of his shirt slightly, and my stomach rolled.

There, behind Dad's desk, were three security monitors, each with live, flickering images of various spots throughout the grounds. However, that wasn't the worst of what we found upon entering my father's workspace ...

A smile formed on Dad's face as he looked between Jensen and me, his deep brown eyes bright and so-very aware. "Oh good, you're both here. I trust everything went well this weekend?"

In unison, Jensen and I both swallowed thickly, unsure of what to expect next.

22
I NEVER SAW IT COMING

Seconds felt like years as Jensen and I stood in the doorway to Dad's home office, staring like a couple of teenagers who just got busted making out on the couch. He looked between us, his eyes dropping to the hand I still clutched Jensen's shirt with. Panicked, I dropped it and wiped it on my soaked shirt like I'd just acquired cooties.

"Dad? What are you doing here?" I asked dumbly.

Cocking an eyebrow, he smirked. "Um, last I checked, I lived here?" His voice rose at the end in question—even if sarcasm dripped from every vowel and consonant. "I think a better question would be: what are the two of you doing here? Especially if you didn't realize I was here. And, *together?*"

Oh, he definitely knew something was up. The way he said "together," all inflected with his super-dad powers of deduction. We were fucked. Jensen hummed behind me as he tried—and failed, I might add—to come up with a story that Dad would believe.

"Invoices!" I screeched at a decibel only dogs should have been able to hear. Dad looked at me strangely. I cleared my throat nervously and glanced down at the floor as I tried to calm myself down. "Um, it's almost the end of August and

I wanted to get a head start on invoicing. You know, have it done for you so you can send them out to the clients. Take on some of the responsibility." *Shit, I hope he buys that.*

"Uhhh," Dad began, cocking an eyebrow at me—I hated when he did that; it made me all nervous and shit. And I was already plenty fucking nervous. "You know you can access the invoices from *your* computer, right?" Dad said, his eyes still showing just how much of my bullshit he wasn't buying.

"She's got a virus," Jensen blurted out, to which I promptly scrunched up my face, feeling slightly insulted as I turned to give him the stink eye. "On her *computer*," he finished, putting heavy emphasis on the last word so I would calm down.

"Right! Yeah, Jensen downloaded some stuff and infected the computer," I rushed to elaborate.

Jensen nudged my arm gently. "I did not. That was all you." His eyes seemed less terrified now as his lips twisted into a smirk as he tried to deny being the cause of my computer's supposed "infection."

"Did so," I countered, narrowing my eyes teasingly.

Narrowing his right back, he refused to take blame. "If thinking that helps you sleep at night."

Our little exchange was doing nothing to throw my Dad off. In fact, he crossed his arms and sat back, listening to us goad each other on. Turning my attention back to him, I offered my most innocent smile. "So, do you mind if I get a start on them for you? I wanted to show Jensen how we invoice."

Dad looked at his watch for a second. "Sure, Madi. I was about to go have a shower anyway." He stood from his chair and stepped out from behind the desk. "You know where everything's located. I'll see you in a few."

Jensen and I parted like the Red Sea to make room for Dad to pass by us. Once the bathroom door closed and the shower started, I bolted for the monitors with Jensen hot on my trail. Seeing the black and white screens up close caused my stomach to lurch. Especially knowing that they were recording and that there was very likely recorded evidence of Jensen and I dry humping each other. Actually, we were soaked from our water fight, so I wasn't sure if that term still applied.

Shaking the image from my head before I forgot what it was we were here to do, I moved behind the desk and started looking at the monitors for where the tapes or discs or whatever-they-were. My search came up empty.

"Damn it!" I whisper-yelled, not wanting to draw any more attention to the real reason we were here. "There's no ..." I paused, still unsure what it was I was hoping to find. "... whatever it is we're even looking for!"

Jensen stood beside me, looking over the monitors himself. When I looked up at him, I saw his brow furrow in concentration. "It's probably wired to go straight to his computer," he mumbled, turning to sit at the desk as he turned on the PC.

The main screen popped up, prompting him for a password. "Do you know his password?"

Smiling faintly, I nodded. "Allison. My mother's name."

"It's a beautiful name," he told me with a soft smile before turning back and keying it in.

I laughed, leaning over his shoulder to watch what he was doing. "You don't have to suck up, you know. However ..." I let the word trail off before kissing his cheek quickly "... if you can find and delete us in the wash stall, I'll owe you. Big."

Jensen chuckled. "I'm working on it, Landry. Don't get your panties in a bunch."

Without even thinking, I said, "What if I'm not wearing any?"

His fingers slipped over a couple keys accidentally, a whispered curse blowing past his lips. Behaving myself, I watched as Jensen opened a few files, searching for some kind of clues that would lead him to the security footage. "Anything yet?" It was a dumb question, but I honestly had no idea.

Much to my disappointment, he shook his head. "Nope. I'm going to have to go in through the back end of the system."

"You can do that?" I asked incredulously. Jensen Davis was a computer genius? The man never failed to impress me as I watched him open up screens with half-words that he treated no differently than English. It was fascinating. "Where did you learn all of this?"

A few more screens flashed by before Jensen located a hidden folder. "In a world as technologically advanced as ours is, I'm surprised you don't know some of this stuff," he ribbed playfully before further explaining. "Back in Houston I worked for a large computer software company that Kaylie's father owns. That was how we met. She had come in for lunch with her father one day ... Well the rest isn't important as you know how it turned out." Then, he smiled wide, double clicking the mouse before the computer screen showed the same images that were on the monitors behind us. "Got it!"

Now that he had accessed the folder, he moved forward and started looking for the footage from the wash stall. The little white arrow rested above the icon I could only assume we were so hell-bent on finding. My heart skipped a beat as he double clicked on it.

We watched the black and white image on the computer monitor. Yup, it was the wash stall. The empty wash stall. There was a time stamp in the upper left corner of the screen, showing us that we were watching from the night before our water fight. "Try fast-forwarding," I suggested quietly.

Nodding, Jensen started skipping the recording ahead until I entered the frame, carrying my water buckets. He chuckled as he watched me set them down, fussing with them until they were perfectly aligned. "A little OCD, huh, Landry?"

I slapped his shoulder. "Oh, shut up," I said with a laugh, keeping my eyes on the screen. There was a small – okay *huge* – part of me that wanted to see what was about to transpire.

I watched as the water flowed over the bucket soundlessly, seeing with perfect clarity my use of the word "shit" when it happened. When I looked up, I knew that was when Jensen had appeared, scolding me for my being wasteful. Words were exchanged between us before he slowly entered the frame and I turned the hose on him. I had to slap my hand over my mouth to muffle my laughter as I watched the scene play out before my eyes. It was quite funny. The way he chased me around in circles, trying to grab the hose, then me, as I continued to spray him.

"I'm glad you find this just as funny the second time around," Jensen teased. I could tell he was smiling by the sound of his voice.

Feeling certain my laughter could be contained, I pulled my hand away from my mouth and kissed his cheek softly. "Come on, you loved it."

"Being sprayed with cold water? Nope, can't say that I did," he said surely, turning his head slightly to capture my eyes. We stared at each other for ages, my eyes dropping to his lips as I contemplated kissing him. It didn't seem to matter that we were in my father's house and could be caught at any moment. If anything, that made it a little more tempting.

Jensen cleared his throat as he watched my tongue peek out to wet my lips. "However ..." he rasped, turning his attention back to the computer.

My eyes followed his, and I gasped when I saw camera-him pin camera-me to the wall, the water from the hose raining down on us. We stared at each other for a moment, and before I knew it, our lips were joined as we practically devoured each other. Just watching the recording of Jensen's hands disappearing beneath my shirt caused my nipples to harden and yearn for his touch.

"Holy shit," I whispered, expelling a soft breath.

"Uh ... Yeah, I should turn this off before your dad walks in here," he suggested, his voice rough and gravelly. "Delete it?"

"Well, I feel better." Dad's voice boomed, startling both Jensen and I before I got a chance to answer.

Several quick clicks of the mouse and Jensen was back to the desktop, opening a file marked "Invoicing." Nodding as he opened the main document, Jensen spoke. "Yeah, I think that makes sense." He lifted his head from the monitor with a wide smile. "Hey, Wayne."

Glancing between us—which wasn't a far trek considering I was still hovering so closely over Jensen that I was practically in his lap—Dad smirked. I straightened up when his eyebrow arched. *Here it comes ...*

"So, I trust you two had a good weekend?" he inquired.

Jensen stood from the chair, continuing to smile. "Everything went fine, sir." The way he called Dad "sir" had me in a near-fit of giggles. He was definitely trying to suck up in an effort to stay on his good side.

Dad grinned. He seemed incredibly happy and not at all put-out by what I thought I knew he knew—that made sense, right? Oh, hell, this entire situation was confusing; I wasn't sure what the hell I knew anymore. All I knew was Dad looked at us with this smile on his face that no longer made me *quite* as nervous.

"Good to hear. Listen, I'm about ready to turn in — long weekend and all. Jensen, would you mind giving Madi and me a minute?" he asked.

Oh no, oh no, oh no. The nerves were back full force, causing my stomach to drop and my hands to shake as the adrenaline that pumped through my body overpowered me completely.

"Of course. I'll head back to the house and start dinner." Without looking at me, Jensen moved around me to leave the office. "I'll see you in a few, Madi."

I couldn't move. Paralyzing fear took hold as the front door opened and closed behind Jensen, leaving Dad and me alone. Alone after finding out he installed cameras. Cameras that caught Jensen and I making out — no, not just making out; there was boob-grabbage and ass-groping. Both things that a father should never see. Ever.

"Daddy ..." I started nervously, finally feeling the need to confess everything I had been keeping from him — well, not *everything*. "I need to —"

"You look good, kiddo," he said, interrupting me. "Happy. It's been a while since I've seen you smile like you have been lately." There was a beat of silence between us before his smile widened even more. "He's a good guy, Madison."

"W — what?" I stammered quietly, dropping my face to the floor before he could see the deep blush that filled my cheeks, absolutely giving away my truth.

"Jensen," he clarified. My head snapped up, my wide eyes meeting his as he stepped farther into the room and pulled me into a warm embrace. "You didn't need to keep it from me," he whispered into the top of my head. "Despite what he's been through — and I'm assuming he's told you about his recent troubles — he's a good guy who just made a bad choice. Even if it was to avenge his sister."

"Dad, we're not together," I told him with conviction.

"But you like him?"

I thought about that a minute. Jensen and I were supposed to be keeping things casual, but yeah. I thought he was a great guy, and if the timing was right, I could see myself wanting to be with him.

"Sure," I replied. "He's a nice guy."

"That's all?"

"Dad, I just got out of a relationship, and Jensen is just getting on his feet. Neither of us is ready for an actual relationship."

Dad seemed skeptical. "Whatever you say, Madi. Just know, you'll have my support whatever you decide. I just want you to be happy."

Melting into him, I wrapped my arms around his waist. "Thanks, Dad." I mumbled. "We've discussed where we're at, and the truth is we only just met a few weeks ago. It's too soon to—"

"I knew your mother for less than a day before I knew she was the one, kiddo. Sometimes, you just know. My advice is to just go with it," Dad said nostalgically. "If you think he can make you happy, why does it matter how long you've been single or he's been back on his feet?"

The man had a point.

"What made you think I liked him?" I asked carefully.

Dad laughed loudly, unwrapping me from his arms and holding my biceps to keep me at arm's length as he met my gaze. "It wasn't until you fell off the second time on his first day that I thought maybe you had a little crush on him," he confessed with a sly smirk.

"In fact," He turned from me and headed out of the office. "When I first heard from Henry that Jensen was in town and having trouble finding work, I thought that maybe the two of you would be good for each other—having both been through so much and all. Has he told you about his ex?" He suddenly seemed nervous that he had told me something he maybe shouldn't have, so I assured him with a nod.

"Yeah. Kaylie. He told me everything." I suspected Dad likely only knew what Henry knew about Kaylie, and that was just that they had ended things. So I honored Jensen's secret and just left my reply at that ... until something he said struck me suddenly. "Wait. Did you set this up?"

While the idea of my own father meddling in my love life kind of weirded me out, it was also kind of sweet. Dad always had my best interests at heart and was sure to stand behind me in any and all decisions. When Dane and I started dating, he had his doubts, but he kept quiet because I was happy — or at least *appeared* happy.

"When you got hurt, and Jensen offered to take care of you? It was then that I knew the two of you had an instant connection," Dad told me. "Sure, you both seemed to dislike each other initially, but I think given your pasts, it was inevitable you'd both be a little stand-offish. I knew that by forcing you together one of two things would happen. You'd find out that you both have a lot more in common than you realized. Or ..."

"Or we'd kill each other?" I dead-panned.

Dad laughed. "I was going to say, or Jensen would have quit, leaving us without the help we needed. But I suppose you could be right." With his hand on the doorknob, Dad paused. "Listen, kiddo. I know what Dane did to you broke your heart."

I inhaled and held the breath, because Dad still didn't know about Dane showing up the night before. How could I tell him? Should I even? Ultimately, I decided against it.

"You deserve to be happy. And from what I've seen, Jensen makes you happy."

Seen? What he's seen? Suddenly my heart started pounding again. The security camera. I wondered if his words held some kind of hidden meaning. Searching his eyes for some answers, I came up empty; I would think that if he had seen what went on in the wash stall that he'd have been slightly more uncomfortable. Right?

"Madison, you seem nervous about something?"

He wasn't kidding. However, there was no way to ask about the cameras without admitting to him that Jensen and I had been recorded. So, I forced a smile and lied through my teeth, hoping he wouldn't call me on it. "Nope, just relieved that you would be okay with my moving on—whenever that happens."

After quickly putting my boots back on, I moved to walk past him and through the door when he stopped me. "Oh, before you go. I'm sure you saw the monitors in the office when you were doing invoicing." I had to bite the inside of my cheek to stay quiet—even if I wanted to cry a little. "I just wanted to let you know that I installed security cameras throughout the premises. The insurance company assured me we would get a discount if we took more precautions. I meant to tell you Friday, I just forgot."

"Oh," I responded, trying my best to act surprised. "That's great." The look in his eyes told me that he likely had no idea about the wash stall with Jensen, and I found myself breathing a huge sigh of relief. "Well, I should get back and help with dinner. Thanks for the talk, Dad."

"Anytime, baby girl. Have a good night."

"You too. I'll see you in the morning."

The entire way back to the house, I basked in the relief that Dad hadn't seen the video. Even more was that he'd be okay if I ever decided I was ready for a relationship.

When I walked into the house, I saw Jensen in fresh, dry clothes, pacing in the entry nervously. I shook my head and smiled. "Jensen?" I asked, closing and locking the front door behind me before taking my still-muddy boots off. "What's wrong?" I realized it was a stupid question; I knew exactly what was bothering him.

Lifting his frantic eyes to mine, he rushed across the small room and pulled me into the house. "What did he say?"

"It was nothing bad," I assured him. "He noticed I've been acting different—happier—since Dane left." Smiling, I placed my hands on Jensen's chest and closed my fists around his shirt, pulling him closer. "He figures it's because of you, and he doesn't seem upset about it."

"Really?"

I nodded. "Really. Now come on. I'm starving. What's for dinner?"

Jensen shook his head, still looking a little out of sorts. "Oh, I don't know. I realize I said I was going to come home and cook, but when Wayne asked me to leave so he could talk to you, I got a little frazzled."

"Okay, come with me," I suggested, pulling him to the living room and pushing him onto the couch. "Have a seat, watch TV, and *I'll* go find something to eat." I had just turned to leave the room when Jensen grabbed my wrist.

"You're happier?" he inquired, focusing on what I told him in the foyer.

With a bright smile on my face, I relaxed onto the couch next to him, my clothes still soaked through and uncomfortable. My knees touched his outer thighs as I kneeled on the cushion with my legs tucked under me. "How can I not be?" I combed my fingers through his hair, trailing my fingers over his scalp and down to the nape of his neck where I teased the hairs there. "He's gone. I'm free to be who I want to be, and date who I want to date … in the future when I decide I'm ready," I clarified when I saw the panic in his eyes. I knew he wasn't looking for a relationship, yet I kept scaring the crap out of him when I spoke like that.

As my fingers tickled and teased the short hair, his posture finally relaxed. "I'm happy too, Madi. After what happened with Kaylie, I didn't think I would ever feel this way again."

My fingers stopped moving. We'd agreed no feelings, yet here he was, telling me he'd done what we'd set out to avoid.

"Jensen ..." My voice was barely above a whisper as I spoke. I was at a loss. Was I supposed to tell him it was too soon for that? That we should end things now before they get too complicated? And, if I did, why did I get the feeling it would crush me?

Everything had changed in a matter of seconds.

The silence must have been too much for him, because he broke our intense stare and leaned forward nervously, resting his forearms on his knees and clasping his hands together. "I'm sorry. I just meant that I haven't been as stressed as I was with her. You're so easy to be around. It's nice to know that things won't get complicated between us."

I felt like I was being kicked from every angle by a herd of horses. But I forced a smile through it all. "Right. Good."

"So," he said in an effort to change the subject. "What's for dinner?"

Trying to mask my sudden doom-and-gloom attitude, I shrugged before standing. "Not sure. I'll go find something easy and then maybe we can watch TV before bed?" There was no need to be upset about the unspoken words between us. We were happy before, so there was no reason we shouldn't be able to move past it and keep doing what we were doing. Right?

Reaching for the remote, Jensen nodded, and I took that as my cue to go change and then start dinner. After putting together a couple of sandwiches, I went back to the living room to see Jensen with his feet up on the coffee table, watching TV. "I forgot to ask, did you delete the recording?"

Jensen looked at me sheepishly. "Um, actually, no, not exactly." My mouth dropped as I handed him his dinner and plopped down next to him. "I may have emailed it to myself before deleting the last forty-eight hours on all of the security cameras—you know, so Wayne didn't ask any questions on why there was only one camera with missing footage."

"Good thinking," I said, nodding before my brain belatedly registered him saying he emailed the footage to himself.

OOPS...I DID IT AGAIN

I was shocked to hear he hadn't deleted it, but I was even *more* surprised to find out he still had a copy. "Wait ... You ... *Why?*"

Shrugging, he smirked crookedly and it made me want to toss my plate on the table and kiss him hard. "I don't know. I guess I wanted a little souvenir of it. From what we saw, I thought it was pretty hot."

"Typical," I muttered teasingly as I took a bite of my dinner.

Chuckling, Jensen nudged my arm with his. "Don't tell me you didn't."

"I cannot confirm nor deny such allegations," I replied seductively.

Jensen and I sat back on the couch, our bodies huddled against one another as we ate and watched a rerun of *The Office*. Since I cooked, Jensen offered to clean up. It was nice how we always shared the household responsibilities that way. It was something Dane never cared to do.

He returned from the kitchen and joined me on the couch. I sidled up to him when he draped his arm around my shoulder, and exhaled when he stroked my hair soothingly.

"I love how that feels," I sighed against his chest as the

ticklish sensations rippled through my scalp and down my neck before spreading across my body. "It's so calming." I raised my face to his, and he leaned down to place a feather-light kiss on my lips. As they lingered delicately against mine, I felt that familiar spark shoot through me, exploding deep within my belly. With a breathless whimper against his mouth, I straddled his thighs and wrapped my arms around his neck. I shivered when his hands moved up my thighs before they came to rest on the curve of my ass.

My fingers moved along his jaw and twisted into his hair, pulling him even closer to me, and it didn't take long for our sweet, innocent kissing to erupt into a full-blown frenzy. Our lips worked fervently against one another's, Jensen's fingers curling into my backside as I shifted my hips into his groin.

Grunting low, he pressed back, meeting my second thrust with one of his own before he began placing kisses along the edge of my lips, down my jaw, until he found his way to the crook of my neck. "Oh, god ..." I moaned quietly, my hips pushing forward again, seeking him out. "Jensen, I ..."

"Yes, Madi?" His voice was low and raspy, sending vibrations through me and affecting me in the most amazing ways. "What do you want? Tell me ..."

So many fantasies raced through my mind. All of which involved sex in some way, and considering I was too forgetful to add condoms to our grocery list, I knew that ninety-seven percent of my thoughts weren't even in the realm of possibilities. "You," I answered vaguely, only to have him respond with a laugh.

Laughing didn't stop him from showering my neck with kisses, gently nipping the more sensitive parts with his teeth. "You know we can't ... It's just ... I don't want to be irresponsible, here."

"Mmm hmm," I hummed, understanding completely. Then I got bold. "What if I told you I'm on the pill?"

Jensen groaned against my shoulder. "Madi, think about that. Don't just say it in the moment because we're both desperate here."

I hated that he was right. We barely knew each other. "You're right," I agreed. "Safety first."

Removing his face from my neck, he cradled my jaw in his hands. "I want you *so badly*." His words created a wave of lust that washed over me, and soon enough, my lips were back on his as I tugged his hair to keep him from pulling away. I didn't care if we ran out of oxygen; it would have been the best way to go.

His hands moved back down my body, grazing my ass again before sweeping beneath my shirt and groping me over my bra. A blast of heat erupted through my body, my skin on fire beneath his touch. His hands left my chest, moving slowly back over my ribs until he gripped my shirt and started to lift it skyward.

I didn't *want* to let go of his hair. I didn't *want* to stop kissing him. But I *did* want to be naked with him. Really fucking naked. With a groan of displeasure, I parted our lips in favor of being topless. Before I allowed him to resume kissing me, though, I scooted back on his lap and started tugging at his shirt, discarding it to the living room floor as well.

Jensen's eyes surveyed my near-naked upper body, his hands rising up, fingers ghosting delicately over my heated flesh. He teased the straps of my bra before hooking his thumbs under them.

Pulling my bottom lip between my teeth, our eyes locked. He seemed to be silently asking permission to proceed. I nodded, of course, whimpering in the process as he slowly slid the straps down my arms, goose bumps appearing in the wake of his touch as he moved the white cotton fabric away from my small breasts.

My breath was shaky as it left my lungs, and Jensen's hands gripped my ribs over the bra that remained fastened around me, his thumbs brushing my nipples softly. "Fuck, you're beautiful," he whispered before tightening his grip on my ribs and pushing himself forward until his mouth found my neck.

Alternating tender kisses with forceful ones, he journeyed down my chest. I cried out when his wet tongue started circling my nipple, causing it to harden in his mouth before he grazed it with his teeth.

Snaking his right arm up my back and clamping his hand down on my shoulder to hold me still, his left hand cupped the breast he was currently tending to, still flicking his tongue over my sensitive flesh. My hands found purchase in his hair again, holding his face against me as my shallow breaths turned to unsteady pants.

Suddenly both of his hands were on my lower back, and I released a startled cry when he flipped us until he had me pinned on the couch. His mouth left its current location, kissing and licking a trail down to my sternum and up over the other breast, which was actually feeling a little jealous of the attention the right was being paid. He didn't do anything different to that one, biting and licking and kissing until the skin puckered in his mouth. Goose bumps erupted all-the-fuck-over my body as I thrust my hips up into his.

"Madi?" Jensen whispered, lifting his face from my chest. I lifted my heavy-lidded eyes to him, trying to focus my hazy vision. "I want ..." placing his right hand on my body, his touch was firm as he moved down until his fingers looped in behind the button of my jeans. I whimpered as the very tips of his fingers tickled the sensitive patch of skin above the apex of my thighs.

A fog of lust rolled in, causing me to lose any cognitive

abilities whatsoever. "Whateveryouwant," I said, my words mashed together as my head fell heavily back to the couch. "Just don't stop touching me ..." With one flick of his wrist, he had my jeans undone, and he moved his hands to my hips as he began to lower them, scooting back from his spot on the couch so he could pull them off completely, along with my panties and socks.

When I heard the denim hit the floor, I was instantly thrown back into what was happening. I quickly propped myself up on my elbows seeing only a flash of white still wrapped around my ribs below my boobs. *I'm practically naked!* It wasn't until I saw the look on Jensen's face as he looked at me with that confident, panty-melting grin on his face, that I felt my sudden anxiety flee. Before I could sit up completely, he lowered himself between my legs again, kissing me hard. The light scruff on his face brushed along my skin, sending shivers of pleasure through me as he left a trail of open and closed-mouthed kisses over my jaw, down my throat, my chest, over my breasts, my abdomen.

As his lips moved over my hipbones, my legs tightened around him. I tried to suppress the desire that had me yearning to drive my pelvis up into him. My need for him to touch me was soon sated as his fingers slowly moved back and forth between my legs, stopping at the top to swirl around my clit and leaving me breathless and weak-kneed. With his fingers gliding with determination, his mouth continued to move inward before continuing their trek down south.

"Oh, fuck," I cried out when his warm tongue darted out to bring me to new heights of ecstasy. His fingers and his tongue worked in unison while his free hand lay flat against my tense abdomen to keep me from pulling away from him as I continued to climb to the peak of rapture, only to fall hard and fast when I climaxed.

Pleasure flooded my body from all angles as Jensen's

fingers slowly entered me. My back arched against the soft leather couch, and I threw my arms above my head to brace myself as every muscle in my body tensed in preparation of my impending orgasm. As soon as Jensen started humming, his mouth still pressed firmly between my legs, I fell. My legs tightened around his shoulders and my fingers dug into the cushiony arms of the couch above my head as I cried out a long string of profanities. There was no time to be embarrassed for my colorful language as Jensen slowly sat up, smiling like the cat who just ate the canary. Or another cat— which would be a euphemism for my pussy.

My breathing was still ragged as bliss rolled in soothing waves over my body. I wanted to sit up, but I lacked the bones in my body as they had all turned to pudding. "Shit," I panted breathlessly, running my fingers through my disheveled hair.

"Yeah," Jensen said with a chuckle. "You said that already."

"Did I?"

"Among other things."

He shifted in his seat, grimacing slightly as he tried to adjust himself without my noticing.

I felt so guilty. There I was, so caught up in what he was doing to my body, that I had completely neglected him. That was all I needed to find the strength to stand. As I stood before him, still ninety-nine percent nude, I grabbed the remote and turned off the television we weren't even watching and held out my hand.

"Where are we—?" he started to ask as I tugged him to his feet before trailing him behind me.

"We're going to go have a shower."

He froze behind me like a stubborn stallion, stopping me in my tracks as well. "Madison, I think that both of us being naked together could lead to something neither of us is prepared for right now."

Turning to him, I offered him a calm smile. "I promise I won't let it go any further than me taking care of you." I stepped into him, my still-pert breasts pressing against his naked chest. "Let me take care of you, baby," I purred. "The way you just took care of me."

Nodding slowly, he acquiesced, and I moved backward down the hall, keeping our eyes locked as I stepped onto the cool tile floor and walked to the tub.

After starting the shower, I turned back to Jensen and unbuttoned his jeans before letting them fall over his narrow hips to the floor where he stepped out of them. Locking my sights on his brilliant blue eyes again, I slid my hands into his boxer briefs just above his ass. Slowly, I worked them over the muscular curve before moving them around front, brushing his length as I released it. Even though I had seen Jensen naked on a couple of occasions, and held him in my hand that very morning, I still felt my cheeks warm as my eyes dropped between us to stare for what was probably an inappropriate amount of time.

The bathroom started to fill with fog. Jensen lifted his feet out of his boxers, removing his socks one at a time, and I let my bra fall to the floor. Together, we moved to the edge of the tub where he offered me his hand, and I stepped over the edge. He joined me a half-second later, lowering his face to mine and kissing me softly as he backed me under the warm spray of water. I rested my hands on his waist, tickling the skin there. It quivered under my feathery caresses, and I smiled against his lips having just found out he was ticklish.

"It's not that funny," he said, unable to contain his own smirk as I continued to tickle his sides. All humor dissipated when he kissed me again, pulling me roughly against him until his erection was pressed between us.

Shifting away from him while our lips and tongues

moved enthusiastically together, I slid my right hand between us and wrapped it tightly around him, pushing down to the base before making my ascent once more.

"Oh, shit," Jensen moaned around my tongue, resting his forehead to mine, but parting our lips as I continued to stroke him firmly. Warm streams of water flowed over us as I pumped him, hopefully bringing his body the release it needed.

When his steady breaths turned to the familiar pants I heard in the kitchen that morning, I knew he was close. With my left hand, I cradled his face, coaxing his gaze to mine as I continued to pleasure him. "God, Jensen," I whispered, our lips just barely touching as I spoke. "I want you. I wish we didn't have to wait. I want to feel you inside me the next time you make me come."

Just as I'd hoped, my confession was his complete undoing as his eyes fought the urge to close. He pulsed in my hand, the water washing away the physical evidence of his orgasm. I moved my left hand down over his neck, and I could feel his quickened pulse as he planted his lips firmly on mine.

"I don't know what I did to deserve you, Madison Landry ..." The corners of his bright, sparkling eyes crinkled slightly as he smiled wide, his happiness absolutely radiating off of him. His confession shocked me a little, but I chalked it up to the bliss one feels after an orgasm and nothing more.

Feeling playful, I winked at him. "Well, I don't know that you *deserve* me just yet, Mr. Davis. You may need to work just a little harder," I teased.

"Mmm ... I think I can do that." He kissed me softly, causing another blast of desire to erupt beneath my skin. He must have sensed this, because he quickly pulled away and pushed me back under the water, running his fingers over my hair to dampen it completely. "We should get cleaned up before we run out of hot water."

I kept my eyes trained on him as he squeezed my shampoo into his hand and worked it between his palms before massaging it into my scalp. Those same delightful tingles that worked their way into my head from his fingers earlier were back, and I found my eyes lulling shut before he rinsed my hair and applied my conditioner in the same manner.

Letting my conditioner sit in my hair for a few minutes, I switched spots with Jensen and repaid the favor by washing his hair. I knew that offering to wash each other's bodies would just lead to trouble, so we opted to take care of that ourselves before we rinsed off and climbed out of the shower.

Jensen wrapped my towel around me, securing it tightly beneath my arms before tightening his own around his waist. "So, your room or mine tonight?" he asked as he led us from the bathroom.

"Yours," I told him, still struggling with the idea of sleeping on my bed. "I like yours."

Nodding his approval, he kissed me quickly. "Okay, go and put your pajamas on. I'll be waiting."

After a moment of deliberation, I opted for a pair of short-shorts and a fitted tank-top. Using my towel, I dried my hair a little before hanging it on the back of my door and heading across the hall where I found Jensen beneath the blankets already. His upper body was completely bare. It was unlikely that the nakedness continued below his waist where his comforter rested, but a girl could dream — and it was likely I would.

With a bounce in my step, I headed for his bed and hopped on, climbing over him to get to the spot he had tacitly designated as mine the night before. I had only made it as far as having one leg on either side of him before he ensnared my barely-clothed hips in his hands.

"I said pajamas. Not your underwear," he groaned, his

eyes growing dark with desire.

"Down boy," I said with a devious smirk, not *just* talking to him. "I didn't want things to get too hot beneath your fluffy blankets." Yeah, I was teasing him. It was cruel, really.

Jensen chuckled, releasing my hips and lightly slapping both sides of my ass. "You're evil. By you dressing this way, it almost guarantees things getting ... *hot.*"

With a crooked smirk of my own, I leaned forward and used my right hand to grip his jaw, squeezing his cheeks together just a little. "You need to learn how to behave yourself." I looked over his naked upper body. "Besides, you're wearing far less than I am."

"Touché," he responded, finally allowing me to make my way over to my side of the bed. "Okay, you win."

"Yup," I concurred energetically as I turned away from him, lying on my left side as I waited for him to gather me in his arms. "And don't you forget it, either, mister."

Warmth surrounded me as soon as I had settled in, Jensen's body pressed flat against my back as his lips kissed my neck where I knew the mark he left was visible to him. A smile spread across my face as I let the feeling sink in, soon imagining the two of us like this years from now when we're old and gray.

I shivered as a shocking revelation hit me like a hoof to the chest. The butterflies in my belly awakened with a vengeance and a shot of adrenaline zipped through my veins.

It was then I realized why I'd been so hurt every time he reminded me what this really was. Without really realizing it—thank you, denial—I'd fallen for him. My feelings had gradually moved past friendship and casual orgasm-buddies to deep and meaningful. I must have been projecting this onto him, misreading him this whole time. Every time I thought he was about to confess his feelings, it was because I was denying my own. Because we had an agreement.

Jensen and I had agreed to keep things between us casual and fun when he first showed up on the ranch, but I was afraid I just messed it up.

I had been in denial the entire time, and I didn't even realize it. But as we lay in bed, his arms around me and his lips brushing the bare skin of my shoulder, it became all-too clear that I had unexpectedly developed feelings for him. We hadn't even had sex yet, and I found I craved more than he was ready to give. How could I not? He had been there for me when I was hurt, he helped me get over what Dane had done, he protected me. I fell faster than I thought I ever could, and it scared me. Not because I didn't trust myself, but because Jensen didn't want this. He'd sais so repeatedly.

"Goodnight, Madison," he whispered against my shoulder, pulling me out of my silent torment.

"Mmm," I hummed, tamping down the fear and nerves for just a moment. "G'night, baby."

When his fingertips danced over my lower abdomen, exhaustion took over, but my mind was still racing with my sudden discovery. I just couldn't let it go. I couldn't stop myself from wondering how long it would be before Jensen found out how I was starting to feel. Or what might happen when he did.

He shifted behind me, and I worried he might have picked up on my anxiety, but he inhaled deeply, and then exhaled with a soft moan. He had fallen asleep.

And I had fallen in love.

Jensen released another soft breath as I hunkered down and tried to shut my brain off, resolving to deal with everything in the morning. Exhaustion had just started to wrap around me like a warm blanket straight from the dryer on a cold day when Jensen started mumbling in his sleep.

He groaned, almost sounding a little distressed, then followed it with random words I couldn't quite piece together.

Trying to solve the puzzle of Jensen's sleep rambling pulled the last shroud of exhaustion over me, and I was just succumbing to sleep when I heard, "Can't feel the same way. Not ready."

My heart sank, but my mind was made up. I would keep my feelings to myself for now. Sure, it would probably complicate things and set me up for heartbreak, but I couldn't bring myself to pull away from him.

Not yet.

CHOMPIN' AT THE BIT

a horse play novel ~ book two

"This is incredible," I said breathlessly. The walls were painted a very pale blue with white trim and crown moldings. There were two windows along one wall with floor-to-ceiling dark brown curtains that were closed. The bed was huge, dressed in fluffy white linens that looked sure to be down-filled, and pillows just as light and fluffy looking that took up half the bed. A sturdy, intricate looking wood headboard with a matching dresser and nightstands completed the room.

I just started to turn to Jensen when I heard a soft thump right behind me and his hands ensnared my waist, completing my rotation before throwing us down onto the bed. I squealed playfully on our descent, and just as I suspected the blanket was so delightfully downy that it nearly swallowed us both.

Once on the bed, Jensen's mouth found mine, his tongue tracing the line of my lips as his left leg found its way between mine. Basking in the feeling of finally being in his arms like this again, I complied more than eagerly. I moaned as I opened my mouth and our tongues met, slowly gliding against each other as my fingers wove into his soft hair. Jensen's left hand moved down my body, a tremor of desire tingling in its wake until he gripped my ass and rolled us over until I was straddling him.

A strong feeling of longing settled between my legs, begging for an overdue release, so I pushed my hips forward in an effort to quell the ache for his touch. Both of us moaned at the friction—even with the two layers of denim between us—and continued to writhe against each other. I slipped my hands between us and started to unbutton the shirt he was wearing as he continued to guide me on top of him, setting the speed. With his shirt now open, my fingers danced over the hard lines of his chest and abdomen until I found his belt and started to unbuckle it. I moved fast, really hoping he wouldn't stop me this time, and had it open, along with his pants button and fly, only seconds later.

Jensen followed my lead, moving his own hands to the hem of my shirt before raising it up my body. I sat up once he reached my shoulders and finished pulling my shirt off before tossing it behind me. Jensen eyed me hungrily—like he wanted to completely devour me—and my body shook with exhilaration.

Coming Soon

ABOUT THE AUTHOR

A.D. Ryan resides in Edmonton, Alberta with her extremely supportive husband and children (two sons and a stepdaughter). Reading and writing have always been a big part of her life, and she hopes that her books will entertain countless others the way that other authors have done for her. Even as a small child, she enjoyed creating new and interesting characters and molding their worlds around them.

To learn more about the author and stay up-to-date on future publications, please look for her on Facebook and her blog.

https://www.facebook.com/pages/AD-Ryan-Author

http://adryanauthorblog.wordpress.com

Sign up for my **NEWSLETTER** to receive updates & exclusive content!

Made in the USA
Middletown, DE
09 May 2016